"How would was your

Caught off guard by the question, Phillip felt a moment of panic. Who was this woman and what did she want?

"I didn't catch your name," he finally said.

"I didn't throw it to you," she replied. "Anyway, my name isn't important. I'm here about the young girl who died because there was no neurosurgeon available to attend to her. What I want to understand," she continued, "is this. While Jenny was riding around in the ambulance, what exactly prevented some-one—anyone—from coming in to save her? You, for example, Dr. Neurosurgeon."

Phillip said nothing.

"As if it isn't awful enough to lose a child," the woman added. "To know that the child didn't need to die…" She glared at him. "You want to know my name? You can call me Concerned. Frustrated. Mad as Hell."

The arrival of a security guard, apparently summoned by his receptionist, saved Phillip from having to respond.

"*Brilliant solution,*" the woman said as a blue-uniformed guard who probably outweighed her by two hundred pounds or so took her arm. "*But you haven't heard the last from me.*"

Dear Reader,

I've often thought—perhaps not an original idea—that writing a book is somewhat akin to giving birth. There is the first germ of an idea that grows and develops and ultimately takes on a life of its own. *Along Came Zoe*, my sixth offspring, was one of those particularly difficult births, the kind where you groan, "Oh, never again."

Fortunately, the joy of creation—books and babies alike—quickly dissolves the pain, leaving only a sense of wonder at what you've produced. I'm tempted here to carry on the analogy and talk about how the wonder only continues until your miraculous offspring gets its first report card—or review—but I think I've followed this thought far enough.

I hope you enjoy *Along Came Zoe*. I'd love to hear from you. Please visit my Web site at janicemacdonald.com, or write to me at PMB101, 136 E. 8th Street, Port Angeles, WA 98362.

Best wishes,

Janice Macdonald

Along Came Zoe
Janice Macdonald

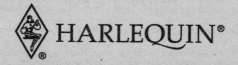

HARLEQUIN®

TORONTO • NEW YORK • LONDON
AMSTERDAM • PARIS • SYDNEY • HAMBURG
STOCKHOLM • ATHENS • TOKYO • MILAN • MADRID
PRAGUE • WARSAW • BUDAPEST • AUCKLAND

ISBN 0-373-71244-8

ALONG CAME ZOE

Copyright © 2004 by Janice Macdonald.

This edition published by arrangement with Harlequin Books S.A.

® and TM are trademarks of the publisher. Trademarks indicated with ® are registered in the United States Patent and Trademark Office, the Canadian Trade Marks Office and in other countries.

www.eHarlequin.com

Printed in U.S.A.

To my editor, Zilla Soriano, for her patience and
understanding during the difficult times I had while writing
this book, and for her unfailing wisdom and guidance. I feel
very fortunate to have the privilege of working with her.

Books by Janice Macdonald

HARLEQUIN SUPERROMANCE
1060—THE DOCTOR DELIVERS
1077—THE MAN ON THE CLIFF
1132—KEEPING FAITH
1157—SUSPICION
1201—RETURN TO LITTLE HILLS

Don't miss any of our special offers. Write to us at the
following address for information on our newest releases.

Harlequin Reader Service
U.S.: 3010 Walden Ave., P.O. Box 1325, Buffalo, NY 14269
Canadian: P.O. Box 609, Fort Erie, Ont. L2A 5X3

CHAPTER ONE

JENNY DIXON WAS SIXTEEN.

Jenny Dixon was a cheerleader.

Jenny Dixon was driving home from practice when her Toyota was broadsided by a drunk driver.

Jenny Dixon is dead.

Dr. Phillip Barry, pulling into the underground garage of his Seacliff apartment, was stricken suddenly with exhaustion. He parked the car in its allotted space, climbed the stairs to the front door, unlocked it and threw himself on the sofa, where he fell asleep almost instantly.

Jenny Dixon is dead.

He sat up with a start, shook his head. The phone was ringing.

"Phillip?" His ex-wife, Deanna. "Were you sleeping?"

"No...yes." He dug his knuckles into his eyes. "I'm fine. What's up?"

"I was calling to talk about Molly. You said you'd have her this weekend, remember?" A pause. "Phillip. Are you okay? I ran into your brother at the market and he said you've been looking like hell lately—"

"I'm fine." He tried to recall exactly when he'd agreed that Molly, their sixteen-year-old daughter, would spend the weekend; not that he didn't want her, but things seemed to be getting away from him lately. Nothing big, nothing outside of the O.R., thank God, just conversations, appointments, things like that. He leaned his head against the couch back and closed his eyes. "So what's the deal? I pick up Molly, or will you bring—"

"Phillip, we've already talked about this…I'm concerned about you. Joe is, too. It's that damn…that Dixon case, isn't it? Phillip, you're human, for God's sake. You go on burning the candle at both ends long enough and something's going to give. Anyway, why should you blame yourself? I don't see Stu going aroung wringing his hands—everyone deserves some time off once in a while, when was the last time—"

"So do you want me to pick up Molly?"

"Okay, you're not going to listen to me, I might as well save my breath. I just want you to think about something. Molly needed you. Needs you. This girl's death wasn't your fault. It wasn't your fault a bus overturned. It wasn't your fault the paramedics had to drive her around…"

With Deanna's voice in his ear, Phillip got up from the couch and wandered over to the opened French doors. Straight ahead, the Pacific stretched endlessly. On either side he could see, in his peripheral vision, the balconies of his neighbors. Smoke from someone's grill wafted briefly into the room.

"…I don't mean to sound callous or anything," Deanna was saying, "but instead of dwelling on the what-ifs, why don't you just think about what it means to Molly that you're available once in a while. Like her birthday, for example…"

Phillip came back inside, slid the doors shut and returned to the couch. The headline in that morning's *Tribune* had asked, Did Jenny Have To Die? Maybe not, he was forced to admit. If he and Stu, his partner, hadn't decided just weeks before Jenny Dixon's accident to suspend emergency neurosurgical services to Seacliff's trauma center…if a tourist bus hadn't tumbled down a mountainous ravine just east of the city, swamping other local centers with injured passengers…if Jenny had been immediately airlifted instead of being driven around in an ambulance… If, if, if. An endless wheel of *ifs* circling unmercifully through his brain.

AS SOON AS SHE HEARD the morning weather report announcing a hurricane in the Gulf of Mexico, Zoe McCann knew that the winds traveling up from Baja wouldn't be the day's only storm. The announcer's voice on the clock radio—specifically his mention of the words *historic surf*—had woken her from sleep.

Adrenaline coursing through her body, Zoe pulled on jeans and grabbed a flannel shirt from the pile of clean laundry that she'd intended to put away the night before and ran, barefoot, downstairs to the kitchen to grab her keys.

"That bastard," she muttered to herself as she climbed into her truck. "I swear to God, I'll kill him."

Ten minutes later—it would have been five but for the morning commuter traffic—she drove her pickup south on Pacific Coast Highway, the car radio blaring something unintelligible. *Jeez.* She punched buttons, searching for something other than the punk rock that always screamed from the speakers after her son Brett had used the truck.

"...and the continued fallout from the tragic death of a local teenager has prompted a Seacliff city councilman to propose financial incentives ranging from five hundred to one thousand dollars or more a day to lure neurosurgeons back into providing on-call services."

Financial rewards to lure neurosurgeons.

Disgusted, Zoe snapped off the radio. Money always took care of everything. A thousand dollars in Dr. Phillip Barry's hot little hand and Jenny Dixon might be alive today.

She glanced out through the passenger window to the ocean where great feathery sprays of foam were shooting into the air. She'd lived her whole life in California, but she never took the ocean for granted. Whether it was that weird churning green it sometimes turned in winter, or the pale blue silk of early summer, the water inspired her. However cranky she might feel, twenty minutes or so watching the waves generally did the trick. Except, of course, if she happened to notice that another small beach cottage along the cliffs had been razed to make room for some hideous megamansion that blocked views for everyone except the self-absorbed morons who lived in them.

Like Dr. Phillip Barry.

The car ahead had Nebraska plates and the driver had slowed to a crawl while everyone in the vehicle rubbernecked at the view. Zoe moved them along with two quick bleeps on the horn. Fingers tapping the steering wheel, she drove past Diamond Beach— where distant black figures out in the breaking waves might, to the uninitiated, be frolicking dolphins—finally slowing down as she reached the bluffs.

The line of parked pickup trucks and battered cars with oxidized paint jobs started halfway up the hill and ended just opposite the power plant on the other side of the street.

Zoe parked at the bottom of the hill, turned off the ignition and drew a deep breath. "Please," she prayed, imagining Denny's goofy grin, "just this once let him surprise me by not being a selfish, irresponsible idiot whose mental development was arrested sometime around the age of seventeen."

She grabbed the key from the ignition, slid out of the truck and walked briskly along the line of vehicles. Breeze from the ocean tossed her hair around, blowing hunks of it across her face. She glanced at her reflection in the passenger window of a parked car and wished she hadn't. On its rare good days, her hair had this long, curly, just-fallen-out-of-bed look about it; the rest of the time it was a dense, kinky uncombable mess that she usually controlled with combs and scrunchies or whatever else was on hand. Today, it looked vaguely like a collie's coat.

Her ex-husband's battered red pickup truck, surfboard sticking up like a dorsal fin from the truck bed, was right where she knew it would be. And so was her ex-husband. Burly—and that was charitable—wearing black-and-gray-flowered Bermudas and a white tank top, his feet encased in flip-flops. A pair of binoculars in hand, he gazed out at the water.

She took another breath. Everything about Denny McCann, from the black tufts of hair on his big toes to his stupid goatee, annoyed Zoe, but what was sending her out of the stratosphere right now was the confirmation of her suspicion. Standing there beside his father—both of them towering above her—was her sixteen-year-old son, Brett, a towel wrapped modestly around his waist as he shimmied into his black rubber wet suit. Neither of them saw her coming.

She noticed Denny had shaved his head, a pathetic attempt to cover a bald spot, but, to give him credit, better than a toupee or a comb-over. He had set his binoculars on the cab of the truck and was tugging at the zipper of Brett's suit. Brett, adolescent skinny, had his back to her.

She tapped her son on the shoulder.

"School?" she inquired, and he whirled around, eyes wide.

"Mom, just let me explain, okay?"

"Get in the car," she said. "Now."

"I'll handle this, son." Denny eyed Zoe cautiously, as one might a rabid dog. "You gotta understand—"

"No, I don't *gotta understand* anything." She jerked her head in the direction of the parked cars. "In the car, Brett. Now."

"But Mom, the surf is, like, historic. Tell her, Dad." He looked at his father. "There haven't been waves this big since—"

"In the car." Zoe stared him down until he headed, slump shouldered and sighing noisily, toward her car. The sight of her son's skinny brown back, knobby spine poking between the unzipped sides of the wet suit, swelled her heart. Brett lived to surf, a passion shared by his father. Slight difference though between a sixteen-year-old kid living for monster waves and a forty-year-old delayed adolescent whose failure to hold a steady job could be largely attributed to his practice of calling in sick whenever surfing conditions warranted it.

"This is the last time he stays with you on a school night," she told his father. "Got it?"

Denny had his arms folded across his chest and a look on his face that said he'd be damned if he'd let his nutcase of an ex-wife dictate the way things were going to go. Still, his eyes lingered long enough on the front of her shirt that she thought maybe a breast had broken free. She was going through a Mother Earth phase, all hips and boobs—a side effect of some recent experimentation with bread baking and, of course, tasting. A quick glance confirmed nothing more revealing than a bunch of cleavage and some strained buttons, but it was vintage Denny to argue with her and ogle at the same time.

"Don't go giving me a bunch of crap, Zoe," he was saying. "I was going to take him to school. He said there was nothing much going on this morning, so I figured it was no big deal if he missed an hour or two."

"Well, you figured wrong." Zoe stabbed her index finger at his chest. "If you *ever* pull this again…if you *ever* keep him out of school—I don't care if it's for five minutes—without clearing it with me first I will personally shove that goddamned surfboard down your throat—and don't think I couldn't do it."

"You need to get a life—"

"And you need to send me last month's child-support check," she shot back. "When can I expect it?"

"If you took him out of that goddamned snob school, you wouldn't always be short of money."

Zoe cupped a hand to her ear. "I can expect it when?"

"What the hell's wrong with public schools?"

"I'm sorry." Zoe smacked the side of her head. "My hearing must be going. You said you're going to write me a check right now?"

"Damn it, Zoe." He opened the passenger door and ducked his head inside. "You're not the only one with expenses."

"Need a pen?"

"Go to hell." He fished a checkbook from the glove compartment and made a big performance out of writing the amount. "And while we're talking about this, don't think I'm footing the bill for some Ivy League university. No reason he can't go to community college like I did." He signed his name with a flourish, and held out the check. "Brett tell you about his girlfriend?"

Zoe took the check. "He doesn't have a girlfriend."

Denny smirked. "Like he's going to tell mommy anyway." *Gotcha,* his expression said. "He's not gonna tell you *nothing.*"

"Well, that's good news," Zoe said. "That means he'll be telling me *something,* right?"

The smirk faded. "Shut the hell up, Zoe. If you were half as damn smart as you think you are, you wouldn't be selling vegetables."

Zoe smiled. "If I were half as damn smart as I think I am, I obviously wouldn't have married you in the first place." She watched the color creep up the side of his neck. She could almost hear his brain whirring as he struggled to regain the upper hand— *Let's see, how can I really zap her?*

"Me and him had a little talk last night," he finally said. "Man to man, like. 'Gotta use a condom,' I told him, 'or some girl's going to trap you just like your mom trapped me.'"

BRETT'S MUFFIN POPPED out of the toaster and he spread peanut butter on it. His mom and Rhea were in the kitchen making soup and reading out loud from a cookbook that was propped up against a clay pot he'd made in some art class when he was a little kid. Rhea had been there when he got home from school.

"I don't see why you couldn't make this with fresh lima beans," his mom was saying to Rhea. "Let's just improvise, okay. I hate following recipes."

Rhea laughed and winked at him. "Rules, recipes...your mom marches to her own drummer," she said.

"Yeah," Brett agreed. Whatever that meant. He screwed the lid back on the peanut butter, put the knife in the sink. His mom was wearing a long yellow skirt—that he'd heard her tell Rhea she'd made out of a tablecloth—and a tight black sweater and her hair was tied up with this Indian scarf. He knew what it was because she had Indian scarves pinned up all over her bedroom, on the ceiling and walls, along with dried roses and big velvet pillows everywhere. Old black-and-white pictures all over the place, lamps with scarves all over them, which drove his grandma crazy because she said it was a fire hazard and one of these days his mom was going to set the house on fire. His grandma said his mom's room looked like a Gypsy caravan.

Everything his mom did drove his grandma crazy, but his mom said that wasn't her problem. His mom was kinda different, the way she dressed and acted and everything, but he was used to it—except like this morning when she freaked out about him going surfing. He was still kinda mad about the way she made him feel like some stupid kid in front of his dad, but when his mom got some idea in her head, forget about anything else.

Rhea looked pretty much like everyone else's

mom. Sweats and jeans and normal hair. Rhea was Jenny's mom. Jenny got hit on her way home from practice by a drunk driver and she died. It was about the worst thing that ever happened in his life. Afterward everyone started talking about how it shouldn't have happened and taking sides not just about the drunk driver, although everyone including his mom got plenty fired up about that, but how it shouldn't be that kids died because they couldn't get taken care of and everything. It happened, like about six months ago, but it seemed like there was always more stuff about it on TV or something.

He still couldn't believe Jenny wasn't just going to show up one day, like she'd played some joke on them or something. He'd known Jenny practically forever. She'd been like his sister. Well, except she was always claiming he'd kissed her when they were in nursery school. *Right*. Girls always claimed they remembered dumb-ass stuff like that, but Jenny was cool. They'd been better friends when he was still going to the old high school. She said he was stuck-up now, which even she knew was a bunch of bull because he couldn't stand stupid Country Day Academy.

Anyway, if it wasn't Rhea in the kitchen with his mom, it would be someone else. People were always coming over to his house. Friends his mom hadn't seen for years who just happened to stop by, neighbors he didn't know but who knew his mom. Some crazy old woman she'd met at the grocery store who had been trying to pay for her stuff with play money.

His mom ended up paying for the old lady's stuff, then bringing her here till some relative could come and take her back home.

He and his mom lived in this big house that his dad said his mom should sell and buy a condominium or something, and it seemed like there was always someone sleeping in the guest bedroom until they got their act together. His mom was pretty cool that way, she'd leave them to themselves—sometimes he wished she'd do that with him, instead of making him feel like some bug under a microscope—listen to them, if they wanted to talk, make them food.

Everyone said his mom had a big heart. For everything. People. Dogs or cats that just showed up one day. *A sheep.* No kidding. Last year they'd gone to the county fair and she'd bought this sheep because some guy said it was going to be dog food. It wasn't even like a cute little lamb or anything. It was this huge, woolly pillow-shaped thing that his mom said looked like Tony Bennett, whoever that was.

She called it Svetlana and sang this dumb song to it. *"I left my heart,"* she'd go, *"in Baabaa Frisco."* And then she'd crack up at how funny she was and all her friends would be laughing, too. Except for his dad, who called his mom a head case, everyone thought his mom was really cool. People were always calling her a character and he guessed she was a pretty good mom, except that sometimes she was also kind of embarrassing the way she just said whatever she thought.

"So, Brett—" Rhea scooped onions up in both hands and dropped them into the frying pan "—are you beating the girls off with sticks?"

"He'd better be," his mom said. "If he isn't, I will."

"Omigod, Zoe." Rhea was looking at the little TV on the kitchen counter. "Look. It's Phillip Barry. He's—"

"Shh." His mom flapped her hands at Rhea. "Listen."

Brett watched the screen. Dr. Barry wasn't really doing anything, just walking along some corridor, dressed in blue scrubs, like maybe he'd just come from surgery. His arms and face were tanned and he had bright blue eyes. It was weird knowing who he was because he looked kinda like an actor on *ER* or something. Now he was taking off this blue paper cap and he had brown hair that was cut way, way short, and some gray in the front. His mom had this thing about Phillip Barry. She knew him from when they were both little kids and she said the whole family was a bunch of snobs. He was some big-shot brain surgeon at Seacliff, and his mom claimed that if he'd been there to take care of Jenny, she wouldn't have died. He had this truly weird daughter, Molly, who was in his class at Country Day and was always following him around and saying dumb things.

"Taking care of high-risk patients requires you to have a bit of an ego…" Dr. Barry was saying.

"No kidding," his mom said, all sarcastic, like, *duh.*

"Mom, when's dinner?"

"Uno momento, sweetie."

His mom was still watching Dr. Barry. She had this vegetable in one hand, like a carrot but whitish-brown, and a knife in the other one.

"Idiot, jerk—"

"Shh," Rhea put her finger over her mouth.

"I have a hot date with a cool babe," Brett said, just to shake things up. Like what did he care about what Molly Barry's dad was saying? "Be back around midnight."

"What?" His mom swiveled around to look at him. "I'll give you midnight." She was trying not to laugh. "Go do your homework. Dinner will be ready when you're through."

"What are we having?"

"Lima bean and summer squash soup." She was watching TV again. "Go. I'll call you when it's ready."

Yech. Like he'd want to know.

Upstairs, he lay on the bed. His mom knew that Dr. Barry's daughter Molly went to Country Day. What she didn't know was how weird Molly was. Like how she was always following him around and saying she was his girlfriend and if he didn't start liking her she was going to kill herself.

"ON MANY DAYS, by the time the staff arrives at the office," the TV announcer was saying, "Dr. Barry and his partner have already performed two surgeries and started rounds at the hospital."

"It's hectic, no question about it." Barry was sitting behind a desk now. "When I first decided to go into neurosurgery, someone I greatly respected said to me, "If you're going to be a true professional, not just do the job, it's really difficult to be a decent husband or a father, and you certainly can't do anything else, like have any sort of social life. It's a real struggle.""

"My heart bleeds." Zoe poured away the water the lima beans had been soaking in, and melted butter in the bottom of a pan. "Turn it off if you want," she told Rhea, now feeling kind of insensitive that she hadn't turned it off as soon as Phillip Barry's face appeared on the screen. That morning's headline still haunted her. *Did Jenny Have To Die?* Imagine picking up the paper to read that. Like it's not devastating enough to lose your child, but then you find out that she's dead because some doctor wants to play golf. She watched as the onions turned transparent. Okay, she didn't know for a fact that Phillip Barry wanted to play golf, but what doctor didn't?

"Hey…" Rhea reached over Zoe's shoulder to turn down the flame. "If you're going to obsess, I'm gonna pack up my tent and leave."

"I'm not obsessing."

"You've burned the onions, you pulverized the carrots. Jenny was *my* daughter, Zoe. If I'm not angry—"

"Okay, okay." Zoe shook her head. "I'm not angry."

"I said if you're going to obsess."

"I'm not obsessing."

"Yes, you are."

"What am I obsessing about?"

"It happened, Zoe." Her voice cracked. "Look, I know you wouldn't purposely do anything to hurt me, but I'm trying very hard to deal with everything and your anger doesn't exactly help, okay? I mean, God, it's difficult enough—"

"Rhee, I'm so sorry." Zoe set down the spoon she'd been using and wrapped her arms around Rhea. "I'm sorry, really, I just get on these rampages and…look at me. What can I do?"

Rhea gave a weary smile and shook her head. "Nothing. Just go on being Zoe, but…maybe a teensy bit less angry at the world?"

Later after Rhea left, Zoe cleaned the kitchen and set out cereal and bowls for Brett's breakfast tomorrow. It was hard not to get angry. She and Rhea had gone over the whole thing so many times. Cried together over innumerable cups of herbal tea, wept over bowls of flax muffin mix, talked themselves hoarse into the wee hours. Rhea, Zoe could tell, was moving toward an acceptance of Jenny's death that she personally couldn't master. She was angry, furious. Did Jenny Have To Die? That was the title of the front page article in the paper today. *No,* she wanted to scream. Not if Dr. Phillip Barry had been there to do what doctors are supposed to do. Reason told her that this was flawed, simplistic thinking, but reason was no match for furious, impotent anger.

CHAPTER TWO

A SWOOSH OF THE AUTOMATIC DOORS announced Phillip's arrival in the operating room. His hands and forearms dripping, he dried them with a sterile towel, unfolded a gown and slid both arms through the sleeves. Without a word, one of the circulating nurses tied the gown behind him; a scrub nurse removed a pair of gloves from their paper-wrapped package and held them out for him.

"Your handmaidens," his ex-wife used to call them.

His first surgery of the day was an eight-year-old boy who had been sleeping in the back seat of his father's pickup truck. The truck had stopped for a red light just as a couple of rival gang members were shooting at each other from opposite sides of the road. The stray bullet had torn through the side of the truck, ricocheted off the floorboard and penetrated the boy's brain. In the blink of an eye, half of his right brain had been destroyed.

The human nervous system is an amazing, even elegant, structure, Phillip often pointed out to patients and their families. It allows us to feel, move, see, hear, smile and taste. It allows us to experience pleasure, as well as pain. It is essentially the organ system that defines us as human beings. And, by and large, we take it all for granted—until a bullet rips through it.

Or, as in the case of his daughter, Molly, something seems to go suddenly and inexplicably awry.

"I'm fine now, Daddy, really," she was reassuring him as they walked along the beach below his Seacliff home that night. "I learned my lesson, I swear I'll never be that stupid again. Why are you wearing shoes to walk on the beach?"

"Shoes?" Phillip glanced absently at his feet, sockless but in a pair of old Topsiders. "No idea." He put his arm around her shoulder and squeezed her close. Molly had attempted suicide just over six months ago. Her second try in a little over a year.

"You really need to loosen up," Molly said. "Quit working so hard. Go barefoot once in a while."

Phillip took a moment to appreciate the irony of what his daughter had just said. And, briefly, to register the glint of orange light on the windows of the houses on the cliffs above them. The tide was out, the sun low in the sky. The evening was cool and gray—a California weather phenomenon TV weather people called June Gloom. Both he and Molly wore heavy sweaters and jeans. Molly, barefoot, held her sneakers in one hand.

By the time he'd arrived at the hospital, Molly was having her stomach pumped. A fleeting sense of relief that paramedics hadn't taken her to Seacliff, where everyone knew him—her boarding school had been too far away for Seacliff to have been an option—left him with a dull guilt that still hadn't entirely disappeared.

His ex-wife, Molly's mother, had been similarly relieved. Ever since her latest self-help book, *My Daughter, My Best Friend,* had begun climbing into the lower reaches of the *New York Times* extended bestseller list, Deanna lived in constant fear of bad publicity.

"I'm serious, Daddy," Molly was saying now. "When was the last time you had any fun?"

"I don't know, Moll." He heard the impatience in his voice. "Let's talk about you first."

"I've figured things out, I told you. I mean I can't believe I tried to end *my* life just because some stupid boy made such a mess of his own life that he'd totally lost touch with reality," Molly said. "I swear to God, never again. From now on, I'm taking charge of my own life."

Phillip thought about the first boy to set Molly's life adrift. Spirit, who Phillip had tracked down one bright summer morning, at work—the sidewalk spot where the kid drew whales and sea horses in pastel-colored chalk for the coins and occasional dollar bills dropped into the coffee can next to his box of art supplies—in the slim hope that he could shed some light on why Molly had set fire to the bed in her dormitory. Phillip had guessed that Spirit, who had green hair and wore a nose ring, was probably in his late twenties.

"I don't know, man…" Spirit's gaze had drifted somewhere beyond Phillip's left shoulder. "No offense or anything, I mean I know she's your daughter and all, but Molly is one seriously weird chick."

Molly's story had been that Spirit, with whom she was "like totally, totally in love," had given her an ultimatum: sell everything she owned and take off with him to Belize, or the relationship was over. It was anger over the unfairness of his demand, she'd explained, that had caused her to set fire to her bed.

But Spirit had claimed at first that he didn't even know Molly. Only after Phillip produced a picture from his billfold, did the kid remember that, "Yeah, I've seen her like a couple of times, hanging out at this coffee place." Once she'd dropped a five-dollar bill into his coffee can and tried to give him her emerald ring, which Spirit, astoundingly and to his credit, had refused to accept.

"I figured she was, like, strung out on something," he'd told Phillip, "and I didn't want problems with, you know, like stolen merchandise or something."

The ring had been handed down to Molly from her great-grandmother.

Molly had been on medication ever since and, until this latest attempt, had been doing fairly well. This time they'd taken her to see a psychiatrist in Santa Barbara. Far enough away from Seacliff to feel comfortable that they were unlikely to run into anyone they knew. The psychiatrist, who had Art Garfunkel hair and round eyeglasses, had offered

Phillip a preliminary diagnosis. Affective schizo-phrenic disorder, the term set out there like a bomb.

"Bull," Phillip had responded. Okay, she was going through a weird period, she had a tendency to overdramatize—as did her mother—but this was his daughter. Bright, pretty, resourceful, a great kid. Everyone loved Molly. She had her life ahead of her. The psychiatrist had leaned back in his chair, the faintest suspicion of a smirk on his face. *So. How does it feel to be on the receiving end of bad news?* Phillip remembered folding his arms across his chest, then unfolding them in case this was inter-preted as resistance.

"Look, I'm ready to try anything that will help Molly," he'd told the psychiatrist. "Frankly, though, I find it difficult to accept…" Hearing himself, he stopped and started over. "My own professional judgment tells me that Molly is going through a con-fused period and would certainly benefit from in-tensive therapy, but I absolutely refuse to accept this diagnosis. In fact, I find it patently absurd." He'd heard his voice growing louder, felt his anger build-ing. "You're probably thinking, denial," he'd said. "I run into the same response myself—no parent wants to hear that their child will never walk again—but Molly's a different matter altogether and I refuse to allow her to be stigmatized by a hastily made diag-nosis."

As a consequence of this latest incident, and over Molly's protests, they'd transferred their daughter to a small and expensive private school that promised

"...a high degree of attention to each and every one of our student's unique and special needs and abilities." Deanna had agreed to cut down on book promotions that required extensive periods of out-of-town travel, and he'd suspended Seacliff's emergency neurosurgical services.

And then a sixteen-year-old girl with head injuries had died in an ambulance.

He hadn't slept through the night since.

ZOE LOVED EVERYTHING involved in growing and selling vegetables, but farmer's market days were the best. Three times a week, she'd load fruit, vegetables and flowers into the back of the pickup truck and drive to whatever town was having their market. Today was market day in Seacliff, which, hands down, had to be the coolest site in California with all the stalls grouped around the perimeter of a grassy park overlooking the Pacific. From where she sat under a blue Cinzano umbrella, Zoe could see the white froth of waves breaking on the rocks below. The jingle of an ice-cream bell and the throb of rock music provided an audio backdrop to the green, blue and gold of grassy verges, cloudless sky and sun-dappled strollers. Artists sat on folding chairs, their paintings leaned and stacked, bright rectangles of color. Flags fluttered from the artisan stalls where some of her friends sold jewelry, pottery, leather belts and sandals.

Zoe never thought of herself as an artist, or, as her mother would say, an *artiste,* but some early, misty mornings, as she arranged her produce she'd feel like a painter contemplating a palette: lemon-colored squash, like little bananas, tiny burgundy beets all cunningly arranged in a bed of bright green parsley. In adjacent baskets, plump green butter lettuce just picked from the garden; huge bunches of red-stemmed Swiss chard, feathery bronze fennel, and silver-blue heads of cabbage. Miniature eggplants that tasted like melon and sweet thumbnail-sized golden tomatoes.

On either side, were the stalls of her friends Roz and Sandy. Sandy grew and sold herbs and different kinds of lavender. Roz made honey—clover, wildflower and lavender, courtesy of hives from Sandy's fields—and always had some hilarious story about bee-related mishaps. Rhea, the fourth member of the group they called Market Mamas, sold bread that she baked herself—intricately braided glossy brown baguettes, soft floury loaves. Rhea hadn't been back to the market since Jenny died, but Zoe had started selling home-baked bread and donating the money to a fund established in Jenny's name.

"Brett wishes I'd sell bread instead of vegetables," she said now. "But check this out." She grabbed the roll of flesh between the dirndl waist of her paisley skirt and the bottom of her white peasant blouse. "Molasses, oatmeal, raisin. I've got a pumpernickel loaf on each hip."

"Jeez, I could have sworn that was the jelly doughnuts you talked us into eating this morning," Sandy said.

"*I* talked *you* into eating jelly doughnuts?" Zoe scoffed. "My arm still has marks from your fingernails."

"Just trying to get my share." Sandy gestured with her coffee cup at a blond surfer type browsing at a nearby stall. "Thirty? Thirty-five?"

"Try nineteen," Zoe said, taking a closer look. Checking out the passersby, specifically the reasonably attractive male passersby on this side of fifty—although they kept pushing up the age limit—was a favorite pastime. They were all divorced and, if not actively looking, at least appreciative. They all had kids, too, teenagers—which was mostly what they yakked about. Sandy's oldest son, Brian, had just gone off to medical school where, according to his mother, he spent as much time chasing babes as he did earning his degree. Dr. Biff, Sandy called him— Biff, the nickname Zoe had always known him by. God, time flies, they were always saying. Before long, her own son would be going off to medical school. The thought always gave her a thrill—she'd be even more thrilled when Brett started getting serious about it, too, but that day would come.

Roz's daughter had, according to Roz, little ambition other than to get married and have babies. Rhea's Jenny had shared her mother's passion for cooking and had been planning to attend culinary school. One of Zoe's favorite memories was of walking into Rhea's kitchen and seeing mother and daughter, their two dark heads almost touching, poring over a recipe, or giggling together over some culinary mishap. Since Jenny's death, so many white hairs had sprouted in Rhea's wiry dark hair that, from a distance, she seemed to have gone completely gray.

No one had confessed to it, of course, but Zoe had detected an almost palpable sense of relief when she'd told the others that Rhea wouldn't be coming to the market for a while. They loved her like a sister and would do anything for her, but it sometimes seemed as though Rhea had contracted a contagious disease.

Would there ever be a time, Zoe wondered, when their thoughts wouldn't inevitably end up with Jenny? For her own part, as soon as she started thinking about Rhea, her mind immediately turned to trying to figure out some way to prevent the same thing from happening to someone else. And there was only one solution: the trauma center *had* to reopen. Everyone knew neurosurgeons made megabucks—more in a year than she'd make in a dozen, so how hard could it be to find a replacement? It seemed all wrong just to sit back and think, God, I hope nothing happens to my family.

"How much is the lettuce?" A woman in a straw hat and a diaphanous turquoise pantsuit interrupted Zoe's reverie. Like a crane in a fun fair machine, one fat beringed hand swooped down on the lettuce, lifted it and dangled it between thumb and forefinger under Zoe's nose.

"Seventy-five cents," Zoe said.

"They're selling iceberg three for a dollar at the stall down there."

Zoe looked at her. "These aren't iceberg."

"What's the difference?"

"Taste." Zoe offered the woman the ice-chilled bowl of samples, and watched her nibble gingerly at a single lettuce leaf. *Dying,* Zoe just knew, to ask if it had been washed. "Pretty good, huh?"

The woman sniffed. "Can't tell the difference, personally."

"Then you should get the iceberg," Zoe said.

The woman set the lettuce down and reached for another one. Holding it aloft, she inspected it from all angles.

It's a damn lettuce, lady. "Picked just this morning," she told the woman.

"So it's two for a dollar-fifty?" the woman asked.

"Yep." Zoe smiled at a couple of teenage girls who had stopped to sniff the pots of basil at the end of the table. "You like pesto?" she asked. "I've got a killer recipe."

"Cool." One of the girls picked up a pot and fished in the bulging straw bag she was carrying. "How much?"

"Dollar-fifty." Zoe took the bills the girl handed her, made change and handed over a recipe card.

"They're not all the same size." The lettuce woman was still checking things out. "You should charge less for the smaller ones."

"Or more for the bigger ones." Zoe imagined hurling an overripe tomato. *Splaat.* Like a caste mark, right in the middle of the woman's forehead

"Typical Seacliff," Roz muttered as the woman walked away.

Zoe grinned. Seacliff might be one of the most picturesquely located farmer's markets, but it had the lion's share of patronizing, demanding customers. Not surprising, really. Seacliff was one of those chichi California coastal communities where you either were very rich, or you worked for the very rich. Phillip Barry's family was very rich, old family money. Until they were thirteen and fifteen respectively, Zoe and her sister Courtney had grown up in a cottage on the Barry family's oceanfront Seacliff estate, where their mother, Janna, worked as the housekeeper for Phillip Barry's family.

These days, Phillip, the oldest of the four Barry sons, was a hotshot surgeon at Seacliff Medical Center, while she grew vegetables that she sold at farmers' markets and occasionally delivered in fancy wicker baskets to oceanfront houses where people like Phillip Barry lived.

Although she didn't live in Seacliff anymore— wouldn't want to even if she could afford to—her son Brett...trumpets and fanfare please...attended school there, the same elite private academy that Phillip Barry's daughter, Molly, now attended. Brett hadn't been thrilled about changing schools, but the classrooms at the high school were overcrowded, the teaching impersonal and his grades had been dropping. After one semester at Country Day, Zoe had seen enough improvement that, in her mind at least, it justified the expense.

To her way of thinking, Brett himself justified the expense. Not to be overdramatic or anything, but

Brett was her life. Plus, he was a terrific kid—bright, popular and destined for big things. And she'd do anything to make them happen. It took endless scrimping and saving, but if sending him to a good school meant starving herself, which, God knows, she never had, or dressing in thrift-shop clothing— which, no problem at all, she did—her son would never, *ever* have to settle for second best.

She'd never met Molly Barry, but Brett said she had been kicked out of the last fancy school she'd attended and only got into Country Day because her parents were big shots in the community. That's what drove Zoe crazy about the excuse Phillip Barry had given for closing emergency services. "We have to protect our families." Huh, if his family came first, she was Mother Teresa.

Maybe that's what got under her skin. Parents *should* put their children first, all the time, and not just after the kids had run so far off the rails that their school expelled them. Maybe she'd organize a protest group. Parents Putting Kids First. PAPUKIFI. Sounded like some exotic Hawaiian fruit.

She grabbed a tube of sunblock from her purse under the counter and dabbed the cream on her nose, which had an annoying habit of turning crimson in the sun. Her shoulders and arms were beginning to freckle, and the tops of her breasts were getting a little toasty, too.

Tonight, she suddenly remembered, was her mother's barbecue. These days Janna was a high-powered real-estate broker. She was also about to become engaged to her boss, Arnie. Zoe had quickly discovered that Arnie knew everything, including what Zoe needed to do to go from growing and selling vegetables as a part-time hobby, his definition, to a dynamic business. Last week Janna had complained that Zoe didn't like Arnie.

"I adore Arnie," Zoe had said. "I worship the ground he walks on."

"You don't like him and he knows it," Janna shot back. "And I don't appreciate your sarcasm. Arnie doesn't understand why he can't…connect with you. He and Courtney get along beautifully. She had us over for cocktails last week and we all had a wonderful time. Arnie gets such a kick out of Brett."

This had prompted Zoe to ask her mother what exactly she'd meant by the remark. Janna had laughed and reached forward to squeeze Zoe's chin. "Oh, honey, you should see your face. I mention Brett's name and you're immediately on the defensive." She'd laughed some more. "It's so cute, you're like a little terrier sniffing out injustice."

"I am not." Her face had gone hot. "I just asked what Arnie found so funny about Brett."

"I didn't say that," Janna had corrected her. " I said Arnie got a kick out of him." Her hand shot out again, but this time Zoe ducked. "See what I mean about you being defensive," Janna said.

Thinking of Arnie now, Zoe decided that what she'd really get a kick out of would be shoving Arnie and his Mercedes off the cliff. For good measure she'd send fancy-schmancy Phillip Barry along for the ride. She felt hot and disgruntled and tired of people in general.

A woman who was inspecting the bunches of blue delphinium that Zoe had picked that morning selected a bouquet and handed her a ten-dollar bill. Zoe forced herself to smile. She knew she should be focusing on her customers, but her thoughts kept wandering to that conversation with her mother.

"Don't tell Arnie that I used to be a housekeeper," Janna had reminded her. Janna's pretensions drove her crazy. What the hell did it matter if Janna had once been a housekeeper? In fact, sometimes she imagined herself walking into Phillip Barry's office and cashing in on the family connection as a way to get a discussion started about the trauma services. *Hi, I used to be the housekeeper's daughter...*

"Parsnip," she said aloud to a surfer type a few years older than Brett as he slowed down by her stall to inspect the cartons of fruit and vegetables. "Here." She handed him a recipe card. "You've probably never cooked them, right?"

He grinned. "I thought they were albino carrots."

"Gotta grate 'em, though, that's the trick."

"I'll remember that," he said.

"And don't forget the honey," Roz said, "which I just happen to have on sale at the next stall."

"Cool."

Zoe watched his face. The kid was about as likely to go home and cook parsnips as she was to invite Phillip Barry to join her in a cup of coffee, just for old times' sake. *And, while I'm here, not to get per-*

sonal or anything, but how could you just let a girl die?

She shook her head. "So, how many pounds you want?" *Focus,* she told herself. On the customer, not on Phillip Barry.

"Uh…"

"How about a pound to start with?" She grabbed a plastic bag and delved into the crate of parsnips, picked out a couple, inspected them briefly, then discarded them. "Gonna find you some real good ones," she told him.

"He's going to find the nearest bin and dump them," Sandy said a few moments later. "Cute buns though." She eased herself up from the chair. "Guess I better go troll for a while."

"IT'S THAT DAMN farmer's market," the real estate agent was explaining to Phillip as she tried to find a spot to park her Mercedes. "Not that I don't like fresh vegetables, but I swear to God, every Wednesday, the parking is a nightmare. And the worse thing is, it brings in the hordes from all around. Let them go to their own markets, for God's sake. Now this first house I'm going to show you is right on the bluffs. You can sip a martini on the balcony and watch the sun set."

"Sounds good." He decided it wasn't worth mentioning that he couldn't remember the last time he'd been home in time to watch the sun set. "It's on Neptune, you said?"

She turned to smile at him. "You know Neptune?"

"My family's place was—"

"Oh, of course." She shook her head. "Silly me. When you told me your last name, I remembered thinking that you were probably one of those Barrys. Well good." She expertly maneuvered the Mercedes between a landscaper's truck and a sports car. "I always say, if you can afford Seacliff, why would you ever leave?"

CHAPTER THREE

"YOU'RE LOOKING in Seacliff, of course," Phillip's ex-wife said when she called from New York to ask about his house-hunting search.

"Seacliff and Seacliff Heights." He'd eaten a dinner of microwaved bean soup and had been dozing off over a pile of catch-up reading when the phone rang. "There was a house in the Heights—"

"*God*, Phillip. The Heights is awful. No ocean view and it's full of those hideous new places that they get away with charging millions for just because of the name. I don't want Molly living there."

Phillip picked up the journal he'd been reading when he fell asleep, realized he was still hungry and wandered into the kitchen. "I'm still looking," he said ambiguously. In fact the apartment he'd lived in since their divorce suited him just fine, but if Molly was going to live part-time with him, as he and Deanna had agreed, he needed something with more room. Which reminded him that his ex-wife had agreed to cut down on her traveling.

"Who is with Molly?" he asked. "I thought you weren't going to New York until next month."

"My mother is staying at the house...much to Molly's chagrin. *'I am not a child, I don't need a baby-sitter.'* Anyway, I wasn't supposed to be here, but they're having a reception for me. I thought it might seem churlish not to show up."

Deanna would never change, he decided, giving up and switching the subject to one that might be more productive. "So what's this about her charging up your credit cards?" he asked. Deanna had mentioned this in an earlier call to him at the hospital, but he hadn't had time to discuss it then.

"The new woman who's handling all of my business affairs called to question some purchases," Deanna said. "Specifically a three-hundred-dollar surfboard. She said she didn't think I was the surfing type."

Phillip carried the phone out to the balcony. The ocean was dark and calm. He sat down, leaned his head back against the glass of the French door. "Did you talk to Molly about it?"

"I'm in New York, Phillip. And, quite honestly, I'm losing patience for all this. What more could we possibly do for the girl? I haven't had a minute and I don't expect things to get better. You have no idea how completely exhausting these tours are. I've said I'll cut back and I will, but for now if you could take care of things—maybe have her for a few weeks, just to give my mother a break—I'd really appreciate it. I told you, didn't I, that I think it's a boy again?"

"*Specifically,* why do you think there's a boy this time?"

"Call it a mother's intuition."

Silence, Phillip decided, was the only tactful response.

"And, I just know it's one of those damn scholarship kids," she went on. "She gets these goofy ideas that it's up to her to save the world. I think she may have pawned my tennis bracelet. Before I left, I turned my room upside down—"

"Did you ask her?"

"No, Phillip, I didn't ask her. I'm striving for tranquility in my life and confronting Molly would be counterproductive—"

"Of course. Hell of a lot easier to let her pawn your jewelry."

"I didn't say she *was* pawning it, Phillip, I just said…oh, never mind. I don't know why I even try to discuss anything with you. All I know is I'm sick to death of it all…I don't care how politically incorrect it sounds, we're paying God knows how much to send her to the best damn school in the area and she's hanging out with…gardeners—"

"Gardeners?"

"I don't know," she said irritably. "The mother's a gardener or something. Molly said something about her selling vegetables. Hold on a second… okay, the boy's name is Brett. He's called several times. Here's his number."

Phillip took a deep breath. "What am I supposed to say? Leave my daughter alone because you're the son of a gardener?"

"Oh, for God's sake, Phillip. You're the brain surgeon, *you* figure something out. I've got a book due at the end of next month and my agent is pressing me for updates. I really don't have time for around-the-clock monitoring, nor, quite frankly, the inclination."

"Give me the number again." He took the phone back inside, jotted the number on the cover of last month's *New England Journal of Medicine,* ended the call and, with no idea what he was going to say, dialed the boy's number before he could talk himself out of calling altogether.

An answering machine.

"Hi, there, you've reached Zany Zoe at Growing My Way," the recording said. *"Asparagus and apples, beets and broccoli, carrots and cauliflower...well, you get the idea. Leave a message if you want to place an order, or drop by our stall at the Seacliff Farmer's Market.*

He hung up without leaving a message.

"OH, THESE ARE LOVELY, honey." Janna, at the door of Arnie's Seacliff Heights condo, took the bunch of mauve and pale blue larkspur Zoe handed her. "Hi, Brett, sweetie." She embraced her grandson in a quick hug. "God, you get more handsome every time I see you. Got a girlfriend yet?"

Brett grinned. "Can't talk about it," he said with a sly glance at Zoe.

"Tell Grandma," Janna said in a conspiratorial whisper. She'd evidently just come from the nail salon. Her nails—French tip—glistened in the sunlight, the aroma of fresh polish wafting all about her. Janna was fifty-eight but told everyone she was forty-five. A stretch, but on a good day, in the right lighting she could maybe pass. Tonight, she wore a cream linen pantsuit that flattered her curves and her hair was short, blond and artlessly unkempt, as though she didn't drop big bucks to keep it looking that way. People were always telling Janna that she looked more like Zoe's older sister than her mother and this thrilled Janna to no end.

"Come on." Janna cocked her head at Brett. "Don't be coy."

"Three," Brett whispered back. "But don't tell mom."

"You little devil," Janna chuckled.

Zoe folded her arms across her chest. "Maybe you can get some of them to help out about the place. Weed the flower beds, clean out the animal pens, stuff like that."

"You're no fun." Janna swiped at Zoe's arm. "Your cousins are in the den watching videos," she told Brett. "And Arnie's barbecuing salmon steaks out on the patio." She waited until Brett left, then brought her face close to Zoe's. "Sweetie, please, please remember, don't get into…you know, the housekeeper thing. Arnie thinks I lived for years in England."

"Was I born there?"

Janna eyed her for a moment. "Please don't be difficult, honey. This means a lot to me."

"I'm not. If we're going to have a revisionist history night, I just need to have my facts straight."

"You know, Courtney was perfectly fine with this. I don't understand—"

"Was Courtney born in England?"

Janna sighed. "Oh, just forget it, Zoe. I'm sorry I mentioned it. I didn't think it was that much to ask. Your skin's broken out, by the way," she said as she carried the flowers into the kitchen. "A big blotch on your neck."

Zoe's fingers moved automatically to her neck. Eczema. An irritating—literally—skin rash that appeared if she ate anything with fish in it, or got stressed about something, like whenever she dealt with her ex-husband. Of course, it was a whole lot easier not to eat fish than it was to avoid dealing with Denny.

Just as she was leaving the house, he'd called to say that he wanted to take Brett to the desert over the July Fourth weekend. She'd said no. One, it wasn't his weekend to have Brett, and two, the idea of Brett tearing around on his father's dune buggy terrified her. Brett, of course, wanted to go. "You never let me do anything fun," he'd complained as they drove over to the barbecue. "It's not fair."

"Life's not fair, honey," she'd said. At that moment, her left arm had started itching. By the time they got to Arnie's place, she had tracks up and down both arms, and the backs of her legs were burning like crazy.

Now she could smell the fish Arnie was cooking on the patio. Had it even occurred to Janna to mention her daughter's allergies? Probably not.

Her sister, Courtney, came into the kitchen, cell phone at her ear. Courtney's two kids from her first marriage, a boy and a girl, were several years older than Brett. The boy, Eric, parked cars at a Seacliff steak house, where his sister, Ellen, was a cocktail waitress. "They're both working in the service industry," Courtney was always explaining, "while they decide upon their future directions."

Translation, they'd both dropped out of junior college after a few semesters, and Ellen had moved in with her boyfriend. Not that Courtney would readily admit that: she'd recently remarried and worked as a receptionist in a travel agency, prompting Janna to describe her—without a trace of irony—as "my ambitious daughter."

"Okay, bye," Courtney said into the phone. "Love you, too. Big smooches, I won't be late." She hung up and gave Zoe a quick hug. "Hey, your skin's all broken out."

"I know."

"Arnie's cooking fish," Courtney said sotto voce, as she adjusted her pistachio-colored sarong and white halter top. To ensure that they showed off her figure to best advantage, Zoe thought. Tall, wheat-colored hair and thin, that was Courtney.

"I'll eat salad."

"Oh, my God." Janna, arranging the larkspur in a vase, clapped a hand to her mouth. "I forgot all about you, Zoe. Arnie wanted salmon and—"

"Don't worry about it, Mom." Janna would self-flagellate for the rest of the evening, and Zoe didn't want to hear it, especially since nine times out of ten Janna served fish when she invited them to dinner.

"Ever tried Benadryl?" Arnie appeared in the kitchen, carrying a platter of salmon. "That would clear it right up."

"Yep." She looked at Arnie, who was wearing white pants, the stretchy waist kind that older men played golf in, and a yellow polo-neck shirt with, naturally, Seacliff Country Club embroidered in discreet small lettering above the breast pocket. "Doesn't help."

"*I* could always keep it under control." Janna had started assembling a salad, overlapping circles of cucumbers, radishes and tomato on a bed of finely chopped lettuce. "I just didn't have time to be constantly after you to do it." She stood back to survey her handiwork. "That's the best I can do with iceberg. I meant to ask you to bring some of your little lettuces, Zoe." She turned to look at her daughter, frowned and leaned over to lightly stroke the top of Zoe's head, much as she might have petted a small dog.

"*Woof,*" Zoe said

"Did you have it cut again?"

"Just the bangs. Did it myself. Attractive, huh?"

"Honey." Janna's expression was strained. "Why do you do this sort of thing? I'd *give* you the money for a decent haircut."

Zoe raked her fingers through her hair. She'd paid last month's overdue feed-store bill with the forty dollars—or however much haircuts cost these days—she'd saved by not going to the beauty shop.

"*I* like it," she said.

Janna shook her head. "You have absolutely no vanity."

"Is that a good thing?"

Arnie was banging around, opening cabinets, setting out glasses. "Pay a million dollars for a place, and the damn doors don't shut properly. Say Zoe, d'you check out that entrepreneur site I told you about?"

Zoe ate a cherry tomato from the salad. "No." Through the tomato, it came out *dlo*. "Hey, did anyone catch Phillip Barry on TV?"

"Zoe's content to just muddle along," Janna told Arnie apologetically. "Courtney's my ambitious one. She takes after me. She knows that success doesn't come seeking you out, you have to actively pursue it."

"They might put me on commission," Courtney explained as she leaned against the counter. "*I* saw him, Zoe. Phillip Barry. Actually, I often see him around Seacliff." She looked at Arnie. "We know the Barrys from way back."

Janna loudly cleared her throat.

Courtney grinned. "Oops."

"The Barrys were neighbors of ours," Janna said. "For a while."

"We used to play with their kids," Courtney said. "Phillip was…what, three or four years older than me?" She looked at Zoe. "Remember cannibal?"

"Vaguely." Zoe turned to look out of the window. Brett and his cousins sat on the edge of a frothing hot tub. Brett was saying something and the other two were laughing. Ellen lifted a leg and splashed hard, showering Brett with a spray of water. The scene, obviously full of good-natured fun, seemed light-years away from her childhood memories.

One year, it seemed the Barry kids and Courtney had spent the entire summer playing cannibal in this great big metal bathtub. She could still see Phillip Barry's hateful smirk. He'd looked straight at her arms with their big red blotches and said, "You'll poison the pot."

And then the other kids had all laughed, even Courtney. "Screw you," Zoe had said. "I wouldn't go in there for a million dollars. I don't like Barry cooties in my food."

Zoe stayed at the window, watching Brett, who had moved to sit next to Ellen. They were all laughing now. She wondered what they were talking about. Had Brett told them about this girlfriend his father had mentioned? Probably. She suddenly felt shut out, and somehow extraneous.

"The other kids wouldn't let Zoe play cannibal," Courtney was telling Arnie. "They thought her rash was contagious. Remember that, Zoe? How you got so mad?"

"Not really," Zoe lied. Even now, she ached for the fierce little kid she'd been then. Locked in the bathroom, crying and scratching her legs and arms until she drew blood. Maybe Phillip Barry was God's gift to medicine, but she could only think of him as a grown-up version of a horrible, snobby boy with a knack for cruelty.

"Oh, her skin wasn't that bad," Janna said. "It just flared up now and then because she forgot to put stuff on it. Remember all those salves I used to buy? If you'd just used them the way you were supposed to, you wouldn't have had the flare-ups."

Zoe turned from the window to stare at Janna. The scaly, oozing outbreaks at the backs of her knees had been so bad that it hurt to walk. Every day had been like that. Sitting on her bike, gears disengaged, a hand against the wall to keep her stationary, frantically pedaling around and around to unstick her legs. Had her mother really forgotten all that?

"Well, let's talk about something else," Janna said brightly. "Arnie, hon, what do you think Zoe could get for that house of hers if she put it on the market?"

"PAM SAID you should take Saint-John's-wort," Brett told Zoe the next morning as she was sweeping up the shards of a coffee cup she'd accidentally knocked off the counter. "She said it helped her when she was getting mad about everything."

Zoe practiced deep breathing. Okay, breaking the coffee mug hadn't been an accident. It was more like leftover anger from the night before. And hearing Pam's name this morning did nothing to improve her mood. Pam, Denny's twenty-eight-year-old surfer-chick bride. Pam wore neon-colored bikinis and bodysurfed. Last week in a late-night phone call Denny had asked Zoe if she could get by with half of the monthly child-support check because he wanted to surprise Pam with a trip to Hawaii to celebrate their three-month anniversary. Zoe had sweetly suggested that he do something anatomically impossible with his surfboard.

After Brett went off to school, Zoe slipped on her gardening clogs and went outside to augment the soil in the flower beds. Physical work to shake the surly, disgruntled aftertaste that family matters tended to leave in her mouth. An hour or so later, she looked up to see a guy in bib overalls and a straw hat pulling down the steep driveway towing a horse trailer behind a battered white truck. By the time she reached him, he'd unloaded a tan-and-white Shetland pony from the trailer and was leading it toward her.

"Heard from the feed-store guy that you keep a few animals." He patted the pony's neck. "This one here's looking for a home. Used to give kids rides in a petting zoo, but she's getting along in years. Ready for retirement," he said with a laugh. "Know exactly how she feels."

"Hold on." Zoe ran into the house, grabbed a carrot from the refrigerator bin and brought it back for the horse who accepted it eagerly. She watched it, chewing contentedly with big square teeth, orange goo oozing from the side of its mouth. Cute, she thought. Blond bangs like a schoolgirl's hanging over big brown eyes.

"You already have four goats, a sheep, three dogs and a litter of feral cats that you need to get fixed," the voice of reason pointed out.

Kenna, Brett's black Lab, was at her side doing

some exploratory sniffing around the horse's hind-quarters. At the bottom of the property, she could hear the two other dogs—Domino, part wolf according to Brett, and Lucy, a big shepherd mix she'd rescued from the animal shelter—barking at the goats. Last weekend, she and Brett had spent three hours stringing up an electric fence around the goats' pen. The dogs were curious more than anything, but they alarmed the goats, which Zoe didn't think could be good for their milk or the cheese she eventually wanted to produce. All those stress hormones.

"Gentle, too." The guy wanted her to make a decision. "Loves kids."

"I'll keep that in mind," Zoe said. "Warn the neighbors."

The guy gave her a look—the same look her sister Courtney always gave her when she figured Zoe had to be joking but she didn't find it especially funny. The horse finished the carrot and Zoe extended her fingers for it to lick.

"Got into some poison ivy?" The guy gestured at tracks that ran down her left arm and bloomed into a red cluster on the back of her hand. A new crop had appeared in the aftermath of Janna's dinner.

"Yeah." She shrugged. Easier than explaining what it really was. Without thinking, she began to scratch and then caught herself. She studied the horse. She was bony, her sides caving with each breath, but her perky cream mane was curiously touching. As if the horse was doing her best to be cute. Zoe realized she was hooked.

"Don't horses need a lot of grooming?" She gestured around at the overgrown lawn, the roses sprouting bright red hips, the vigorous crop of dandelions. Brett was supposed to keep the grass cut, but constantly getting after him to do it was sometimes more trouble than dragging out the mower herself. "I've got more than I can do just to keep up with all this."

He shrugged. "Get someone to help, why don't you?"

Zoe eyed him briefly. "Money?"

"Oh, that." His teeth, when he grinned, were roughly the size and color of the pony's. "Yeah, what's it they say? A necessary evil."

She stroked the pony's nose. "What does she eat?"

"Alfalfa, Bermuda. Some feed. Nothing fancy."

"Expensive?"

"Nah."

"What d'you think, Kenna?" She scratched the dog's neck. "Think your master will groom her? Feed her? Keep her pen clean?"

"She's yours for fifty bucks," the guy said. "And I'll throw in a bale of alfalfa."

"Thirty," Zoe said, visualizing her checkbook balance.

"Done."

Nothing like buying a cheap horse to make you feel better, she decided later as she raked straw across its pen. It was things like this, unexpected gifts almost, that confirmed her belief that even if marrying Denny McCann hadn't been the smartest move she'd ever made, it was also no cause for regret.

The biggest reason, of course, was Brett, but, shortly after Brett was born, Denny had managed to convince her that buying three acres of undeveloped land in northern San Diego County would be a good business investment.

The plan at the time had been for Denny to build houses on the property, one for them and then three others that he'd sell. "We'll be set financially, babe," he'd gloated. "I won't ever have to work again."

Omit the words, "have to," and the second part at least was true.

Back then though, blissed out by the joys of new motherhood, not to mention sleep deprivation, she'd been pretty much indifferent to the idea of buying property. If Denny thought he could make it work, then fine.

While the first house—their house—was being built, she and Denny and Brett had lived in a trailer. Before ground was broken for the second house— actually before Denny had completely finished their own house—he'd succumbed to the charms of a young bank teller.

Zoe had kicked him out. He hadn't taken a whole lot of convincing and, in a fit of conscience or guilt, had signed over the property to her. "You're going to have to make the payments though," he'd told her.

But of course.

The house, a gray two-story wooden structure, vaguely ramshackle New England in style, with a long back deck and steeply sloping roof now seemed so completely hers she could hardly remember her ex-husband's role in its inception. Kind of like his role in creating their son, really.

Three acres of land and she knew every inch of it, from the gully at the bottom of the property that sometimes flooded after a heavy winter rain, to the faint pale green sheen on the distant brown hills that appeared after the first rains of the year. By early spring her land turned as lush and verdant as Ireland, lasting until about June, when the green faded to gold.

She loved it in every season. Like right now, walking through the beds of tomato plants, the pungent smell of ripening fruit, the sun warm on her back, Kenna trailing at her heels on the off chance that some food might be involved.

"You are getting way too smart for your own good," she said.

"Woof."

"Sit." The dog sat, almost quivering with anticipation, her eyes on Zoe's hand as Zoe reached into a huge old mailbox on the potting table in the middle of the garden. *Dog biscuits.* Kenna's tail was going crazy now, her front feet dancing a little jig. "We're happy, huh Boofuls?" Zoe threw the biscuit and watched the dog carry it off. She always got a kick out of how furtive Kenna looked as she trotted off with the prize. *Gotta hide this real good,* she could imagine the dog thinking. *Never know when someone might get a taste for Old Roy peanut-flavored dog biscuit.*

Some of the branches of the plants were so heavy

with tomatoes that they were touching the ground, and she decided now was as good a time as any to do a little cleanup. As she went into the garage for twine and nippers, the phone rang from inside the house.

"Hello," she said, breathless from running to catch it.

The line went dead.

Zoe stared at the phone and felt her newly improved mood begin to slump. This had been happening a lot lately. Nothing there when she picked up the phone. Once a girl had asked for Brett.

"May I tell him who's calling?"

"Oh, he'll know."

"Maybe I'd also like to know."

Click.

Brett tell you about his girlfriend?

She and Brett seemed to be fighting over everything lately.

You want to end up like your father, Brett? Is that what you want?

If she had a dollar for every time she'd stopped herself from blurting that question, she'd be a wealthy woman. And as much as she'd like to credit her restraint with something high-minded, like fairness at all costs, the main reason she never asked her son if he wanted to end up like his dad was a suspicion that Brett might say that turning out like his dad would be pretty cool. A garage full of toys—surfboards, water skis, a cluster of dirt bikes; summer weekends vrooming across the water in a sleek white powerboat, winter weekends snowboarding in the local mountains. A hot-looking babe for a wife. How bad could that be?

A more pertinent question might be *Do you want to end up like me?*

Last month she'd attended her twentieth high-school reunion. Reluctantly. Her friend had practically had to drag her there. "Come on. It'll be fun."

Right. Wearing heels was never fun and neither was anything else about the evening. Like the emerald-green silk dress she'd bought from Second Time Around that clung like a fretting child to her legs, or the large, laminated and hideously embarrassing picture of herself at eighteen, or Evelyn Something-or-other, Ph.D., former class valedictorian, who had droned on about how reunions were a chance to catch up on one another's lives.

"A reunion is an opportunity to examine our own life narrative," Earnest Evelyn had told the assembled crowd in the San Diego Hilton ballroom. "A chance to consider the stories we tell ourselves about who we are and how we became that person. Always remember though," she'd cautioned, "reunions can also threaten the integrity of those stories by subjecting them to the scrutiny of others, to friends and acquaintances whose memories of the past and of us may be altogether different from our own."

That bit at least had gotten Zoe's attention. In fact she'd fallen asleep thinking about it. Less about how she got to be the person she was—she could pretty much work that out—than why her version of who she was, which she was quite satisfied with, thank you very much—seemed so out of whack with the way everyone else saw her. Who exactly was fooling whom?

CHAPTER FOUR

AFTER HE'D TRIED TWICE to reach the boy's mother and got Zany Zoe's recorded message, Phillip decided he'd talk to Molly before he tried the number again. He reached her from his office, between surgeries.

"Hello?" a young, female voice responded.

"Hi." Was this Molly? Embarrassing, but he couldn't be sure. "Moll?"

"Dad?" It *was* Molly. "Something wrong?"

"No," he said. "Why would you think that?"

"Uh, *duh,* Dad. Why do you usually call me?"

Phillip exhaled through this mouth, slumped in his chair. In his peripheral vision, he saw Eileen motioning to him. He covered the receiver. "Eileen?"

"Hospital administration on line two."

"I'll call right back." He spoke into the receiver. "What's up?"

"You called *me,* Dad."

"I know I called you, Molly, I—"

"Well, you're making it sound like I called you."

"I'm not making it sound like anything." He forced himself to relax. Exactly when they'd gone from being friends to adversaries, he couldn't say, but lately every conversation with Molly seemed to go this way. "I just called—"

"What time is it?" Molly demanded. "I was still asleep."

"It's after noon, Molly."

"So?"

"You were sleeping when I came to take you out to lunch last week."

"So what?" Her voice had escalated a notch. "I was tired."

"You don't have school?" he asked, looking up as Eileen tapped on his door. "Hold on a minute, Moll. Yes?"

"That reporter from the *Tribune*. He has a follow-up question."

"Tell him I'll call him back."

"He asked me to interrupt you. He said he's on a deadline."

"Hold on again, Moll." He clicked the hold button and pressed the other line. "I have a question for you," he said to the reporter. "What if you'd caught me in the middle of surgery?"

The reporter laughed. "I'm tenacious."

"Okay," Phillip said. "So what's the question?"

"Confirmation really. You said on a typical day, you usually do four surgeries.

"Scheduled surgeries. There could be one or two emergency surgeries."

"But not after-hours?"

"We've suspended twenty-four-hour coverage." Phillip repeated the statement he'd given to every press query received since he and his partner had made the decision. Repetition didn't make it any easier. Tonight, if there was a head-on crash in or around Seacliff, he didn't say, or the gun and knife contingent went on a rampage, head or spinal injuries needing neurosurgery services would be airlifted to a center to the north, a potentially deadly delay. Worse, they'd be taken to the nearest E.R. where the chances of being misdiagnosed or undertreated by a sleep-deprived second-year resident…he stopped the thought.

"Any chance you'll be starting up again?"

"Not until we find a third partner," Phillip said. The green hold light had gone out; Molly had hung up. He finished with the reporter and redialed her number. It rang four times before she answered.

"Sorry, Moll."

"Yeah, right."

"Molly…"

"Well, it's not like I'm used to having your undivided attention. Like I'm suddenly thinking, 'Whoa what's with Dad? Omigod, his mind doesn't seem to be on what I'm saying. I wonder what's wrong—'"

"Knock it off, Molly. Let's talk about you running up your mother's American Express card."

She sighed noisily. "I needed stuff, Dad. That's why Mom said I could use the card in the first place."

"Fifteen hundred dollars buys a lot of *stuff*. What *stuff* did you need?"

"Fine, forget it. I won't use the damn card again. I don't want to go through some stupid inquisition."

"This isn't an inquisition, Molly. I'm just asking you to account for the fifteen hundred dollars you charged this month."

"I'm buying drugs."

"Drugs?"

"You know, cocaine, heroin. Whatever I can get my hands on."

"Very funny." It *was* a joke, right? He might reject the psychiatrist's diagnosis, but Molly frequently baffled him: her mercurial moods, the sudden and inexplicable obsessions—was it last month that she'd gone on, endlessly it seemed, about wheat grass? And before that, fasting as the cure to any medical problem. That one had driven him nuts. But, as Deanna had pointed out, whacky ideas were part of being seventeen. Drugs, though, hadn't really occurred to him as a serious possibility. Molly wasn't losing weight, she had no needle marks, and her eyes didn't show any signs of drug use.

Denial? The psychiatrist smirked. Phillip pushed away the image.

"Anyway, fifteen hundred dollars," Molly was saying now. "Big deal. Mom spends that on her facials."

"We're talking about you."

"I needed clothes, Dad."

"For yourself?"

"Of course for myself. What d'you think?"

"Your mother said something about a boy."

"What boy?"

"That's what I'm asking you."

Silence on the line.

"Moll?"

"I don't want to talk about it right now, Dad."

"Is there a time you *would* feel like talking about it?"

More silence. "We could get something to eat at Swaami's."

"When?"

"I don't know, like in an hour."

"I'll be in surgery in an hour, Molly."

"Whatever," she said.

The line went dead. In the outer office, he heard a phone ringing, then Eileen's voice. "Next Thursday? Mmm…let me take a quick look at his schedule, but Thursdays are really booked tight." He heard the tap of computer keys and then Eileen laughed. "True, Dr. Barry's one busy man."

"Dr. Barry." Eileen's voice now came through on the intercom. "Mrs. Barry on line two."

He picked up the phone. "Yes, Deanna?"

"Tell Deanna she can wait," said a voice from the doorway.

"Hold on," Phillip told his ex-wife. The woman who'd just spoken was now walking into his office. He stared, slightly stunned, as she seated herself in the chair opposite his desk, watching him with a faint smile as though perhaps she knew him. He was quite sure he didn't know her. He wasn't in the habit of thinking in artistic or literary terms, but the term Rubenesque came to mind. Needs to lose a few pounds, Deanna would have sniffed. Voluptuous, he thought. High color, a great deal of fair hair and…breasts. Full and white, they seemed in imminent danger of tumbling from the low neck of the yellow blouse she wore. Not perky, twenty-year-old breasts, but full, lush, sensuous breasts. He mentally shook his head.

She crossed her legs. She wore sandals with thin leather straps that tied around the ankles. The hem of her long yellow-and-red skirt brushed the top of her left ankle. Beads and bracelets circling both arms created a constant small symphony of sound.

In his peripheral vision, he could see Eileen frowning in the doorway.

"I couldn't stop her," she explained.

"Phillip," his ex-wife said. "I don't have all day."

"Just a second." He addressed the woman. "What's the problem?"

"Hi." She gave him a long look. "How are you?"

He waved a hand, dismissing the formalities. "Do we have an appointment?"

"No." She looked mildly amused, as if she knew something that he didn't. "I guess that's the acceptable way to gain access to your inner sanctum, huh? An appointment. Kind of weeds out the crazies. Sorry, I've never been very good at that kind of formality.

"Dr. Barry." Eileen motioned from the doorway, and pantomimed dialing a phone. Security? she inquired, silently mouthing the word.

Phillip shook his head. As soon as he learned what she thought she was doing here, he'd send her on her way.

The woman pulled a newspaper from her bag, slapped the front page on his desk. Did Jenny Have To Die? the headline read. "I don't know what kind of whitewash job you did on this reporter, but we both know this doesn't even come close to telling the real story."

He looked at her. So this was the problem—the Todd Bowen article about Jenny Dixon. "And, what in your opinion, *is* the real story?"

"Okay, so you closed the emergency neurology services, but you didn't stop being a neurosurgeon, right? You *could* have come in." She nodded her head toward the newspaper he had just moved out of her reach. "I'm sure you had some terrific reason, I just thought maybe you'd do me a favor and share it with me."

Phillip could hear his ex-wife calling his name. "I'll call you back," he told Deanna, and put down the phone.

"I'm sorry," he said to the woman. "You'll need to talk to someone in administration." She didn't appear convinced, so he stood up. "Look ma'am—"

"*Ma'am.* God, I hate being called 'ma'am.'"

And he hated the fact that he was having the damnedest time keeping his eyes off her breasts. Words he'd long forgotten he ever knew ran through his brain. Wench. Moll Flanders. He forced himself to look up at her face. Amber eyes and a full mouth. Her clothes, he thought, would just slip off. Her breasts already appeared in danger of escape.

She noticed his focus and tugged at her blouse. As

he marshaled his thoughts, it occurred to him that perhaps she was part of a gag perpetrated by one of his partners. Last year, on April first, he'd walked in to his office to find a temporary secretary in a fringed buckskin jacket sitting at Eileen's desk, snapping gum and filing her nails. Eileen was sick, she'd told him. After several hours of horrendous inefficiency, he'd finally asked for the name of her temporary agency so that he could send her back. Just then, his partner, Stu, an inveterate prankster, had walked into the office, laughing uproariously as he confessed to the joke. Later, Eileen confessed, too; Stu had roped her into it. Stu might have struck again. Frankly, he would prefer that she was the latest of Stu's jokes, rather than someone completely on the level.

"I didn't catch your name," he finally said.

"I didn't throw it to you," she said.

He folded his arms across his chest and waited.

"Defensive posture," she said.

"Excuse me?"

"Arms crossed like that." She folded hers in the same way. "Denotes guardedness. Keep out, that's what it says."

He looked beyond her shoulder, hoping to spot Eileen. "So your name is…" he prompted.

"Um…" She appeared to be thinking about the question. "You don't know, huh?"

"Should I?"

"Course not." Another pause while she seemed to be thinking things over. "Anyway, *my* name isn't important. I'm here on behalf of Jenny. The girl who died in the ambulance. All the Jennys and all their parents and families, who assume that if they need emergency room services, they'll receive appropriate medical care."

"Are you a relative?"

She looked at him. "Not relevant. Jenny could be a perfect stranger and her death would still be tragic and unnecessary."

Phillip said nothing. He couldn't. After the Bowen article, the hospital's legal team had been crystal clear—he couldn't discuss Jenny Dixon. Maybe he should send the woman down to legal.

"As if it isn't awful enough to lose a child," she said, "but then to know that this child didn't have to die. You want to know my name? I'll tell you what. You can call me Concerned. Frustrated. Mad as Hell."

Or Crazy. Phillip reconsidered calling security. Last week in L.A., an angry family member of a former patient had walked into administration and fatally shot the assistant hospital administrator. The woman sitting across from him had a large yellow straw bag at her feet. Could be a gun inside for all he knew.

She leaned forward and jabbed at the newspaper on his desk. "How would you feel if this were your daughter?"

Caught off guard by the question, he felt a moment of panic. Did this woman know Molly? Just then his secretary appeared behind the woman's shoulder. "Dr. Samuels on line one, Dr. Barry. Administration on line two and you need to get down to conference—"

"Yeah, yeah, yeah." The woman nodded her head. "We get the idea, Dr. Barry is one busy dude. But I think, we, the Jennys of the world, deserve some answers. Why *wouldn't* you come in that night—"

He needed to stop her questions. Now. "First of all, this isn't about me. The trauma-system problem is a nationwide issue…" He wanted her to leave. The mild curiosity he'd initially felt had subsided along with his patience. She was, he was certain now, just another run-of-the mill crackpot. Her concern was probably genuine enough, but her methods needed work. "Second, unless you understand all the facts—"

"Exactly why I'm here." She settled into the chair in a way that clearly meant to say she had all day. "What I want to understand is this. As Jenny was riding around in the ambulance, what exactly prevented someone, anyone, from coming in to save her? Really, I'm trying to imagine. You, Dr. Neurosurgeon, are asleep in your multimillion-dollar oceanfront house when the phone rings. A girl will die unless you come in to save her. What do you say? 'Too bad, that's the breaks,' and just roll over and go back to sleep?"

The arrival of a security guard, apparently summoned by Eileen, saved him from having to answer the question, but not from feeling the bite of her anger.

"Brilliant solution," the woman said as a blue-uniformed guard, who probably outweighed her by two hundred pounds or so, took her arm. "But you haven't heard the last from me."

SOMETIMES BRETT FELT he was surrounded by crazies. Like his mom, for instance, when she made him go sit in the car like he was some little kid while she ragged to his dad about taking him surfing.

Or like last week, when he got home from school and she was reading this magazine article.

"Watcha reading, Mom?" Like he cared, but he was trying to be nice. So she gives him this guilty look like he's caught her doing something wrong.

Just because she looked so sneaky, he took a look over her shoulder to check out what she was reading. A full-page ad.

"It's a moment all parents dread. The first time they hand over the car keys to their teen driver." He read some more. *''Drivers in the sixteen-to-twenty-two-year-old age group are involved in more accidents and fatalities than…"*

Then he figured out what the ad was all about and stopped reading.

"Jeez, Mom."

"What?"

"See, that's what I mean about you making a big deal out of everything. Roger's folks are buying him a car—"

"And you can use the truck…"

"To go to the store. Big deal." As soon as he said it, he knew he'd made a mistake. A few weeks ago, he'd driven the truck to pick up some stuff for her from the market and then, just because it felt so cool to be sitting behind the wheel, even if the truck was kind of a dump, he'd driven over to Roger's, which was only three blocks from the market, but then Roger wasn't home so he'd driven to another friend's house and hung out there for a while. His mom had climbed all over him for that. She'd been standing at the door waiting as he pulled up.

"Three hours for a five-minute trip to the market?"

"Come on, Mom. I was just hanging out at—"

"*Just hanging out.* How did I know you hadn't had an accident? How did I know you weren't lying in an emergency room somewhere?"

He'd been grounded for a week, which he pretty much expected but then when she didn't mention it again, he thought she'd forgotten all about it. *Right.*

"It's a tracking device." She was looking at the ad again. "When you're driving, it will send me reports on your location, whether you're speeding…"

Yep, his mom was definitely crazy, all right. And now, today, he walks in and she's in the kitchen, standing over a screeching kettle. Just standing there, her back to him, with the kettle hissing and screeching away. *Screech…rattle…hsssssssssss.* Standing there, like she had no idea it was practically falling off the stove, it was shaking so hard.

He coughed so she would know he was there, but she didn't turn around.

"Mom?"

Finally. She turned off the gas, banged a mug on the counter and dropped a tea bag in it.

"What's wrong?" he asked.

"The world." She poured water into the mug. "Skewed priorities, inequity." With her thumb and finger, she fished the tea bag out of the mug and threw it toward the trash can. Missed.

He bent down, scooped it up and tossed it. That's how his mom talked: big words, big concepts. "Gotta overcome that genetic predisposition," she'd say if she came in and caught him watching TV. *Genetic predisposition.* Translation. *Don't be like your father.* "Skewed priorities" meant she'd probably been to see Rhea and got all fired up about Jenny dying while doctors played golf or something.

"I'm sorry, honey," she said now. "I'm just in a very bad mood. Give me a few minutes, okay?"

"Sure." He wondered what was for dinner.

"Getting people to pay attention," his mom said. She was sitting at the table now, staring into her mug of tea like it was a crystal ball or something. "That's the first step to creating change."

Sure, Mom, he thought. Whatever you say. If anyone could make people pay attention, it was his mom. Sometimes she made him feel tired, like he'd been caught up in a hurricane and pushed around by all the noise and movement. Once Hurricane Zoe got rolling, no one thought for a minute she wouldn't do what she'd set out to do. She'd get on these kicks…like right now it was getting the trauma services started again. The last one was getting a stoplight put in on this street where some little kid got run over, and before that it was getting a new trial for this black guy who was in jail for murdering a girl. Now the guy was out, back to working as a schoolteacher and telling everyone that he owed it all to Zoe McCann.

She'd even gotten herself arrested once for protesting against something. He couldn't remember what it was now, but they'd shown her on TV being dragged across the street by a couple of cops. That's how she was. Grandma said her own mother had led some kind of protest about women not being allowed into this bar where all the men were playing darts. Grandma and Aunt Courtney weren't like that, though, but Grandma said these things sometimes skipped generations.

All he knew was that he didn't want that gene, or whatever it was, lurking inside him waiting for a chance to make him act obnoxious. Not that his mom would call it obnoxious though, she'd say it was standing up for herself. Don't let anyone push you around, *ever,* she was always telling him. You're as good as anyone. Just remember that.

Like he could forget when she reminded him practically every day? Not that he wasn't kind of proud of his mom, even though she sometimes drove him nuts the way she sucked him into all her energy. Like she was so big on him being a doctor, he even told the school counselor that's what he wanted, too. Except that he didn't know what he wanted to be, maybe a carpenter or something, like his dad—not that he'd ever tell her that. Plus, he hated chemistry and the other science stuff.

He watched her, still sitting there looking into her mug of tea. *Uh, Mom? Dinner? I'm only like starving to death.* He had a secret stash of burritos behind his mom's bags of frozen whatever it was that she was always digging up from the garden, but with her in the kitchen there was no way he could get to it without her making this big, humongous deal about it. She'd grab the burrito box from him and start reading the list of ingredients. Picking out these long words that didn't even sound like something you should put in your mouth. "Where did you get this disgusting thing from anyway?"

Then she'd fix him with a look that said she knew damn well where they'd come from. Pam, his father's new wife, who looked more like a cheerleader than a stepmom and couldn't cook to save her life, was always giving him stuff to take home with him. He knew she did it mostly to bug his mom, but, hey, he liked frozen burritos. When his mom made Mexican food, she always tried to put in stuff like zucchini.

"I am so furious at myself." She brought her fists down so hard on the table that the mug jumped and the tea splashed all over the place. "God, I'm an idiot."

He stopped thinking about how he could get a burrito from the freezer and microwave it without her noticing, and sat down at the table. "Why? Granny Janny?" His grandma always put his mom in a bad mood. *Aunt Courtney this and Aunt Courtney that,* he mimicked his mom's voice in his head. Once he'd asked his mom if she was jealous of Aunt Courtney and then she'd really blown up.

"No. I told you, I'm mad at myself."

"What's for dinner, Mom?"

"Dinner?" She looked up as though she'd suddenly noticed he was sitting there. "Oh, honey…I'm sorry, I got so caught up in…I'm so sorry, sweetie." Now she had her arm around his shoulder. "God, I didn't realize the time, you must be starving—"

"Mom, it's no big deal." He thought about his stash in the freezer. "I could fix myself something."

"Uh-uh." She was in the fridge now, opening the vegetable drawer. "Cauliflower. Look at these, sweetie, they're not from our garden—it's the wrong time of year for cauliflower, but I got this at Organic Foods. Look." She held it out for him to see. "Pure, pure white. Not a single blemish."

Burritos. Drippy orange cheese. Beef and beans. Green chili and corn.

"Don't look at me like that, Brett. Sandy gave me this recipe for cauliflower mashed potatoes, except it's not potatoes, it's cauliflower. But you'd never know it, I swear. And veggie burgers. How about that?"

Maybe he'd ask if he could use the truck, then drive down to Angelo's for a double monster burger. Except he didn't have any money. And his mom was zipping around the kitchen now, bringing out stuff from the fridge—*toss me one of those burritos, Mom*—grating cheese, cutting the stupid cauliflower.

"…and of course, I had to go through his secretary first," his mom was saying. "*Important* people always want you to make an appointment, and they have secretaries who are like sentries, or something."

"Whose secretary?"

She frowned like she didn't understand the question. "What d'you mean, whose secretary? Phillip Barry's."

"Dr. Barry?" Weird Molly's dad? That's why she was all bent out of shape? He started to ask what he'd done to make her mad, but then he decided he was too hungry, plus he didn't really care. He yawned.

"Hey. Try to at least *act* interested, okay?"

"Please, oh, please, dear Mother..." He cupped his hand to his chin, stared right at her like he was listening as hard as he could. "Please, oh, please, tell me your story. I beg you."

Zoe swiped at his head. "Wiseass. Anyway, Ms. Guard Dog tried to tell me he was busy, but he was taking a personal phone call, for God's sake, so I just ignored her and walked in. He looked kind of surprised at first, and I kept waiting for him to recognize me...you know, growing up together and everything."

Brett nodded, wishing she'd just get on with the story so he could go up to his room. He was always hearing stuff about how she and Aunt Courtney and Granny Janna used to live in some cottage that Dr. Barry's family owned. Once he'd almost told Weird Molly about it because it seemed kind of like a strange coincidence, but Molly was so freaky she'd probably say it was a sign they should get married or something. Same reason he didn't tell his mom about Molly. She'd make some big deal of it and then Granny Janna and Aunt Courtney would start teasing him and making him look like a total jerk.

"…so anyway," his mom was saying now, "Dr. God—"

"Dr. *God.* You called him that?"

"Not to his face," she said. "Give me a little credit. Anyway, he didn't recognize me. I thought he would, but he didn't. So when he asked me what my name was, I started to tell him and then…I don't know, it was spooky. Like all the bad feelings about not feeling good enough and everything…"

"That's crazy," he said. "You're just as good as he is." He was about to say something else, but she was staring at him, all bug-eyed like he'd grown two heads or something and then she started laughing, this great hooting laugh she had. Laughing her head off practically and then she got up and stuck her arms around his neck and started kissing his face. "Knock it off, Mom." He pushed her away. "Quit acting weird."

She was still laughing. "Oh, honey. You really think I'm weird?"

"Sometimes. Like right now."

"But it's better than boring, right?"

He shrugged. "I guess. So that's why you're in a bad mood? Because of Dr. Barry?"

"Why I *was* in a bad mood."

"Okay." He didn't know what he'd said to make her not in a bad mood, but suddenly it was like the sun was shining in Zoeland again. "Can I go now?"

"No." She caught his hand. "I want to talk to you some more. What you just said is exactly right. Of course, I'm as good as he is. And I hate it that I even have those feelings."

"So don't."

"It's not that easy, honey. See that's why I want so much more for you. Why I'm always nagging you about school and everything. I want you to feel good about *all* the decisions you make in life. When you're forty, I want you to be able to look at anyone, no matter how successful they are, and not feel apologetic for your own life."

He didn't say anything. It freaked him when she said stuff like that, like there was some secret part of her that wasn't really his mom. It was all kind of weird and mixed-up, like looking into a bowl of soup or something and trying to guess what some of the bits were supposed to be—vegetable, meat or whatever.

"Hey, Mom, can we just have pizza or something?"

"You eat enough junk at your father's." She jumped up from the table and ran out of the kitchen. "Watch the cauliflower, sweetheart," she yelled from the stairs. " It needs to be really soft and squishy and then you add sour cream to make it yummy, yummy, yummy and I have something to show you."

He opened the freezer and checked his stash.

"Hey, Brett," his mom called from upstairs. "Where did this leather jacket on your bed come from? It's not yours, is it?"

"Damn it," Brett muttered. He slammed the freezer door shut. "Damn it, damn it, damn it."

CHAPTER FIVE

As HE STOPPED on the way home to pick up something for dinner, Phillip thought he saw the woman who had barged into his office a few days earlier. She was standing at the dairy counter, examining a package of cheese. The breasts might have identified her, but she had her back to him. Still something about her, the tousled hair, the generous hips. He'd been headed in the same direction—he needed Parmesan, in the event that Molly ever made good on her promise to make the spaghetti carbonara for his birthday last month.

As the woman turned, Phillip ducked down the nearest aisle and walked out of the market empty-handed. He'd eat out, he decided as he drove from the parking lot.

During their marriage, it had been Deanna's claim that when he was focused on anything work related, bombs could go off and nothing would disturb his concentration. Usually that was true, but between Molly's latest problems, the continued closure of emergency neurological services and that damn woman barging into his office, his concentration was shot.

"Ah, don't let it rattle you," his partner had said when Phillip told him about the incident. "The press is playing up the story—they love that sort of thing. Kids dying while greedy, heartless doctors play golf. Did you tell her there are two sides to every story?"

Not really, Phillip thought now. He'd tried, but mostly, he'd just wanted to get her out of his office. Maybe if she hadn't been so damned confrontational, he could have tried to help her understand. He could have said, quite truthfully, that there were no easy answers to address the issue. He could have pointed out that escalating malpractice rates were driving specialists out of practice in droves, hence the shortage—and not just at Seacliff.

He could have paid less attention to her breasts.

His life, he thought as he waited for the electric gate to allow him entrance to his apartment building, was filled with things he *could* have done—*should* have done he amended, thinking of Molly again.

IT WAS NEARLY MIDNIGHT and Brett was lying on his bed, dressed but under the covers so that his mom wouldn't start asking questions if she came in and found him still awake. He was thinking about Weird Molly. She was small and skinny like some stray cat that just showed up on the doorstep. She kind of moved like a cat, too, quiet and…what was that word? Stealthy. Plus, she was a big pain in the butt. He was sick of her hanging around him, getting him in trouble with presents and stuff.

Like the other day, when his friend Kevin had

given him a ride home and Molly had followed in her car, but they hadn't seen her. This was one seriously weird chick. She kept going on about how his house was so honest and unpretentious compared to hers. Translation. Molly lived in an oceanfront house in Seacliff where even tear-down shacks went for millions and he lived ten miles or so from the ocean in Bellavista, where migrant workers lived in apartments and run-down houses and there were Mexican take-out places on every corner and billboards in Spanish advertising the services of immigration lawyers.

Not that he was ashamed of where he lived or anything. His mom had worked hard to make this a pretty neat place, the animals and the flowers and vegetables and everything. Trouble was, she was always at him to help more. "The flower beds need weeding, Brett," or "You know the funny thing about plants, they actually need water occasionally." His mom was real big on sarcasm. Whenever he complained to his dad about his mom making him do things, his dad would tell him to tell his mom to go get stuffed. "You're not her slave labor," his dad would say.

Anyway, yesterday, he was raking the goats' pen. Gertie and Gordy were African pygmies, gray and black and totally into butting each other. Cantankerous, his mom called them. *She should know.* The other two, Fred and Freda, were Nubians. They were light brown and taller than the pygmies and they had soft floppy ears like cocker spaniels. They were both pretty friendly. His mom fed them the old telephone directories. It seemed pretty weird to him, the first time he saw Freda munching away at the Yellow Pages, but his mom said the print on the paper was made with soy and that's what they liked. Go figure.

So he was thinking about stuff, like going to the desert with his dad, and he looked up and there was Molly, just sitting on this bale of alfalfa watching him rake like it was the most fascinating thing she'd ever seen. Molly usually wore black clothes. Big army boots, faded jeans—only today she had on these camouflage pants—and a black tank top. Her hair was short and spiky, and dyed black.

Sometimes he wondered what his mom would think of Molly, but most of the time he didn't want to deal with that idea. Zoe would think Molly was a bad influence and bug him constantly about her. Or she would like Molly and bug him constantly about her. Lose-lose, whatever way it went.

After Molly had sat there for a while, not saying anything, she'd suddenly dug something out of her backpack. "This is what your mom should grow," she said.

A freakin' marijuana plant.

She'd started laughing when she saw his face. "It's not what you think it is."

Right. But then she went on and on about this industrial hemp and how it was confused with marijuana and how great it was. All he knew was that it looked enough like a pot plant that his mom would totally freak out if she saw it and she was going to be home anytime.

"We should go live in Humboldt County where people aren't so narrow-minded," Molly had said. "I hate my parents, they're the phoniest people you've ever met. Like my dad has this patient who's my age who has a brain tumor and I swear to God, you'd think she was his daughter the way he goes on about how brave she is and everything. And my mom's either writing her stupid books or going on tours to talk about them. I'm just a pain to her."

"Molly, you gotta go." He'd gone on raking out the goats' pen like he hadn't heard and then she jumped down off the bale and started watching the goats.

"Check out their eyeballs," she said. "The pupil is horizontal."

He shrugged. "So?"

"Goats are a sign of the devil. You can tell by their eyes. They're yellow."

He'd started getting really freaked then because his mom could drive up at any second. She'd left him a note to say she'd gone to Rhea's but would be back to make dinner. Of course. His mom always made dinner. Molly claimed her mother never cooked. Either they ate out, she said, or they ordered in.

"Listen," he said after he'd finished with the pen. "I've got stuff to do and my mom's going to be home."

"So?" She smiled up at him. "I'd like to meet her."

"No, you wouldn't," he said.

"Why?"

"Just because…"

Molly laughed. "Well, that explains everything."

She'd finally gone though, about a minute before his mom drove in.

Jeez. Now he was hungry. He reached for the bag of chips he'd stashed under the bed. His mom hated him eating stuff like that so he had to hide it. Anyway, he'd figured out what to do to get Weird Molly to stop bugging him. First though, he had to wait till his mom was asleep.

When he went up to bed at ten, she'd been cleaning out the pantry. *Ten at night, and she's cleaning out the freakin' pantry.*

She bought food in these huge cans from some discount restaurant supply place. He'd go into the pantry, looking for something to eat—chips or cookies like his dad kept—and find, like five-pound cans of mushrooms, or a fifty-pound sack of rice. And she was always finding marked-down bargains—potatoes, tomatoes, peppers that were *this close* to going moldy so they had to be used up, which meant he even had to check his breakfast cereal to make sure she hadn't chopped up some tomato in there or something. Plus the top shelves were crammed with glass jars of what she grew herself.

So anyway, the pantry was always jammed and she'd keep adding more stuff until you could hardly get inside. It would go on like this, until she'd start bitching about how she couldn't find whatever it was she needed and then she'd haul everything out—*everything*. Jars and cans and sacks of stuff, all of it out and piled all over the kitchen floor while she swept and cleaned. His friends' moms watched TV at night, *The West Wing* or whatever, but not his mom.

He lay there listening and then he started getting sleepy. When he looked at the clock again it was almost one in the morning. He got out of bed, crept across the room, pulled his door open a crack and listened. Nothing. His mom must have gone to bed, finally.

Kenna was under the blankets, doing her dead-dog act. The other two were on the floor, Domino under the bed, Lucy on the rug. He sat on the edge of the bed and put his sneakers on. The other two were cool about staying at home, but Kenna always wanted to go everywhere he went. The thing was her toenails tapped on the wooden floors, so he left her sleeping—she'd just think he'd gone to the bathroom or something—and walked downstairs. Then he remembered why he was going and went back for the surfboard and the jacket. Slowly, quietly, holding his breath so his mom wouldn't wake up and start freaking out.

In the kitchen, he found the truck keys on a hook above the pantry door—the pantry looked real tidy—and snuck out through the back door. Outside it was pitch-dark and kinda windy, the warm Santa Ana kind of windy, which was a good thing because it covered any sound he might make. Another bit of luck was she'd bought goat feed on the way home, so the truck was parked down by the goats' pen instead of in the driveway where she'd hear him starting up.

There was no traffic on the 78, not much on the 405. At the Seacliff off-ramp, he exited and drove down Seacliff Village Drive. He'd been to Molly's house once before to pick up this book she'd borrowed. She lived on Del Mar, the most big-bucks street in a whole town of big-bucks streets and her house was this awesome place on the edge of the cliffs. His mom would call it ostentatious and talk about how taxpayers always ended up paying for places like that because they were built too close to the edge and they were always falling into the water every time it rained.

He parked outside, cut the lights, turned off the ignition and grabbed the jacket and board. The house had these security lights everywhere and as he crept around the side, he got kinda freaked, thinking he might set off an alarm or something. For a minute, he thought he heard something and he flattened himself against the wall. Underneath Molly's window, he picked up a pebble and tossed it up.

The clink it made when it hit the glass was way louder than he thought it would be. Jeez, what a dumbass. He half expected to hear police sirens coming down the street. Maybe he should just split now. No, he didn't want the jacket and stuff getting him into more trouble.

He waited. No police cars, no barking dogs. Cool. From where he stood, the waves sounded kind of like freeway traffic. He moved away from the wall to look up to Molly's window. Out at sea, it was pitch-black except for the phosphorescence on the top of the waves. He reached for another pebble, tossed it up at the glass.

"Molly."

Nothing.

Crap. He scrabbled at his feet for something bigger. *Clink.*

Nothing.

"Molly!"

He was thinking that he'd have to talk to her at school tomorrow, which sucked because she'd get all emotional and make some big scene and everyone would think they had something going. Right. Last time he was ever going to feel sorry for some girl again.

"Brett."

He looked up. She was hanging out of the window.

"Hold on," she said. "I'll be right down."

A few minutes later he heard a door softly close and then Molly was standing there hugging her arms and grinning like they were boyfriend and girlfriend and he was about to kiss her or something. Her feet were bare and she was wearing plaid boxing shorts and a baggy T-shirt and he thought it was too bad she was so flat-out weird, because she was actually kind of cute.

"You wanna come in?" She hunched her shoulders, tucked her hands in her armpits. "It's kind of cold."

"Where are your parents?"

"My grandma's staying with me. She's so deaf you could set off a bomb or something and she wouldn't hear." She caught his hand. "Come on."

He pulled away. "It's okay, I'll stay here."

"What's up?" she asked. "You couldn't sleep, because you missed me so much?"

"Dream on." He looked at the truck keys in his hand. "Look, you gotta quit it, okay?"

"Quit what?"

"Everything. Calling me, following me around, giving me things." He nodded at the surfboard that he'd set against the wall with the jacket draped over the top of it. "I don't need all that stuff."

"You're so grateful and polite," she said.

"I didn't ask for the freakin' things. I don't want you spending money on me."

"You didn't like the leather jacket?"

"Sure, I liked it, who wouldn't? But I had to make up something to tell my mom. If she'd found the surfboard, too, I'd be totally busted."

"Why didn't you tell her they were from me? Girls give their boyfriends presents, what's wrong with that?"

"What's wrong with that is you're not my girlfriend," he said. *Plus you're too freakin' weird.* Oh, jeez, now she was going to cry. "Come on, Molly—" he put one hand on her shoulder "—don't do that."

She sniffed. "What?"

"Look all sad like that."

"Shit." She flung his hand off her shoulder. "I am sad, goddamn it. You would be, too, if your parents wished to hell you were dead so they could get on with their precious little lives and not have to be bothered with you."

"Molly." She'd started running and he chased after her. "Hey." He grabbed her arm to stop her from running away. "Look, maybe you need to talk to them or something."

She looked at him for a minute as though maybe she was thinking about what he'd said, then she jerked her arm free.

"Thanks for nothing," she said. "Go to hell, why don't you?"

ZOE STOOD IN FRONT of the bathroom mirror looking at her reflection. Her hair was wet from the shower and clung to her head like a skullcap. She leaned forward to take a closer at her face. She looked…pasty and pinched, like maybe she hadn't slept well, but she had—other than being woken briefly from an erotic dream about Phillip Barry, of all people. Embarrassing, because she knew she'd start thinking about it the minute she walked into his office.

That was her plan for the day. To go and see Phillip Barry. *"Hi, I'm Zoe McCann, I don't know why I didn't mention it last time, but…"* Maybe if she blow-dried her hair, it would calm down a bit. Did she even have a drier anymore?

"Brett," she yelled from the bathroom. "Time to get up."

No answer.

In the bedroom, she tossed clothes all over the place looking for something to wear. *"Hi."* Big friendly smile. *"Long time, no see. I'm Zoe McCann. What am I up to these days? Oh…"* Demure smile. *"Where to even start? I'm in the commercial landscaping business. I own property up north. Gourmet vegetables, incredible how in vogue they've become."* Offhand laugh. *"I know. Who would have dreamed lettuce could lead to wealth? Anyway, about this pesky emergency on-call thing..."*

She held up a pink dress with pearl buttons that Janna had talked her into buying to attend a wedding last year. The bride's mother was one of Janna's tennis partners and Janna had nearly driven Zoe nuts over the whole thing. "Please, I beg you," Janna had said, *"do not put any weird color on your hair."*

No sound from Brett's room.

She threw the dress down on the bed, tied her robe and knocked on his door.

"Rise and shine," she called.

Nothing.

"Brett, come on. Wake up. I've got things to do today."

Nothing.

She opened the door and stuck her head around. "Brett?"

A grunt from under the blankets.

"Come on." She reached to yank away the covers and he pulled them back. "I mean it, Brett. Let's go."

Back in her bedroom, she settled on a red cotton sundress that she hadn't worn for a year or so and checked herself in the dresser mirror. Her hair was already drying, frizzy of course. No point in looking for the blow-dryer. She dug in a dresser drawer for a lipstick, found some sandals at the bottom of her closet and decided she'd done the best she could.

When she went to check on Brett's progress, she found him sitting on the edge of the bed, elbows on his knees, head in his hands.

"The Thinker," she said.

"Shut up, Mom."

"It's a famous sculpture, Rodin I think." She started downstairs to fix breakfast, then thought of something and went back in his room. He didn't appear to have moved. "Hey, Brett, did you hear a noise last night?"

"What kind of noise?" he asked without looking up.

"I don't know, a noise noise. I was sleeping and something woke me." From a dream of tickling Phillip Barry senseless with a blade of grass as a matter of fact.

"What time?"

She studied him for a moment. He was bleary-eyed and seemed unusually tired and she wondered whether he was coming down with a cold. "I don't know what time. Midnight? Maybe a little later."

He shook his head. "Didn't hear anything."

"Huh." She shrugged. "Well, I guess Kenna would have barked...."

"How COME you're all dressed up?" Brett asked as she drove him to school.

She smiled. "Because I'm planning to drop in on Phillip Barry and I didn't want to walk in with dirt under my fingernails and straw in my hair."

"How come?"

"How come I didn't want to walk in with dirty fingernails?"

"No, how come you're going to see *him?*"

Something about the way he'd asked the question made her turn her head to look at him. He'd been surly at breakfast, but he now looked so disconsolate, shoulders slumped and head bowed that she leaned over to put her arm around him. "Honey? Is something wrong?"

"No."

"It doesn't look that way."

He shrugged.

"I'm going to see Phillip Barry about…the whole thing with Jenny," she said. "Getting emergency neuro services started again."

"Can I go to Dad's this weekend?"

"You were there last weekend, Brett. I thought we were going to rebuild the goats' pen this weekend. You know how Gertie keeps escaping."

"I'm sick of hanging around the house all the time."

She reached a bank of traffic lights just as the one facing her went from amber to red. She braked, and the truck shuddered to a stop. What was going on with him, she decided, was a little preparatory buildup to a request to use the truck to go somewhere alone. She'd started to detect a pattern. Start with a big show of unhappiness that prompts Mom to ask what's wrong, then play to Mom's insecurities by mentioning Dad, then make her feel guilty about trapping poor kid in the house doing chores when everyone else was out driving their own cars, not their mother's freakin truck, their own car, but not him, he hated this, he wanted to go live with his dad. This would make Mom feel awful enough to let kid use the truck. Presto. Wheels.

They drove along in silence for a while. Well, that was one explanation. But there was that girl who'd called and wouldn't give her name. And the disconnect calls that seemed to only happen in the evening when Brett was home. *Brett tell you about his girlfriend?*

"His daughter is so freakin' weird."

"Whose daughter?" she asked. "You mean Phillip Barry's?"

"Yeah. She's crazy."

"How d'you mean?"

He shrugged. "She just is."

Was this the girlfriend? Zoe tried to recall whether Brett had said anything about Molly Barry that might provide a clue that she was more than just a girl in his class. All she'd ever heard, though, was that he thought Molly Barry was weird. But teens were unpredictable: weird today could be wonderful tomorrow.

"Your dad said something about a girlfriend…."

"Yeah, right."

"What does that mean? Yeah, right, you do? Or, yeah, right, you don't?"

"I don't know," he said irritably. "Quit bugging me about it."

"Is it Molly Barry?"

He shot her a look. "Get real."

CHAPTER SIX

THIRTY MINUTES LATER, Zoe was driving around the Seacliff Memorial Medical Center's visitor lot with three other cars, all circling like sharks for an empty spot. Screw this, she decided and drove over to the physicians' lot. As she pulled her battered black truck in between a Mercedes and a Beamer it struck her that it looked kind of like a bad tooth in a mouth of gleaming chompers. Phillip Barry would probably have a fit if he found himself parked next to her heap. Probably check for dings and scratches, wonder to himself why just the proximity hadn't set off his security system.

In the hospital lobby, she ducked into the ladies' and checked herself out. The dress was kind of creased in the rear and, because the truck had no air-conditioning, her face was pink from heat. Brett had kind of distracted her from feeling that she needed to set things straight with Phillip Barry and now, with her mind working on whether Weird Molly was in fact the mystery girlfriend, she stood at the mirror and wondered if she really wanted to see him after all. Phillip Barry wasn't the only way to resolve the on-call problem; she could talk to the administrator, or do something like start a letter-writing campaign to the *Tribune*'s editorial page.

Her hair looked as though each and every strand and split end had decided to go off in its own direction. *Hi, I'm Zoe McCann. The housekeeper's daughter. Kind of look the part, don't I?* The rest room door swung open and a statuesque blonde wearing a figure-hugging black suit, the sort of dual-message thing Courtney would wear—*Hi, there. I'm great in the boardroom and grrrreat in bed*—swanned over to stand by Zoe at the mirrors. Zoe immediately grabbed her purse and left, before she could become so demoralized that she'd skip Phillip Barry and head to the nearest salon for an extreme makeover—or the nearest saloon for a consoling beer.

Beautiful, she reassured herself as the elevator took her up to the tenth floor, Neurological and Neurosurgical Service. *You, rootin' tootin' Zoe McCann, are the fairest in all the land. Men fall at your feet, smitten by your sheer loveliness. You are…exquisite. Got that?*

"I'M SORRY, this is Dr. Barry's surgery day." The same secretary who had told Zoe that Phillip was busy was now giving her a long, disapproving look. "Did you have an appointment?"

"No." Zoe smiled. "I'm sorry I didn't. Actually, I'm an old friend of Dr. Barry's… That business about security escorting me out? Just a joke. Such a prankster, that Phillip." The secretary seemed unconvinced. "We go back a long way," Zoe said. "A very long way."

"Yes, well, whether you're a friend or not, it doesn't matter. You always need an appointment to see Dr. Barry. He's extremely busy. May I give him a message?"

Zoe hesitated. That was tempting. Leave the ball in his court and if he wanted to get back to her, fine, if not she'd proved that she had no hang-ups about past or present. But no—she had no guarantee that Ms. Bulldog here would pass on the message.

"I'll just try later," she told the secretary. "Any idea what time he'll be out of surgery?"

"I'm sorry, I don't."

"Or whether he'll be coming back here?"

"Sorry. May I give him your name?"

Courtney Brownstone, Zoe almost said, just for the hell of it. "No that's fine. Thank you."

She left and walked down to the elevators, thinking about her next move. The secretary probably knew pretty much everything about Phillip Barry, including the time he was likely to be out of surgery, but short of a gun held to her head she wasn't about to give it up. Darn.

A few feet away, a group of suits were clustered around a tall guy in blue scrubs who was leaning against a wall. The guy in scrubs had his arms folded across his chest and was nodding at what someone was saying. The folded arms registered before she realized it was Phillip Barry, the man himself.

Without giving herself time to think about it, she walked briskly down the corridor until she was on the edge of the group, facing him. One of the suits was saying something about a million-dollar donation and Phillip was still nodding, but staring off into the distance as though he had other things on his mind.

She was about to get his attention with a little wave, when he looked directly at her. Looking, she could tell, yet not really seeing. But suddenly his eyes widened. She smiled. Now her heart was skittering like one of Brett's hamsters.

"…to create a foundation," the same suit who had mentioned the million dollars was saying.

Phillip turned his head away and said something to the suit guys that she couldn't catch. The suits all nodded and Phillip glanced at his watch and they all trickled away. Now Phillip was giving her this wary look. She smiled again and he walked over to where she stood.

No return smile.

"Don't look so panicked," she said. "I'm not going to bite you."

THAT WOMAN AGAIN. Phillip tried to rally his thoughts. Last night he'd dreamed about her. Ambulance sirens, paramedics wheeling a girl into the trauma bay, a sheet covering her face. Molly. But he'd whipped away the sheet and the woman now standing in front of him, appearing faintly amused by his reaction, had been staring up at him, hazel eyes wide-open. Seeing her now, she didn't look quite as he'd remembered. Less...combative somehow.

"We go back a long way," she said. "A *long* way. You don't recognize me, do you?"

He shook his head. He didn't have time for guessing games. Back in his office, the medical-center administrator would be waiting to talk to him about reestablishing emergency neurosurgical services with third-year neuro residents. The idea made Phillip uneasy and he'd been mentally reviewing his opposition even as he listened to a couple of trustees talk about an endowment.

"I'll give you a clue," the woman said. "Casa Del Mar."

Casa Del Mar had been his family's home in Seacliff. The place was sold after his father died, but he passed the sprawling and gated grounds almost every day on his way home. It was less than five minutes away from the house he and Deanna had bought together and where Deanna still lived. Both places had the same kind of sweeping oceanfront views and evening vistas of the sun melting into the Pacific.

He was drawing a blank, though, on placing the woman there. He glanced at his watch. "You're going to have to tell me."

"Remember the guest cottage? The housekeeper?"

She was smiling at him as though any minute now recognition would smite him like a thunderbolt.

"Her two daughters?"

"Vaguely." The breasts, although less on display,

were still eye catching. He felt a surge of irritation—at himself for noticing and at the woman for…just being. She disturbed him and he wasn't entirely sure why. Molly was always talking about *vibes* she'd get from people. Good vibes, bad vibes. Vibes apparently were never neutral. He was definitely getting vibes. He rallied his thoughts. "You're one of the daughters?" he guessed.

"Yep."

"Wait," he said, snapping his fingers. "Long blond hair, you used to run around all summer in this bikini—"

"That was my sister, Courtney."

"And the other one—"

"Was me."

He scratched his head, thought for a minute. "God, it's coming back to me. Scrawny little kid, knees and elbows always covered with scabs and scratches. But I thought…that was a boy?"

She laughed. "No."

"That was you?"

He smiled and felt his irritation melt. He tried to convey good vibes, then felt vaguely ridiculous at the thought. Something told him she'd buy into the whole vibe thing.

"Do you still play tennis?" she asked.

"Very seldom these days, unfortunately." He was trying to reconcile past and present. "So that boy I remember…was you?"

"Yep. That's why I asked if you still played tennis. I used to hide behind a palm tree to watch you.

You were always tanned and you wore very white shorts."

"God, I can't believe…how old were you when you left?"

"Thirteen. But I looked about ten."

"That must explain it."

"Thank you. I guess."

He started to check his watch again and stopped himself. He was having dinner at his brother's next week. He'd have to ask John if he remembered the housekeeper having two daughters.

"To be honest, I don't remember you very well at all," he admitted. Then something struck him. Deanna. He remembered now that whenever she came to see him, she'd complain about one of the housekeeper's kids following her around and bothering her. "Did you let the air out of my girlfriend's tires?"

"Twice. I also found a picture of her in the newspaper, some debutante thing, and I blacked out all her teeth and stuck the picture under her windshield wipers. She was a snotty-nosed bitch. I hope you ended up dumping her."

Phillip raised an eyebrow. "Actually, I married her."

"We all do dumb things, I guess."

He laughed, he couldn't help himself. He had the feeling that she censored nothing before she said it. Disconcerting, but intriguing, too. Part of the whole off-beat package. Her left hand, he noticed with a quick glance, was bare. "Actually we're divorced now," he said. "Now what about—"

"Courtney. She's the family success story."

He nodded. That hadn't been his question, but it was interesting information. He remembered having this thing for Courtney, although he'd known better than to create trouble with his parents by showing interest in the housekeeper's daughter. Even though he'd always suspected that his father had actually had something going with the housekeeper.

"So...what brings you here, now?"

"The same thing that I came for last time, only this time I'm going to be more diplomatic. I decided that I probably came on a bit strong."

"But you were memorable."

"Yes, well, Jenny—the girl who died—is, was, the daughter of my best friend, and I...it's so incredibly important to me that it doesn't happen again..."

Phillip blinked. *Jenny Dixon.* "You knew her? Jenny Dixon?" He saw her face color slightly and she nodded, but said nothing. He felt himself scrambling for the right words to say. He wanted suddenly to just level with her, to let her know how the tragedy had affected him. "I have a daughter, Jenny's age," he wanted to say. "I have nightmares about the whole thing," he wanted to say. "There are no easy answers," he said instead.

"Lots of things have no easy answers," she replied levelly. "That doesn't mean we should stop looking for them. Even just making people aware. Before this happened to Jenny, I figured that if you needed emergency care, whatever it was, you'd get it. So what *is* going on with the trauma services? Are you doing anything to get them started again?"

Phillip thought of the administrator waiting in his office. "We're looking at a number of possibilities," he said.

Her eyes flashed. "That's exactly the kind of BS answer—"

"This is the diplomatic version?"

"Yeah, well…" She laughed. "Diplomacy isn't one of my major talents. Look, I'm sorry. I'm really concerned."

"Listen…"

"Zoe."

"*Zoe?*"

"Zoe. What? You look as though you've never heard the name before."

"It's not a name I hear very often. You're not Zoe McCann, by any chance?"

"That's me."

"You have a son called Brett?"

"Yes." Her chin had gone up, her eyes were narrowed. "What about it? How do you know him?"

"He attends the same school as my daughter."

"I know."

"So your son has mentioned Molly?"

"A few times."

Something he hadn't expected to hear in her voice—at least in relation to their respective offspring—a certain…cockiness, made him want to question her about the context in which her son had mentioned Molly's name. *I love her, Mom. Molly Barry is the girl of my dreams.* No, he couldn't see that. *She keeps buying me all this stuff, expensive stuff. She's nearly maxed out her mom's credit cards.*

He felt a sudden wave of fatigue—the effort of making the switch from the medical world, where he went around saving lives, to the baffling world of his daughter, where he never seemed to come up with the right answers.

He didn't want to deal with this.

"So?" Zoe jumped into the void. "Is there something I should know about?"

"No, no…" *Coward,* Deanna's voice sneered in his head. *Cop-out. When we have to send Molly somewhere to dry out, you better remember that you didn't even have the guts to talk to her.* "I, um…"

"You what?"

Phillip nodded at a colleague who had slowed to talk to him, eyed Zoe briefly then walked on. He wished to hell someone would page him, call a code or something. Irritation at his ex-wife prompted a decision. He'd call Deanna tonight. *You're the one with the suspicions, you call the mother.*

"Okay, you've farted around long enough," Zoe said. "Obviously you know something I don't." A pause. "Your daughter's pregnant."

"What? Molly?"

"You have another daughter?"

"No. *God, no,*" he said, not meaning to sound quite so emphatic. "Just Molly." He felt sweat on his brow. "She's pregnant?"

"That's what I'm asking you."

"No..." He shook his head. "No, not as far as I know."

"Would she tell you?"

He exhaled. "Of course."

"Does she...like Brett, or something? I mean, is she...seeing him, dating him, whatever kids call it these days?"

Phillip shook his head. "I don't know," he said. "Molly's mother seems to think that there might be some sort of...relationship."

"But Molly hasn't said anything to you?"

"No.

"Have you asked Molly herself?"

"Not...directly." He felt an almost frantic need to get out of this conversation, but plunged in just to get it over with. "Look, Molly's been using her mother's credit card to...buy expensive gifts."

"And you think they're for my son?"

"Maybe, I don't know for su—"

"What kind of expensive gifts?"

"I, uh...I think my wife mentioned a surfboard." Zoe just stared at him.

"I'm not accusing your son of anything, Zoe, I'm just—"

"It sounds to me as though that's exactly what you're doing. Listen to me, *Dr. Barry*." She drew closer and prodded his chest with her index finger. "And listen really, really well. One, my son doesn't *need* expensive gifts. Two, he doesn't *want* expensive gifts. Three, if I find he's accepted expensive gifts from your daughter, I will personally see to it that they're returned immediately. Four, tell your daughter to stay the hell away from my son. And five, please convey all of this to your ex-wife, because I damn well don't intend to have this conversation again."

CHAPTER SEVEN

SATURDAY, PHILLIP TOOK Molly to lunch to get to the bottom of things. Unfortunately, as well as he understood brain function, he found his own doing a disconnect. He absolutely could not reconcile the woman whose breasts he'd recently ogled with the skinny, pathetic child he'd thought was a boy. Zany Zoe, the vegetable seller. Small world. Quite a coinkadink as Molly would say. Perhaps not quite so surprising though. Zoe had grown up in Seacliff, still worked there. Clearly, she wanted the best for her son, and Country Day, if you could afford the tuition, was definitely the best.

That thought brought him back to the reason for this lunch.

He couldn't decide how best to address the issue of Brett McCann and, while he mulled it over, he realized that he'd completely lost track of what Molly had been saying. Which, he thought with a stab of guilt, was apt to happen even when he hung on to her every word.

"...and, Daddy, this is *so* mind-blowing, I mean it could literally change civilization as we know it today." In her excitement Molly leaned so far across the rough wooden tabletop that her chest hit the ginger wheat-grass smoothie she'd been sipping. The glass wobbled precariously for a moment before Phillip reached to steady it. Molly grinned. "Sorry, I just get so…like totally stoked by this whole thing. I mean the possibilities are endless. We can save forests, end world hunger and, Daddy, this will blow you away. *'Stop heart disease altogether.'*"

Phillip nodded, but his mind was drifting again. This was one of the few nonworking Saturdays he'd taken in the past month. Last night, a colleague had called to ask if he wanted to make up a golf foursome. He'd declined. "Sounds good, but I'm taking my daughter to lunch." His colleague had laughed. "Wish you hadn't told me that, Phil. My wife's always complaining that I need to do more with the kids. Once I asked, 'What d'you want me to do with them? Fry them up for dinner?' Boy, did I catch it for that, she didn't see anything funny about it." Phillip hadn't seen much humor in it, either. He fell short of being the perfect father in all sorts of ways, he thought as he looked across the table at his daughter, but he'd never taken his responsibilities lightly, never thought of them as a laughing matter.

This Brett McCann, for example. What *was* his interest in Molly? Another Spirit maybe. "A drug dealer…" Deanna had suggested last night "…and he's trying to get Molly hooked." Phillip hadn't responded. Deanna's flights of fancy didn't always have a logical basis.

He looked at Molly. Her eyes were glistening with an almost…there was no other term for it, fanatical zeal. *Industrial hemp.* Was it normal, this obsessive focus on something so…bizarre, so removed from the things he imagined most teenage girls obsessed about?

Affective schizophrenic disorder. Bull. He still thought it was bull.

Who did he know with daughters Molly's age? Max Winn in cardiology had a daughter, didn't he? Sure, he remembered Max complaining about the cost of prom night. Had Molly ever been to a prom? Deanna would have mentioned it, surely, if for no other reason than the expense.

"…and here's the *truly* amazing thing," Molly was rhapsodizing. *"People have been growing hemp for thousands of years.* George Washington grew hemp. So did Thomas Jefferson." She engaged his eyes. "Pretty amazing, huh?"

Phillip, whose knowledge of hemp, until Molly had set him straight, had been of the variety he'd smoked a couple of times in college, saw her eyes grow distant, as though perhaps she were looking back through time and seeing Washington strolling through his plantation. Maybe deciding whether he should uproot some of the tobacco crop and put in more hemp. "Wooden dentures are history, Martha," Phillip imagined George telling his wife. "Hemp. That's the way to go."

"Get this, Dad. *The Declaration of Independence was signed on hemp paper!"*

"I didn't know that," Phillip replied truthfully as he considered again how to bring up the Brett Mc-Cann thing. Talking to Molly was akin to repairing an aneurysm. One wrong nick and all hell could break loose.

He decided that a direct approach was the safest. "Tell me about Brett McCann," he said.

Molly's brow furrowed. "Daddy, I'm trying to explain something." She slid out of the booth and stood. "Be right back," she called over her shoulder before heading in the direction of the rest room signs.

Phillip pushed away his untouched mug of chicory coffee and glanced up at the clock behind the cash register, where a girl about Molly's age with silver rings dangling from her eyebrows, nose, lower lip, both ears and, probably, other body areas not visible to him, had just told a boy, similarly pierced, that her body was a temple. "Totally," the boy said. "I am *so* with you on that one."

Probably another industrial hemp fan. He read the menu offerings chalked on a blackboard above the counter for anything he might be remotely interested in eating. Anything other than sprouts, brown rice and tofu. A double cheeseburger with bacon and fried onions, for example. *Nada.*

This Brett boy. Son of Zany Zoe the vegetable peddler. Not a big leap, from vegetables to hemp. Was it? Could that explain the fifteen hundred Molly had racked up on Deanna's American Express? Fifteen hundred bucks worth of hemp seed? Where would you even buy hemp seed? He tried to imagine presenting this theory to Zoe McCann. She'd have his head—or worse.

Molly returned to the table. She'd outlined her eyes again. Sooty-black lines above and below her eyes. Her hair, dyed black as a bat's wing, was wet, dripping almost, as though she'd dunked her head under the tap and combed it straight back off her forehead. She looked weird, he thought. Alien, somehow. He felt guilty for the thought and smiled at her.

"So, Moll," he said as though they'd just sat down. "Let's talk about you. What else is happening in your life?"

"This *is* my life, Dad. I am totally, totally into changing people's beliefs. If I can just convert just one person—"

"Sweetheart." Phillip tried to keep irritation from his voice. "You're obviously enthusiastic and that's good." Molly, smiling, nodded her agreement and started to speak, but he held up his hand. "I haven't finished. It's very important that you temper that enthusiasm with some objectivity."

"Absolutely," Molly agreed. "It's the lack of objectivity that causes politicians and the police and all the other fearmongers to resist change."

This was going nowhere, Phillip decided. He pushed up his shirtsleeve to glance at his watch. Not surprisingly, it was fifteen minutes ahead of the one above the cash register. "Molly." He met her eyes. "Listen to what I'm going to say. If this stuff...hemp, was really the miracle you claim it is, don't you think we'd be growing it commercially?"

"But that's just the point, Dad." She leaned across the table again. "The antidrug forces are creating this witch hunt so that farmers are terrified to even talk about growing hemp. There was this third-grade teacher in Idaho or somewhere who lost her job just for saying that people should be encouraged to grow it." Her face impassioned, she lay almost prone across the table. "Dad, you've got to believe me. I swear to God, this is the most important movement in my lifetime—yours, too. It's like so huge—"

"This…interest." He paused, easy does it. Not so direct this time. "It seems very sudden. When…how did you get so involved?"

"Oh…" She bit her lip, frowning now. "Well, it's kind of a weird story. My friend, Brett?" Now she looked up at him. "Okay, listen to me, Dad, and don't say anything until I'm finished. See, he lives on three acres, or something like that, up in the north county. His mother has a nursery, she grows vegetables and stuff."

Phillip sensed where this might be going, but he said nothing.

"Dad, if we grew even one acre of hemp, we could save an entire forest. Think of it, Dad. All those trees saved. But that's not all. We could weave our own clothes, produce our own source of nutrition. I mean, it's totally amazing."

As Molly continued to reel off all the potential benefits, Phillip imagined his next conversation with Deanna and felt an ache in his temple. A sudden yearning to be in the O.R. doing brain surgery made him glance at his watch again.

"And Brett shares your enthusiasm?" he asked. "And his mother," he added, thinking of Zoe McCann.

"Well, not yet."

"You've discussed it with him?"

Her expression impatient, Molly waved away the question. "Dad. What have I been telling you? This is a revolution. Every part of it has to be carefully thought-out. We need a strategy."

"We?"

"The movement." Molly extracted a cell phone from her canvas backpack and glanced at it. "I'm outta time, Dad. I need to be somewhere else." She reached for his hand. "Listen, I know you and Mom are all freaked-out, but everything's cool, really. I am so, *so* happy. Dad, please, please stop worrying. All these negative vibes you guys are sending totally, totally, screw up my karma."

Phillip put some money on the table and made a mental note to call Molly's psychiatrist first thing Monday morning. He also gave some consideration to calling Zoe McCann to discuss their respective offspring and to alert her to his daughter's newfound agricultural interests.

ZOE STARED into the window of Pierre's Patisserie. Trays of Napoleons, macaroons, cream puffs and tiny fruit tarts were calling her name. The sugar would go straight to her head and hips, but it might make her feel better. Vegetables were very healthy and she had some fantastic recipes, but the mood she was in called for sugar.

She was frustrated. Phillip Barry wouldn't leave her alone and she didn't know what to do about it. He walked beside her as she pushed a cart through the market, hovered around the vegetable beds so she couldn't even garden in peace. He made nightly guest appearances in her dreams and now, here he was standing beside her, looking cool and condescending. Get out of my head, she wanted to scream. But he wouldn't.

Scrawny little kid, knees and elbows always covered with scabs and scratches.

She stared down a slice of tiramisu. A second on the lips, two months on the hips. At least he couldn't call her scrawny anymore. A macaroon winked at her. She went inside, picked out a chocolate-covered cream puff, stuck the paper bag in her shoulder purse and walked down the street in search of a place where she could think and gorge.

After leaving Phillip Barry, she'd stalked out of the hospital to find a ticket tucked neatly under the windshield wiper. Offense: unauthorized parking in the physician's lot. Ten dollars. She'd ripped it up, got in the truck and tried to start the ignition. Her hands had been shaking so hard she couldn't insert the key.

She kept walking. After a while, the cream puff began broadcasting messages from her purse. *Eat me,* it commanded. *Eat me.* She reached into her bag, fished around in the paper sack and stuck her finger into a mound of cream. She licked her fingers. Yum. She decided that she would think while she walked. Walking would burn off some of the cream-puff calories, right?

She thought about the jacket on Brett's bed.

They'd had a huge fight over the jacket.

He'd been down in the kitchen and he tore up the stairs, grabbed the jacket from her and tried to squeeze past her and into his room. "I'm sick of this," he'd yelled, his face red and angry.

"Hey, hey, hey." Taken aback by the vehemence of his outburst, she'd grabbed his arm and looked into his eyes. "What's this all about?"

"You're always snooping around in my room. I hate it."

"I am *not* always snooping in your room, Brett," she'd said quietly. He needed a haircut, she'd thought, and a new crop of pimples had erupted on his chin. "I *don't* snoop in your room," she repeated. "The door was open and I just happened to notice the jacket on your bed. What are you getting so mad about?"

"I'm sick of you treating me like some freakin' baby. I can't do anything, except what you want me to do. *You can't go surfing, Brett,*" he said, his voice pitched high. *"You can't do this, Brett. You can't do that, Brett. Be a doctor or a lawyer, Brett.* Well, maybe I don't want to be a freakin' doctor or a lawyer. Maybe that's just what *you* want."

She retrieved another fingerful of cream from the bag. Maybe she should just stop and eat the damn thing. Except she was now walking down Seacliff's main drag with all its expensive shops and well-groomed women who appeared to be in advanced stages of starvation. Earlier, she'd delivered a basket of salad greens to one of the oceanfront mega-mansions and she'd been headed north again when she decided she needed emotional sustenance. From experience, she knew that Pierre's always filled the bill.

Okay, so the jacket most likely came from Molly. Probably all the phone calls and hang-ups, too.

She broke off a hunk of cream puff. So, what if he did have a girlfriend and it *was* Molly Barry? Weird Molly. She should have told Dr. Phillip Barry that's what her son called his card-charging daughter. *Weird Molly.* Brett could have his choice of girls. Why her? But just say it was true. Okay, let's think this through. Girls buy boys gifts, that was a given. And maybe Molly *had* gone overboard, charging up her mother's credit cards and now her father was just trying to get to the bottom of things.

Let's think about that for a few moments.

What was your immediate reaction when you heard Phillip say Brett's name?

Her mother's voice in her head provided the answer. "I swear to God, Zoe, when it's anything to do with Brett, you go on the attack."

A month ago, over an otherwise pleasant lunch, Janna had hinted that she and Arnie both thought that Zoe was overprotective with Brett.

"That's crap," Zoe had shot back. "What the hell does Arnie know anyway? How does he think I'm overprotective? Did he give you an example?"

Janna had sighed, clearly sorry she'd mentioned it. "Could we please drop this? I wanted us to have a nice lunch and now I'm feeling tension in my shoulders. Let's talk about something else." She'd bent to retrieve a credit card from her purse. "I'll get this."

But Zoe pressed anyway. "*Did* he give you an example?"

"God, Zoe, you're relentless. You're just like your grandma. Once you get an idea in your head, you're like a terrier with a bone. Can't we just talk about it later?"

"No, tell me now."

"Well—" Janna scratched the back of her head "—remember when we were over a few weeks ago and you wouldn't let Brett go surfing with his father?"

"Which time?" Zoe asked before she realized she'd inadvertently proved Janna's point. "You mean when he wanted to go right in the middle of a storm? Well, of course I wouldn't let him go. There were all these warnings about dangerous surf."

"I know, but Arnie felt you should have let Brett's father make that decision."

"Brett's father is an idiot," she shot back. "And so is stupid Arnie. Did you stick up for me? Did you say, *Oh, well, maybe Zoe's overprotective because she grew up knowing what it was like to have someone who cared more about her boyfriends than she did her daughter?*"

Recalling the way Janna's face had sort of frozen,

Zoe felt her eyes sting with tears. She'd apologized, of course, but deep down, she had no doubt that the urge to shelter her own son from the harsher realities of life sprang from a fierce anger that she'd never felt protected herself.

And so, for the second time, she'd made an idiot of herself with Phillip Barry. He had to think she was a complete head case. Starting to feel really depressed now, she stopped walking, took the paper bag from her purse and demolished the rest of the cream puff, staring down a Gucci-dressed skeleton walking in the opposite direction.

Back home again, she petted Kenna, who left absolutely no doubt that Zoe's arrival was the highlight of her day. The other two dogs came bounding up, clearly of similar opinions.

"Yeah, you don't think I'm nuts, do you girls?" She fed them all biscuits. "No, you think I'm the tops. As long as I give you biscuits, huh?"

At the sink, she washed her hands, made herself a mug of tea then went upstairs. Brett wasn't home yet. Outside his closed door, she paused, tempted to go inside and seek out clues to other parts of his life he wasn't disclosing to her. She walked on to her own room, lay down with her sandals still on and let herself cry.

Her baby was no longer her baby. Hadn't been her baby for some time now. Wouldn't let her kiss him when she dropped him off from school, complained when she called him her baby. He had his secrets now, pieces of his life she knew nothing about. Weird

Molly. She would have to stop saying that. Perhaps he was in love with the girl. Maybe she and Phillip Barry would become in-laws. His snob ex-wife wouldn't approve, of course, but Janna and Courtney would be delighted. "My grandson is married to the Barry daughter," she could hear Janna saying. And Courtney could flirt with Phillip Barry at the wedding. *That is* so *funny about you thinking Zoe was a boy,* she would whisper as they danced together.

Sometime later, the phone rang, and when Zoe glanced at the clock, she realized she must have drifted off to sleep. Her mouth tasted like copper and her hair was damp and stuck to the side of her face. "Hello?"

"Mom…okay, now don't blow up, just listen to me first—"

"Blow up at you because?"

"I'm over at Dad's. I called Grandma and she said it was okay. Mom? Are you okay?"

"I'm fine." She wanted to spill out everything, to question him and understand what was going on. "You'll be home tonight?"

"Can't I just stay at Dad's?"

"Brett." She lay back against the pillow. "Tonight is a school night. The last time you stayed at your dad's on a school night, you went—"

"I know, I know." He exhaled noisily. "Jeez, I never get to do anything."

"I could weep for you," Zoe said. "Ten o'clock, back here."

"Yeah, yeah."

After he hung up, she stood in the room for a minute thinking about him accepting expensive gifts from Molly Barry. She went into his room, pushed open the door. *The jacket, which had been hanging on the end of the bed for days, was gone.* She closed the door, went to her bathroom and splashed water over her face. Then she went downstairs, gathered her keys and purse and drove to the market.

"...WHOEVER DID her previous surgery put a shunt in through the right side," Phillip's brother was saying as he and Phillip sat on the redwood deck of Joe's Seacliff home drinking beer and watching the sun dissolve into the ocean. Joe rose, checked the albacore steaks slowly turning opaque on the grill and sat back down again. "Huge amount of scar tissue. Anyway, it was bizarre. I started to worry about anomalous venous—"

"Are you guys going to sit there talking shop all night?" Joe's wife Caroline appeared on the patio, a long-stemmed glass of sparkling water in one hand, her face tinged pink by the brilliant red glow off the water. Eight months' pregnant with the couple's first child, she wore a sleeveless white cotton dress that skimmed her smooth, tanned knees, her long dark hair pulled up into a ponytail. "I'll only sit out here if you promise not to discuss surgery."

Phillip grinned. Joe was a cardiac surgeon, like their father. The old man had maintained a full day's operating schedule until the day he died, ironically from undiagnosed heart disease, and liked nothing more than what he used to call "a good old chin-wag" about his work.

"You're both just like Pops," Caroline said. "And when the two of you get together, I could be sitting here stark naked for all you'd notice. So Phillip." She put her elbows on the table and regarded him across an expanse of hand-painted Italian tile. "Tell me what's going on. Anything fun?"

He drank some beer and tried to think. Nothing occurred to him that could remotely be construed as fun. Shrugging, he spread his hands palms up. *"Rien."*

"Oh, come on." Caroline wasn't buying it. "There's got to be something interesting." His beeper lay on the table where he'd set it earlier. She picked it up, flashed an arch smile. "In case your girlfriend calls?"

"Of course."

"What girlfriend?" Joe asked.

"Her name slips my mind," Phillip said. "I've got so many that I've started referring to them by number. It's less confusing."

Joe shook his head at Caroline. "Quit grilling him."

"It's self-protection," Caroline said. "If I don't guide the subject matter, we'll end up talking surgical techniques." Folding her arms across her stomach now, she fixed him with a sly smile. "Did you ever talk to Deanna about anything except work?"

Joe laughed. "He's divorced, isn't he? That should tell you something."

"Yeah, but…" She grinned disarmingly at Phillip. "If you want to know the truth, I never really liked Deanna. I know it's an awful thing to say, but she seemed so…shrewish. That tight little smile—"

"Moving on…" Joe looked at Phillip. "What else is going on?"

"Phillip's not offended, are you, Phillip?" Caroline pressed, clearly reluctant to move on. "It's not like you're still in love with her, right?"

"How's that on-call situation playing out?" Joe asked.

"We've got a prospect who might fit," Phillip replied, relieved to have the conversation take a new slant. "I'm talking to him tomorrow. Stu's had several phone conversations and he's quite impressed with the guy—"

"I'm warning you two," Caroline said. "I hear shoptalk rearing its ugly head and I'm about to scream…come on, Phillip. Tell me something. How's Molly doing?"

Phillip drank some beer and, as he set his glass down, caught Caroline's quick glance at Joe. His mood suddenly plummeted. After yesterday's confrontation with Zoe McCann, he'd gone back to his office to call Molly at his apartment, and got his own recording. With a glance at the clock, he'd realized that Molly would still be at school. Later, she'd claimed an upset stomach and cloistered herself in her room.

Joe and Caroline were watching him, waiting for a response. "I keep telling myself it's typical teenage behavior," he said, "but, I don't know."

"Deanna's still in New York?" Caroline asked.

"Just until next week, she says."

"Molly's staying with you?"

Phillip nodded. "Deanna used to say bombs could go off all around and nothing would distract me from work, but between Molly and…" He'd started to mention Zoe McCann and stopped himself. He hadn't quite sorted out in his own mind why, apart from Molly and the on-call connection, he was spending a hell of a lot of time thinking about Zoe.

"I'll tell you, Phillip," Caroline said. "I saw Molly a couple of weeks ago and she seemed…I don't know, manic. We were outside that health-food market in Leucadia and she was telling me about soybeans or something and the words were coming out so fast, she was kind of tripping all over herself. I wanted to take her arm and say, 'Slow down. Take a deep breath.'"

"She's a teenager," Joe said. "That's how they all talk. Life's exciting at that age."

Phillip stretched out his legs. The air had cooled since the sun set, and a candle Caroline lit earlier had been extinguished by a strong gust off the ocean. Joe was talking, words obviously intended as a balm to his own concerns for Molly. "Good kid," Joe was saying. "High-spirited. Just the way we were. Remember that night we liberated Dad's Jaguar?"

He nodded. They'd borrowed the car and charged up fancy dinners for themselves and their dates. The old man had been apoplectic.

He wanted desperately to believe that Molly was

just doing now what her old man had done years earlier. But he hadn't set his bed on fire. Or attempted suicide. Twice.

Caroline shivered and announced that she was going in to get a jacket. When she returned to the deck, she was carrying a tray with a coffeepot and heavy glass mugs.

Phillip waited until Caroline had poured the coffee, then looked across the table at Joe. His brother's face was now in deep shadow. "Hey, Joe. Remember that housekeeper who used to live in the little guest cottage? Mom hired her, but she and Dad were always fighting about her."

"Janna Parsons." Joe grinned widely. "I had a crush on her." He looked at his wife. "A Mrs. Robinson kind of thing."

Caroline eyed him for a long moment.

"Hey, she was a foxy older woman and I was seventeen," Joe said, then turned back to Phillip. "What about her?"

"Did she have kids?" Phillip asked, testing his brother's memory now.

"Two daughters. One was a little knockout, long blond hair and she ran around in a bikini all the time. She would have been what? Fourteen, fifteen."

"What about the other one? Girl or boy?"

Joe scratched his ear. "Girl, I think." He thought for a moment. "Yeah, a little scrawny kid. Give me a minute and I'll remember her name. Hold on…Zelda? No, it's coming…sss…zzz…*Zooey*. Oh, jeez." Laughing, Joe slapped the table and looked at

Caroline. "That's what we used to call her, I mean I swear to God that kid was a mess. Once I almost made her believe she had a bird's nest in her hair."

Caroline shot Joe a reproving look.

"What?" He looked at Phillip. "Remember, she had some kind of rash all over her legs and she was always scratching."

"I didn't even remember there was another daughter," Phillip said. "I thought she was a boy."

"Well, you'd have to look real close," Joe said, still laughing. "The only reason I remember was playing cannibal. Remember that?"

Phillip shook his head.

"Well, you were always off somewhere with Deanna. We had this old metal bathtub behind the tennis courts. You don't remember that? Anyway, we called it the cooking pot. I was the chief cannibal so I could say who got to climb in. The cute girl, whatever her name was, always got to go in, but Zooey had scabs all over her knees and elbows so we didn't let her get in. God, she was so mad. She spit at me."

"That's the saddest thing I've ever heard," Caroline said angrily. "Where was her mother? Why wasn't she taking care of the kid's rash?" She got up from the table. "I'm sorry, but I hate that story, I really do."

Joe grabbed her arm. "Come on, honey, this was years ago."

"I don't care," she snapped. "Why do people have kids if they can't take care of them?"

"Hormones," Joe said after Caroline left. "These

days anything sets her off. So how come you were thinking about all that?"

"Zoe McCann, that's her name now, McCann," Phillip said. "Anyway, she came to see me last week."

CHAPTER EIGHT

THUMP THUMP THUMP.

The sound of Brett's stereo in his bedroom reverberated downstairs to the kitchen where Zoe was sitting. She walked into the hallway and stood at the foot of the stairs. "Brett. Turn that damn thing down."

Thump thump thump.

Back in the kitchen again, the microwave *pinged*. She tasted the tea and grimaced. English Toffee. Worse even than the box of Honey Almond Mocha she'd been suckered into buying last week, lured as she always was by the delectable names and colorful packaging. They all tasted horrible and synthetic, but she kept buying them anyway. Gingerbread Cookies. Honey Almond, Cherry Apple, Mango. This one *would* be good. There was a thought there. Like marrying Denny McCann because the packaging looked good. *Scrawny little kid...* Phillip Barry's voice said. She was scratching her left hand now, rubbing her knuckles hard against her hip to relieve the itch. In her case, maybe even the packaging wasn't so hot.

Thump thump thump.

She carried her mug of tea out onto the back porch to escape the sound. It was dark and she could smell orange blossom and jasmine. The goats had heard her and they started bleating and hoofed it over to the fence, the pony right behind them. She'd decided to let the pony share their pen until she found time to build a separate enclosure. Cradling the mug in both hands, she walked barefoot across the damp grass to where they were all congregated awaiting her arrival. That was the great thing about animals—they loved and respected you, no matter what.

Until she felt calm enough not to make some big humungous deal, she'd decided not to mention the Molly thing to Brett. Call it her midyear resolution, decided upon after the Phillip Barry fiasco. She would take some deep breaths, put her brain in gear before she blurted out whatever was on her mind.

She watched the goats. In the dark night, the white patches at the throats of the pygmies looked luminous. From inside the house, she heard the phone ringing. Her tea splashing, she ran to answer it.

"Brett, please."

"Excuse me?"

"Brett."

Zoe didn't care for the girl's snippy tone. Molly? She didn't care. "His social secretary has the evening off," she said. "I'm filling in for her. This is his mother. May I tell him who's calling."

"He'll know."

"How about you tell me anyway."

"Screw you."

Zoe heard the sound of the receiver being replaced.

Thump, thump, thump from upstairs. She got up and yelled from the bottom of the stairs again. "Hey, Brett. Turn that off and come down here."

Thump, thump, thump.

"Brett." Why, she wondered as she ran up the stairs, do people mindlessly do the same thing over and over when they know damn well it hasn't worked in the past, it's not working now and all indicators are it's not going to work in the future? "Brett!" She pounded on his bedroom door, then flung it open. "How many times have I told you—"

"Huh?" He sat on the floor amidst the litter of his room, peering up at her as she swooped in to turn off the boom box. "*Hey.* How come you did that?"

"Because the walls were beginning to crumble around me. Keep it down to a dull roar, okay?"

"Can I go to Dad's this weekend?"

"Didn't we already talk about this once?"

He hung his head. "Forget it then."

"A girl just called for you."

"Who?"

"That's what I was wondering."

He eyed her warily.

"She said you'd know who it was."

"Weird Molly."

Zoe sat on the edge of his bed. "That's who gave you the jacket?"

"How d'you know?"

"Her father told me. When I went to the hospital.

That wasn't why I went there, though. I didn't even plan to mention you. But when I told him my name was Zoe, he asked me if my last name was McCann. And then he said that his daughter goes to school with you. He said Molly's been charging up her mother's credit cards, buying expensive gifts."

He nodded. "She bought me a surfboard. A really cool one.

She tried to keep her voice level. "What did you do with it?"

"I gave it back. The jacket, too."

Relief washed through her and with it a huge surge of love. Doubt and speculation vanished like smoke. Of course he would do the right thing. Why would she even doubt him for a minute? She smiled and wrapped her arms around him. He endured it briefly, before pulling away. Still she couldn't keep the smile from her face. Okay, so her life's narrative might have a bunch of flaws, but it also had at its very heart something so incredible and miraculous that sometimes she'd get almost superstitious that some malevolent fate would discover she'd been unfairly rewarded and try to wrest her treasure away.

The treasure was giving her a look. "What?"

"I love you, Brettypoo."

"Don't call me that, Mom. I'm not some baby."

"You're not *some* baby." She caught his face in her hands. "You're *my* baby."

He mumbled something that sounded like "Love you, too."

"Brett, sweetie. You *can* talk to me about this."

He eyed his boom box. "Okay."

"So this girl. Molly. Is she…do you—"

"Mom, I already told you. She's not a girlfriend or anything. She's just weird. I wish she'd quit bugging me."

"When you say she's weird…how do you mean?"

Brett yawned. "I don't know, she just is."

Zoe stood. He'd talk to her when he was ready, she decided. "Well, sweetie. Try to be nice to her anyway. Maybe she just needs a friend."

AFTER HIS MOM LEFT, Brett was lying on his bed thinking about stuff. Even when there was nobody else around, it embarrassed him when she did that cootchy-cootchy baby-talk stuff. Kenna was on the bed beside him, snoring again. He watched her for a minute, the way her sides moved in and out. He didn't want to hurt his mom's feelings or anything. Except for being kinda hyper, she was a pretty good mom. They did fun stuff together, like when they went down to the beach at midnight to watch the grunion run, or going cross-country skiing. His friends' moms didn't do that kind of stuff. Still, sometimes she was hard to figure out. Like how weird it was the way he could just say one thing and suddenly she'd be in this great mood again. Or the other way around. He'd tell her something that was, like, no big deal and she'd be slamming cupboard doors, asking him a million questions. Like if she ever found out he'd taken the truck out at one in the morning and gone over to Molly's. Man, that would get her going forever.

Or if he told her what Molly said yesterday. Totally out of the blue she asks him if he could ever imagine killing one of his parents.

"Like say, they'd done something truly disgusting," she'd said, "and it would make the world a better place if they weren't around?"

Right now though, his mom was in a good mood. He could hear her downstairs, singing. She was always singing and she had the worst voice you ever heard. Like a combination of a screeching cat and a car with bad brakes. And loud. His mom never hummed softly to herself, like his friend Joe's mom. No, *his* mom belted out the songs and sometimes she'd grab him and try to make him dance with her or something.

"'Make *someone* happy,'" she was singing now, real loud like she felt pretty happy herself. "'Make just *someone* happeeeee.'"

He picked up the phone and called his dad.

"Hey, kid, what's up?"

"Nothing much."

His dad laughed. "Same old, same old, huh?"

"Yeah."

"So you comin' here this weekend?"

"Dunno. Mom kind of wants me to help her do stuff here."

"Aw jeez, Brett. When does your mom ever not want you to help her do stuff there? Tell her to bag it. If she sold that place, got a condo or something and found herself a regular job, she wouldn't need to use you as a freakin' day laborer."

"It's not like that, Dad. I mean, she doesn't make me do stuff every weekend and it's kind of fun feeding the animals. We got a horse."

His dad made this sound like he was disgusted or something. "Whose idea was that? Like I don't know. Your mother, son, I swear to God. Always poor-mouthing, she doesn't have money for this, she doesn't have money for that and she buys a damn horse—"

"Dad…" He hated it when his dad got on some tear about his mom. Some of the things he agreed with, like about his mom always making a big deal of everything, but mostly, if he talked about her to his dad, he always ended up feeling so guilty he couldn't look at her. "There's this girl at school?"

"Huh?"

"The weird girl I told you about?"

"Oh, yeah, right. So d'you tell her to take a hike?"

"Kind of."

"What d'you mean, kind of?"

"Well, she started crying and everything."

His dad laughed. "Son, that's a chick's biggest trick. Don't let her sucker you."

"Well, see the thing is yesterday, she said she'd kill herself if we broke up."

"Broke up? What are you talking about? You're telling me now she's like a girlfriend or something?"

"No. It's not like that. And she says other freaky things, too. Like she's always following me home from school and looking at the goats and saying she knows how to slit their throats."

"She Mexican, or something?"

"What does that have to do with it?"

"They eat goats. Birri something or other, I forget. There's this Mexican food joint where Pam likes the carnitas." He laughed. "Carnitas with hot sauce, a couple of margaritas and that babe is *vavavaroom*."

Brett imagined his stepmom. Last time he'd been over, Pam was wearing headphones while she cooked dinner. She had on these silky yellow shorts and a white tank top. It was pretty obvious she wasn't wearing a bra or anything underneath and every time she said anything to him, he'd be trying so hard not to look at her boobs that he kept missing what she was saying. Once Pam said that she thought his mom smothered him. He'd made the big mistake of telling his mom. "When Pam has children of her own, she might be qualified to give me child-rearing advice," his mom had said. "I doubt it, but anything's possible. Until then, I'd prefer that when she shares her bubblegum-colored insights with you, you didn't pass them on to me."

"I don't think Molly wants to eat the goats, Dad," he said now. "It's like she's kind of into devil worship or something."

"She put out for you?"

"Hell no. I wouldn't even want her to. I told you, she's like really freaky."

His dad laughed. "Okay, you're kind of confusing me, Brett. You're not getting any action, she's not your girlfriend, you say. What the hell is there to break up?"

Brett rolled onto his stomach, the phone jammed between his ear and shoulder. Now he kind of wished he hadn't got into this with his dad. His dad was good to talk to in lots of ways. Like he understood about why going to some fancy private school where he had no friends and all the kids were snobs was the pits. But in other ways it was just as bad as dealing with his mom. "See, no one likes her. She doesn't have any friends."

"Son, that's not your problem."

"But what if she kills herself and it's my fault?"

"Okay, you gotta listen to me, son. She's not gonna kill herself."

"She said she tried to do it before."

"You wanna know what I think? Either she's lying or she's nuts. Whatever, it's not your problem."

"Even if she kills herself?"

"Sure. Let her kill herself. You've got your own life to think about. You don't need to get mixed up in her crap. Listen, son, Pam ordered pizza, and the delivery guy just got here. Tell your mom you want to come here this weekend, don't let her lay any guilt trip on you. We'll do some fun stuff. Take the dirt bikes out to the desert or something."

"Okay. Bye, Dad."

His mom was still singing downstairs. "'One smile that cheers you…'" Now she was coming up the stairs. "'One face that lights when it's near yooooo…'" She knocked on his door.

"Yeah?" He sat up, grabbed his backpack and pulled out some papers and a book.

"Can I come in?" She opened the door an inch or two and stuck her head around. "Hey, you are one very good boy." She put her arm around his shoulder, buried her face in his neck. "You're doing your homework without me nagging you."

He shrugged and turned over a page of his book, like she'd just caught him in the middle of something fascinating.

"Listen, sweetie." She sat down on the edge of the bed. "I know you're all grown-up and it's embarrassing to be seen around with your old mom, but I was just thinking about how we used to ride our bikes around Mission Bay. Remember how much fun that was? What do you say we pile them into the truck and take a spin around the bay on Saturday?"

"Yeah, maybe." He didn't look up from the book.

"Well, think about it anyway, okay?" She got up from the bed and went back downstairs.

Brett shoved the book on the floor. *Man.* Now he was going to get this guilt trip. Why did everything have to be so freakin' screwed? All he wanted was just to be a kid.

CHAPTER NINE

ZOE WAS SITTING on a deck chair under a red-and-blue Cinzano patio umbrella behind a long wooden table massed with freshly picked vegetables and flowers and eating an ear of roasted corn when Phillip Barry surprised the hell out of her. One minute she'd been squeezing some lime and chili powder on the corn and thinking how if there was a better food going, she didn't know about it, the next she'd looked up and there he was smiling at her.

First she choked on a corn kernel and went into this huge coughing fit that didn't stop until someone— Phillip Barry—handed her a cup of water. Her face, already red, went a few shades redder—she could feel the heat—and her eyes and nose were streaming. She ducked under the table to grab a paper towel, leaned over too far and fell off her chair. Fell off. Right on her butt. When she glanced up, she could see him peering over the table looking concerned, actually more amused than concerned. With all the dignity she could muster, she rose. Her eyes were still gushing, ditto her nose. She blew hard, tossed the paper towel and smiled politely.

"And for my next act, I inhale the entire corn cob."

"Are you okay?"

"Superb."

He looked at her, long enough that she wondered whether maybe something gross was sticking to her face. From the stall to her left, she could hear Sandy telling someone how to make *herbes de Provence*. "It's a blend," she was saying. "But those little jars you pick up in the market are no good. They don't use lavender. Big mistake." It struck Zoe suddenly that Phillip Barry was very attractive. Too Ivy League, buttoned-down, *GQ* for her taste, but still…

"Do I have corn stuck in my teeth?"

"Show me."

She bared her teeth and he bent his head to take a look.

"All clear."

"I always figure it's better to ask than to sit there wondering the whole time," she said. Her mind was racing. She'd replayed their last exchange so many times, changing what she'd said to what she should have said. Changing her tone from combative to politely concerned, changing it again to witty but biting. Now here he was on her turf and she felt completely thrown off track. And he seemed kind of awkward, too, a whole lot different from the Dr. God at Seacliff.

"That's beautiful," he nodded at the vegetable display. "Looks good enough to eat."

She smiled and they both stood as though transfixed by the sight.

"So," she said when the silence stretched on uncomfortably. "What brings you here? Going to try a little alfresco brain surgery? The guy in that stall over there could use a total extraction. Hey, Jim," she yelled across the aisle. "You about ready to get rid of that nonfunctioning thing inside your head?"

Jim, an old guy who trucked his vegetables in from the Imperial Valley, lifted a hand to his ear. He hadn't heard. Now she felt like an idiot and Phillip was looking as if he wanted the ground to swallow him up, and if anyone needed a total brain extraction, it was her.

He held out a brown paper bag. "Any idea what I do with this?"

She peered into the contents, then up at him. "Escarole. It makes a great frittata or you could cook it with white beans. I have a fantastic salad recipe with Gruyere cheese."

"It doesn't have to be cooked?"

"Nope." She reached for a card with the bean-salad recipe. "This is easy. You just toss the beans in a mustard vinaigrette." She peered into his eyes. Very blue. "There's no way in hell you're going to make a mustard vinaigrette, is there?"

"No."

"Why d'you buy it?"

He laughed. "Good question."

"My goats would enjoy it. If you want to unload it, that is."

"Tell them *bon appétit*." He handed her the bag. "How many goats do you have?"

"Four."

"What do you do with them?"

"Oh, I take them to the movies, to the beach, that sort of thing."

"I'm serious. Do you raise them…keep them as pets?"

"Right now. Eventually I want to make goat cheese."

He shook his head, as though at a loss for words.

"Goats are fun to have, though." She felt compelled to talk. "I feed them the old telephone directories."

He didn't know whether to believe her, she could see it in his face. She is one strange chick, he was thinking. And she was doing a bang-up job living up to his opinion.

"Also a pony, sheep, three dogs and some feral kittens that I need to get fixed," she babbled on. "Want one?"

"No thanks."

"So." She glanced at her watch. Nearly four. "No skulls to drill?"

"Not today. I have a meeting in an hour and I was going to grab something to eat from the cafeteria. Then I looked outside and the sun was shining and I thought I'd take a walk over here instead."

She looked directly at him.

He rubbed his jaw.

"Liar," she said and his face reddened.

"I've felt uncomfortable about the way we left things last week," he said after a moment. "I think I offended you and—"

"Actually, I've thought a lot about that, too." Zoe saw Roz approach the stall, spot Phillip and move on. "It's possible that I may have overreacted a tad. Brett's…well, he means everything to me and I go on the attack if I think he's threatened in any way. I should have listened before I blew up."

He nodded as though agreeing with her, but his mind seemed elsewhere. "Molly's going through a difficult time," he said. "I'm confident she'll pull out of it, but…just so you know, I'd also appreciate it if you would let me know immediately if…well, if you learn about anything…untoward in regards to Molly."

"Untoward. " Zoe raised her eyebrows. "Want to explain that in easy-to-understand language?"

His brow furrowed, and he seemed to be thinking about the question. "As I mentioned," he finally said, "she's going through a rough patch. She has a tendency to…spin tall tales, exaggerate."

"She lies, you're saying?"

"Well yes, but it's not as simple as that. I can't really go into detail, but since she seems to have… formed a friendship with your son, I'd appreciate it if you hear of anything that you think I, as a parent, should know about."

Watching his face as he stumbled through the request, Zoe felt a surge of compassion. This was a man clearly concerned about his daughter but, she recognized, scrambling around for the right thing to do. He might have grown up with advantages she hadn't had, might be Dr. God at Seacliff Memorial Medical Center while she eked out a living selling vegetables, but when it came to their children she was so damn fortunate it almost brought tears to her eyes.

"Look, I keep a pretty close watch, but Brett isn't too communicative with me when it comes to girls. He tells his father, but he clams up if I ask questions." She stopped, surprised by the acknowledgment. "Is there…do you know whether—"

"Is Molly his girlfriend?" Phillip gave a wry laugh. "My daughter is about as hard to fathom as your son probably is. I tell you what though, if I learn anything, I'll let you know.

"And I'll do the same," Zoe said.

"Discreetly, of course."

"Of course." Then she laughed. "Well discreet behavior isn't exactly my bag—as you've already found out—but I'll do my best."

"Thanks, I appreciate that." He eyed the vegetables on the table, glanced over at the buckets of flowers, checked his watch. "Well…"

"Back to work, huh?"

"Back to work." He nodded, but paused. "By the way, about the on-call services. We might have that resolved very shortly. A third neurosurgeon."

"Fantastic," Zoe said. "So the emergency neurosurgery services will open up again?"

"It's looking that way."

"That's wonderful. Really. I know I was kind of a pain about that…"

He grinned. "Well, let's say you were a burr under the saddle."

The remark stopped her. She had the odd feeling that she'd been engaged in a tug-of-war and the other side had suddenly given up. But it was great news anyway. "Now I'll have to find another cause," she said.

"I'm sure you won't have any trouble in that regard."

"Probably not."

"They'll be sending out a search party if I don't get back."

She fluttered her fingers at him. "Bye."

"Bye, Zoe." He started to move away, then stopped. "By the way, I must have been a very stupid or shortsighted kid. To think you were a boy, I mean."

ON AND OFF for the next week or so, the image of Zoe McCann fluttering her fingers at him would flit across his brain and he'd find himself smiling. Thinking of her was like a sudden light cast into a dark room. Molly, back with him again while Deanna was out of town, was sullen and uncommunicative; his patient load was merciless; even the prospect of a third neurosurgeon didn't cheer him a great deal. He felt weary and overburdened, not fully there for anyone, including himself. So he'd think about Zoe and feel brighter somehow.

"DO YOU REMEMBER the housekeeper who used to work for my parents?" Phillip asked Deanna when she dropped by on her way home from the airport to pick up Molly. "She had two kids, one was maybe twelve or thirteen, a couple of years younger than us, I guess. The other one—"

"Two girls." Deanna sat on the edge of the couch, back straight, ready to fly the minute their daughter finished gathering her clothes from the dryer. "Why does she wait until the last minute to do laundry? I've got so damn much to do." She pursed her lips. "Why? What about the housekeeper?"

"What do you remember about the girls?"

Deanna gave him an absent look. "What girls?"

"The housekeeper's girls."

"Oh." Her brow furrowed momentarily. "I know one of them was always running around in a bikini and the other one looked like a boy."

"I thought she *was* a boy."

"She was an ugly little horror." She got up from the couch, moved across the room to the hallway that led to Molly's room. "C'mon, Molly," she called. "I've got things to do." She sat down again, leaned toward Phillip. "How has she been?" she asked in a lowered voice.

Phillip stretched his legs out. Deanna had adopted the inquisitorial look she frequently got when they discussed Molly and he resented it. Book tours and appointments could keep her away for weeks at a time, but she'd return to criticize and complain about everything he'd done while she was gone. "She didn't keep her last doctor's appointment," he said levelly. "His office called to let me know. And she admitted yesterday that she's not taking her medication."

"Oh, for God's sake, Phillip." Deanna glanced at her watch. "Well, all that's going to change, I can tell you. I've asked for an extension of the deadline on my next book and told my secretary to keep my schedule to a bare minimum. We've allowed Molly a free rein for too long. Molly!" she called. "I'm not waiting here all night. What about that boy?" She addressed Phillip again. "Did you talk to the mother?"

"Yes."

"And?"

"She was adamant—" he thought of Zoe's angry face that day and felt a stronger word was probably needed "—that her son didn't need or want expensive gifts from our daughter and that if she found he'd received any she would immediately return them. And she asked me to convey all this to you."

Deanna, watching his face, had apparently read something in his expression. "She was offended?"

"Highly."

"Well," she said, and shrugged. "Maybe it was the way you presented it to her. Did you talk to her in person, or on the phone?"

"In person."

"And? This is the vegetable seller, right? What was she like?"

"Quite a character, actually." He smiled, thinking about Zoe. Lately he'd been thinking quite a lot about Zoe. One memory dredged up from the murky past: a gray rainy day, cold for California. A boy— Zoe, he now realized—in knee socks that kept sagging around her ankles, lugging a huge, battered suitcase down the driveway and out to the street. He'd watched her from the window, stopping every minute or so to pull up her socks or switch the suitcase to the other hand. She'd eventually reached some kind of compromise—a two-handed grip, the suitcase bumping across her body as she trudged out of sight. Where had she been going?

Deanna gave him a sharp look. "What are you sitting there grinning about?"

"Nothing."

"Doesn't inspire a lot of confidence, Phillip. A brain surgeon smiling at nothing. What's the joke?"

"The reason I asked whether you remembered the housekeeper, is that this woman turns out to be one of the daughters."

"You're kidding. Hold on. Molly!" she yelled again. "Which one?"

"The one I thought was a boy."

"The brat. She was always sticking stuff under my windshield, pictures of me with my teeth blacked out. I don't know why I didn't have her mother fired." She checked her watch again. "*Her* son goes to school with *our* daughter? How the hell can she afford Country Day? Even if the kid has a scholarship, which I'm sure he does, there are still expenses. God, what an insane coincidence."

"Not really." He chose to ignore Deanna's putdown of Zoe and her son. "Seacliff's a small community. People don't usually move far away."

"Don't tell me she lives in Seacliff, too?"

"I don't know about that." He thought for a moment. "No, she's got some property up in the north county, I think."

"Go figure," Deanna said. "Out of all the kids that attend Seacliff, how is it that our daughter gets mixed up with a gardener's son?"

"Maybe because he's the most real person in that whole snobby school," Molly said from the doorway. "Maybe because he thinks about things besides how much money people make. Maybe because he needs protection."

"Protection from what?" Phillip asked.

"His mother. Who happens to be totally insane."

THE CELL PHONE RANG as Zoe was hammering the last fence post for the pony's new pen into the rock-hard clay soil.

"What are you doing this weekend?" Courtney asked.

"Finishing the pen for the horse I bought."

"A horse." Disapproval in Courtney's voice, but no surprise. "You need another animal like you need…horses cost a lot of money, don't they?"

"Thirty bucks," Zoe said. "And she came with a bag of alfalfa."

"Thirty dollars? For a horse?"

"I know, it's a ton of money. But once she starts racing at Del Mar, I'll get it all back."

Silence on the line. Courtney wasn't amused. Either that, or she wasn't sure that was a joke. Zoe grinned up at the pale blue sky. Sometimes it amazed her that she and Courtney were related. No doubt it amazed Courtney, too. Actually, she felt pretty good about the horse. At least it would have a good home. She felt pretty good about quite a few things right now. Like Phillip Barry coming to see her at the market.

"Is Brett going to his dad's?"

Zoe felt her mood plunge. This time last year, Brett could still be persuaded to join her for a bike ride around Mission Bay. No more. When she'd suggested taking the bikes for a spin, he'd looked at her as if she'd suggested a nice root canal. He really wanted to go out to the desert with his dad, he'd told her the next day and then worried aloud that he'd hurt her feelings. "No, you haven't," she'd assured him. "I'm a tough broad. Be kinda nice to have the house to myself." He hadn't believed her any more than she believed herself. "I don't know what's he's planning to do," she said.

"That means he's going to his dad's right?"

"Probably."

"Zoe—"

"I'm fine." Zoe cut her off before Courtney could suggest remedies to fix her life. Internet dating had come up once. A real job was a fixture on the list of solutions to her "hippy-dippy existence."

Hammer in hand, Zoe glanced around for somewhere to sit. All around her, clumps of wild artichokes with huge purple thistles vied for space with yellow mustard that grew so tall and in such profusion she and Brett used to play hide-and-seek in it. The phone wedged between her head and shoulder, she dropped to the ground and stretched out onto her back. Clouds of yellow flowers filled her vision, the sky a perfect blue backdrop.

"Mom worries about you," Courtney said. "Have you called her lately?"

"No."

"Arnie was talking about how property is going sky-high…okay, now don't blow up. You can't even buy three acres of open land in San Diego County, everything's built up. He said you're sitting on a gold mine. The house alone is worth three hundred thousand, and then all the land…"

"I'm one lucky girl," Zoe said.

Courtney sighed. "Mom's right, you're impossible. If you don't want to help yourself though…anyway, that wasn't really why I called. I have this guy I want you to meet."

"No thanks." Courtney was always trying to fix her up. With a guy and with a new look to meet the guy. A total makeover, Courtney called it. Depending on how bored she might be, usually when Brett was spending the weekend with his father, she'd sometimes go along with it, mostly for the hilarious stories she always got to tell Roz and Sandy afterward. Like the guy who took her to this Mexican restaurant where the mariachis were singing "Guantanero" and after they'd finished, the guy had looked at her and said, "You're in the produce business. Any idea why they're singing about one-ton tomatoes?"

Courtney was yakking on about how this guy was "really special. A genuinely nice man." They were all genuinely nice.

"Actually, I have a date with Phillip Barry," she said. The words had just popped out, probably because she'd been playing and replaying the mental video of the look on his face when he'd apologized for thinking she was a boy. She still felt a tingle every time she recreated it.

"A date with Phillip Barry," Courtney scoffed. "Get real."

"Why would I lie?"

"Oh, shut up, Zoe. You think I'm stupid or something?"

Zoe sat up, shoulders high in yellow flowers. A bee was doing its thing in a blossom and she watched it for a moment. "Why would you think it's so amazing that I'd have a date with him?"

"If I have to spell it out for you, you're more out of touch than I thought."

"He's a big-shot surgeon and I'm a lowly gardener?"

"I didn't say that and you know it. I just mean you move in different circles and, well let's face it, Zoe, he's this *GQ*-looking guy and you take some weird satisfaction in looking like…"

"A bag lady?"

"*God,*" Courtney exploded. "I honestly don't know why I bother."

"Neither, do I," Zoe shot back. "Why don't you and Mom just find a new cause and stop trying to change me? I'm fine with myself—"

"If you were fine with yourself, Zoe, you wouldn't be so defensive."

Zoe said nothing. Shadows were falling over the

fields, which meant it had to be around four. Brett would be home from school anytime now.

"You walk around with his huge chip on your shoulder," Courtney was saying. "So what if we grew up in a housekeeper's cottage? If you'd make something of your own life you wouldn't need to keep dwelling on ancient history."

"I happen to think that I *have* made something of my life," Zoe said.

"Oh, come on, Zoe, you live through Brett. You dress like some bag lady so that you can afford to send Brett to Country Day."

"I send Brett to Country Day because I want him to have a good education."

"I'm not saying that isn't true," Courtney said. "But you send him to a school you can't afford because if you can't feel good about yourself, you're damn well going to feel good about your son."

"Shut up, Courtney. I don't need this crap—"

"Yes, you do. You need to hear it. You go around doing all this hippy collective gardening schtick, taking on one cause after another when what you really need to do is make something of *your* life."

"How can I ever thank you for opening my eyes, Court? Here I was, blithely assuming I was doing just fine, but you've set me straight. Words can't express—"

"So you don't want to meet this guy?"

"Thanks, but I really don't."

"Zoe?" Courtney's voice was tentative. "Just let me ask you one thing, and don't give me some smart-ass answer. It's not like you…I mean I'm wondering why you said that about Phillip Barry. You don't have…I don't know, some sort of thing about him or something?"

DR. MALCOLM THOMASSON HAD a round, slightly shiny face, a soft body and a smile that struck Phillip as condescending. He also had impeccable credentials, and had just agreed to join the Seacliff Neurosurgical Group. Although Phillip hadn't particularly warmed to him, relief overshadowed his reservations. As of next weekend, the group could resume emergency on-call services. He'd been living in abject fear of another Jenny Dixon.

They were in the doctor's lounge eating a quick lunch before afternoon surgery. Thomasson was slowly and methodically chomping at a cafeteria cheeseburger. Still uneaten were a side of fries and a slice of apple pie. He was divorced, he said. No children. Phillip ate a tuna sandwich and tried to put his finger on what it was about Thomasson that he didn't care for. It didn't matter, he decided. Reestablishing on-call services topped his personal Issues and Concerns list.

Until Deanna had returned, Molly had shared the top ranking, but Deanna was now insisting that Molly would benefit from consistent and close monitoring from one person. "Frankly, Phillip, she's aware that she can twist you around her little finger and it's not conducive to her emotional progress. Given that I'm the author of several books on mother-daughter relationships and, in all modesty, have a little more understanding of the subject than you, I would appreciate your cooperation in this." In other words, back off while I take over.

Even worse, Deanna had temporarily taken a place in Los Angeles—breaking Molly away from "the wrong influences," she'd explained. And probably furthering Deanna's career on the talk-show circuit, Phillip thought.

"I'm fine, Daddy," Molly had insisted when he'd asked her if she was okay with the arrangement. "Whatever."

Not exactly reassuring, but he was willing to let Deanna try—with one exception. He'd overruled Deanna's stated intention to "straighten out this god-damned gardener's kid mess," and insisted that he would take care of it. Molly had refused to elaborate on her statement about Brett needing protection from his mother and he intended to have a discussion with Zoe.

"Well, do it quickly, Phillip," Deanna had said. "If he gets her pregnant, we'll all be in an even worse mess. I can just see the media. 'Now, you write about mother and daughter relationships,'" she mimicked an announcer's modulated tone, "'but your own seventeen-year-old daughter is pregnant. How do you feel about that?'"

Thomasson finished his cheeseburger and patted his mouth with a paper napkin. He eyed the fries momentarily before looking at Phillip. "About the on-call arrangements? Weekends, I imagine, are the busiest time in the E.R. They certainly were in my previous practice."

Phillip nodded. "They can be brutal. It's difficult to predict, though. One weekend will be bedlam, the next not a call. Unfortunately, it's more of the former. Typically, Stu and I will see half a dozen or so urgent patients and do two to four surgeries—in addition to checking on patients recuperating in the hospital."

"And how do you handle it?" Thomasson asked. "Alternating weekends?"

"That's what we were doing when we decided to suspend the services, but it got impossible."

"You took quite a pounding from the press on that, didn't you?" Thomasson smiled faintly. "Poor kid with a head injury dies while a neurosurgeon who might have saved her life is out playing golf."

Phillip pushed his plate away. "The press got it wrong," he said curtly. "But, in any case, with three of us, it should be a lot easier. Stu's thought is, and I agree, that we'd prefer our free weekends to be completely free. The arrangement we've arrived at is that the on-call takes all phone calls, sees emergencies and make rounds on everyone's patients from Friday evening to Monday morning."

Thomasson frowned. "One man takes everyone's cases?"

"Yes. Otherwise, even if you're not on call, your weekend won't be free if you have to do rounds on hospitalized patients."

"Hmm." He considered for a moment. "In my

previous group, each of us made our own weekend rounds."

"Yes, well." Phillip finished his sandwich. "This is the arrangement we've decided upon for this practice."

He would have to ask Stu if he found anything disturbing about Thomasson, he thought as they headed for surgery. Scrubbing up, his thoughts moved to Zoe McCann, and not just in terms of their respective kids. No ring on the left hand. He squeezed Betadine down his arm and wondered what it was about Zoe McCann that had wormed so thoroughly into his thoughts.

AS SOON AS BRETT HEARD the phone ring he knew whose voice would be on the other end of the line. It rang two more times, but then he thought it might be his dad, so he picked it up.

Molly. He thought about his dad, what his dad had said about telling her to take a hike. She was crying. *That's a chick's favorite trick.* Sobbing into the phone. *Don't let her sucker you in.* Crying so hard she couldn't get the words out.

"What's wrong?"

"I'm going to kill myself."

"No, you're not."

"You don't know what it's like. My mother is keeping me a prisoner. She's hired this evil witch who watches everything I do. And they're making me go to this new school where I don't know anyone and I'm not allowed to leave the house, except

to go to school and then she takes me." More crying.
"Help me, Brett, please."

It's not your responsibility, son.

He heard his mom yelling from downstairs.

"Please, Brett," Molly sobbed.

*She's not going to kill herself. Don't let her sucker
you in.*

"Brett," his mom called. "Come and give me a
hand, please."

He hung up the phone.

His mom was hauling a gigantic bag of goat food
out of the truck. He grabbed it from her and carried
it over to the animal pens. His mom followed him,
yakking about the traffic and everything. In his head,
Molly kept saying she was going to kill herself. One
of the pygmy goats was butting her head against an
old rubber tire that was strung up on a line. He
watched her for a while, but he couldn't get Molly's
voice out of his head. What if she did do it?

"Hey." His mom flicked her finger at his arm.
"You're kind of quiet. Something wrong?"

"No."

"Are you worried about something?"

"No." He could see her out of the corner of his
eye. Watching him, the way she did when she knew
there was something going on he wasn't telling her.

"Quit looking at me like that. I said nothing's
wrong."

"How was school today?"

"Fine."

"How's chemistry going?"

"Fine."

"Would you like to engage in a lengthy discourse on the political situation in—"

"Shut up Mom. It's so dumb when you do that."

"So nothing's wrong. You're just standing at the fence contemplating the wonders of nature?"

He sighed. "Jeez, Mom. Quit making such a big deal out of everything. You're always looking at me and asking me stuff. It's like I'm some bug and you're this microscope."

This made her laugh. She circled her thumb and finger and held it up to her eye. "Hmm, I see a piece of something on your bottom lip, let me take a closer look. Ahh…" She brought her face up close. "Smells like burrito."

"Quit it, Mom. I'm serious."

"Okay." She put her elbows on the fence. "I'll leave you alone.

She didn't leave though and they both stood there for a while, watching the goats. Gertie had quit butting the tire. Now she was lowering her head at the other goats, like she was thinking about butting them, too.

"Mom?"

"Yes, my darling."

"Don't go making a big deal about this, okay?"

"Depends on what it is, but I'll do my best."

"You know that girl Molly?"

"Molly Barry?"

"Well like, you know how I said she was weird and everything?"

"I remember you saying that, yes."

"She's always saying she's going to kill herself."
His mom was standing real close to him and he heard
her make this sound, kinda like a cross between a
sigh and a groan. "So Dad said people who say
they're going to kill themselves never do and, like, I
should just ignore her. But she just called and said it
again and she was crying really hard and everything
and asking me to help her."

"What did you do?"

He kept watching the goats. Now Gertie was chasing the others around the pen, her head down like
she'd butt them if they didn't go where she wanted
them to. *It's not your responsibility.*

"Brett?"

"What?"

"When Molly asked you to help her, what did
you do?"

"Hung up on her."

CHAPTER TEN

"...BULLET GRAZED THE SKULL, above the left temple," the resident was telling Phillip. "The other one went through the back of the neck, CAT scans indicate it penetrated the spinal cord..."

"I don't want to hear any more of your damn excuses," Molly had screamed at him the night before. *"You've always got some reason that's more important than me. Just let me come home, I hate it here."*

"...C-three vertebral segment, the guy should be dead."

"Why did you even have a kid?" Molly had demanded.

Phillip took the X-ray envelope from the resident, pulled out the films and pinned them up on a lighted viewing box. The degree of damage done by a bullet to the back depended largely on where the bullet entered. Nerves were usually severed below the injury—a shot to the lower back would probably paralyze the hips and legs, but not the arms. A bullet in the thoracic region would paralyze the chest. As he looked at the films, Phillip slowly shook his head. The bullet had entered near the base of the neck, traveled upward through the spinal column, lodged through the skull and into the back of the brain. The resident's assessment was right on the mark.

Phillip walked over to look at the patient, who lay on a gurney in the middle of the trauma bay squinting at the bright overhead lights. With a quick glance at the clipboard at the foot of the bed, he leaned over the stretcher so the boy didn't have to turn his face. "Tim," he said, "I'm Dr. Barry. We're going to do a few tests, okay? Can you move your right arm?"

Thirty minutes later, he stepped out to the waiting area to look for the family. They were huddled in a corner. The father, probably about his own age, had his head back, eyes closed. As soon as Phillip approached, he opened his eyes.

"It doesn't look good," Phillip said. "Unfortunately, the damage was very high in the spinal column. At this point, we're not sure he will survive. During the next few days there could be any number of complications that could kill him."

"But if he pulls through…is he going to be okay? Will he walk?"

"I can't tell you that for certain, but I think it's very unlikely."

The family sat silently and listened. From experience, Phillip knew that they weren't hearing or understanding most of what he was saying. That's why he'd learned to keep these speeches simple, short. For now, all they could do was let the words wash over them. Reality would sink in soon enough.

"PHILLIP, IT'S ZOE MCCANN." Zoe sat at her desk in the kitchen, a cup of coffee precariously balanced on a pile of seed catalogues. He had been in surgery when she called the first time and she'd left a message for him to call her as soon as possible. An hour later when he hadn't called, she tried again and caught him in his office between surgeries. "We agreed that we would keep each other informed about our kids. Brett and Molly," she added as though he might not know which kids she meant. "I wouldn't have called you at the hospital, but—"

"That's fine," Phillip said. "What's going on?"

"Hold on." All three dogs had wandered over to her desk, tails wagging like whirligigs. She grabbed her cup of coffee just in time to save it from being knocked to the floor. "Sit, girls," she told them. "All of you." All sat, looking up at her expectantly—dog biscuits usually followed such commands. She stuck up her index finger. "Stay. My dogs," she explained to Phillip.

"How many are there?"

"Three. They like to sit at my feet while I'm working, but…I'm not exactly a neat freak and they come barging in and send everything flying." She knew she was rambling to put off telling him about Molly. Then she heard another phone ringing on his end. "Do you have to get that?"

"My secretary will get it."

"Of course." Had that sounded snotty? It might have. She shook her head, clearing the thought.

"Phillip, I'm calling because Brett told me something Molly told him that I thought you should know. She, uh…" God, there was no easy way to say this. "She's talking about taking her life."

"When was this?"

"Brett told me about it this morning, about ten."

He said nothing for a moment. And then he continued. "She's staying at her mother's right now and she's not happy about it. She doesn't like the new school. I'll call over there. Thanks."

"No problem. And Phillip, I hope everything's okay with Molly. I'll be thinking about you."

He thanked her again and she heard the click of the disconnect.

For the next hour, she alternated between staring blankly at her computer screen and staring blankly at the pile of unpaid bills bundled in a rubber band on top of the seed catalogues. How must it feel to hear that your child no longer wanted to live? She couldn't imagine Phillip's thoughts right now, any more than she could Rhea's after Jenny died. No, that wasn't exactly it. She couldn't even go down the road to exploring those feelings.

Yesterday, she'd gone by Rhea's to give her the news about the emergency services being started up again and to drop off some vegetables—Japanese eggplant, baby squash and a couple of pounds of very ripe tomatoes. They'd grilled the vegetables for lunch and sat outside on the patio, talking about everything but Jenny. Rhea had gone into the kitchen to get iced tea and when she came out to the patio again, her eyes were red rimmed.

"Oh, Rhea." She'd wrapped her arms around her friend, Rhea's wiry black hair tickling the side of her face. "It's tough," she'd murmured. "I know."

She'd hugged Rhea tighter, music from the radio in the kitchen drifting out to where they sat. If she closed her eyes, she could see Rhea's kitchen. Full of bright colors and well-used utensils: a daffodil-yellow jar of wooden spoons, copper-clad pans hanging from a rack above the window, blue-and-yellow pot holders, a shelf of cookbooks. On the refrigerator, a scrawled note held up with a magnet. *Mom. Gone to practice. Won't be late. Love you bunches, Jen.*

No, I don't know, she'd thought, a superstitious chill running through her. *Please, God, may I never know.*

And now a father was facing a different kind of tragedy. Elbows on the desk, Zoe placed her fingers over her mouth. Thoughts, like arrows, darted here and there. Jenny had been like a daughter to her. She'd never even met Molly Barry. Phillip's stumbling words the day he'd come to the market to talk to her. *"Molly is going through a difficult time."* Her own voice asking him, "What if this was your daughter?" Her heart was racing now. Little red flames of panic edging closer, licking at her skin. She picked up the phone, set it down again. *Is Molly okay? Is Brett okay?* She'd lingered at the curb that morning, watching as he walked into school. He'd grown so tall. Navy backpack. Blue jeans. Why had the image burned in her brain? She felt terrified. *Won't be late, Love Jen.*

She was hyperventilating, she realized. She shook her head. Okay, think. No, don't think. Stay calm. Everything's fine. *Going through a difficult time. Difficult time. Difficult time. Come on, Mom.* Brett's voice. *Why can't I go to Dad's? Drivers in the sixteen-to-twenty-two-year-old age group are involved in more accidents and fatalities than any other group. Fatalities. Come on, Mom. Come on, Mom. You're smothering him. Smothering him.*

Her skin began to itch, an angry pulse of heat on the knuckles of her left hand. Tendrils of irritation spread up her arms, across her shoulders, snaked down her back. Itching, she'd once read, was a low threshold form of pain. Something like that. Don't scratch, Janna would tell her. Think of something else. As a child, she'd wake up in the night to find her hands bound to either side of the bed. You'd tear yourself to pieces otherwise, Janna explained years later. God, she could tear herself to pieces right now.

Okay. She sat up straight, trying to clear her mind. There was no reason for this. Phillip had not sounded especially alarmed. Brett would come home from school. Eat a peanut-butter sandwich. Play with the dogs. She would drop her resistance and let him go to his dad's. That was clearly what he wanted to do. There would be no wrecked dune buggies or dirt bikes. No freeway fatalities. No crazed killers would burst into his classroom or climb through the window of his bedroom. More kids survived the six-teen-to-twenty-two age group than didn't. She would live to a ripe old age, surrounded by her son's children and grandchildren. *Her son, the doctor.*

From where she sat in the kitchen-cum-office, she could look out through the window above the sink at the brilliant green leafy tops of the trees, and past them to the red roof of the playhouse she'd built for Brett's fourth birthday. Three tall gray-green Torrey Pines—she'd got them as seedlings in tiny white pots, a gift for opening a new account at Torrey Pines Bank—blocked her view beyond that, but she could close her eyes and feel the cool spiky grass under her feet, smell the dusky mingling of orange blossom and nasturtium.

Okay. That was better. The itching had stopped. She picked up a seed catalogue. The cover showed a kitchen garden surrounded by picturesquely faded wooden storage sheds, slumping stone walls and an ornate greenhouse. A round, moss-encrusted ornamental pool formed the center of the garden. The raised beds were arranged into tidy, colorful rows. Lime-green butter lettuce, with frilly heads like miniature tutus. Perfectly round heads of silver red cabbage.

With a sigh, she set the catalogue aside. One peek at the pages inside and she could kiss the day goodbye. The bills would be overdue if she didn't get them out today. The fingers of her right hand moved involuntarily to the patch of exposed skin on the back of her left wrist. A bank statement. Insufficient funds. Nails raking, back and forth, faster and faster, drawing blood now. Scarlet beads on her wrist.

The phone rang. "Hello?"

"Zoe. It's Phillip. You sound breathless. Are you okay?"

"Fine." She rubbed her palm over the inside of her wrist. "I had to run to catch it," she lied. "How's Molly?"

"She's okay. Apparently, she called Brett right after Deanna had laid down a new set of rules."

Just trying to get attention maybe. Zoe felt sympathy and a vague whiff of resentment. Brett had clearly been troubled or, she conceded, he probably wouldn't have confided in her. But this wasn't the kind of burden a sixteen-year-old should have to shoulder. Imagine the guilt he'd have felt if Molly had gone through with her threat. On the other hand, if Brett had followed his father's advice, guilt would never trouble him for a moment.

"Molly says she wants to be with me," Phillip was saying, "but Deanna has a theory that Molly's difficulties are the result of lax parenting, so she wants to try her own hand at improving things."

Zoe tried to imagine her reaction if Denny got it in his head that her parenting skills were lacking and Brett would be better off with him. It would bear no resemblance to Phillip Barry's, she knew that much. "Are you okay with that?"

"I want what's best for Molly," Phillip said. "We both do. So I'm willing to give it a try."

Zoe unclenched her fingers, which had been

locked in a death grip around the receiver. She heard an overhead page in the background for a doctor with an unintelligible name, so Phillip was calling her from the hospital. Everything must be okay, or he wouldn't still be at work. "You must be relieved," she said.

"For now anyway. This isn't the first time she's tried."

Her heart skipped a beat, and her resentment toward Molly faded. "God, I'm so sorry, Phillip. I had no idea."

"How's Brett?" he asked.

"Oh, fine." Her panic attack seemed inexplicable now. What exactly had brought it on—Brett or Molly or everything in general and nothing in particular— she couldn't say, but she felt okay again. In perspective. "He's going to his father's this weekend, so I'm going to get some work done."

"What kind of work?"

"I need to replace some of the raised flower beds. The wood is rotting because it's so old. I keep patching them, but it's time for major surgery."

Phillip laughed. "We'll both be busy then."

"Oh, right." She'd used the expression without thinking and it took a moment before she understood his response. "My kind of surgery gets your hands a whole lot dirtier though."

"I have a surgery scheduled Saturday morning," he said, "but the physician who just joined our group will be on call for the rest of the weekend. Could you use a surgical assistant?"

Zoe blinked. He had to be joking. A moment passed while she decided how to play it. Smart-ass was always a safe bet. "Sure, come over and plow the lower forty acres," she said, "And when you're through with that, I need a new barn built and, if you still have time, I'd love a pond and maybe a waterfall flowing into it, too."

"That sounds a tad ambitious," he said. "My thoughts were more along the lines of hammering together some boards, that sort of thing."

"You're serious?"

"Absolutely."

"Sure, why not?" She was trying to sound casual and offhand, like brain surgeons were always dropping by to help out around the yard. "I'll round up a spare hammer."

After they'd said goodbye, she walked into the living room and flopped down on the couch as though she'd just run a marathon. This was incredibly weird. She wanted to call Courtney and tell her. *Tomorrow? No, I have plans. Phillip Barry is going to help me build new flower beds.* And then she remembered she'd already told Courtney that she had a date with Phillip Barry. Except she'd been tweaking Courtney's chain before, but this was for real.

Now she couldn't sit still. She got up from the couch and put some clothes she'd washed that morning into the dryer. After that, she went back to her desk, stared at the pile of bills and thought about Phillip Barry offering to help.

Why? The only answer she could come up with

sounded crazy. *He likes me.* It's kind of a date, but
not quite. She decided she was hungry, so she got a
slice of turkey and some provolone cheese from the
refrigerator, peered around for the package of English muffins she'd bought last week. She found
them, made a sandwich and carried it upstairs to her
room. With the sandwich in one hand, she studied her
reflection in the mirror.

Emotional eating had taken its toll. From her head
down to her waist she looked okay. Hauling boxes
and bags of fertilizer were as good as the gym for
shaping upper arms. Extra poundage had made her
boobs bigger, but that wasn't really a problem. She
took a bite of the sandwich, realized it needed may-
onnaise, ran down to the kitchen, smeared on the
full-fat kind and ran back upstairs to the mirror. The
problem lay below her waist. Hands on her hips—
plenty of room for her hands to rest there—she
turned this way and that. Jeans made her look heavier than skirts and dresses, especially billowy peasant skirts and dresses, but he was coming to work in
the yard, so a skirt wouldn't work.

The denim shirt she'd pulled on that morning was
buttoned wrong, she realized. As a result, the neck
was lopsided and one side of the shirt hung lower
than the other. Her boobs looked like blue pillows.
Maybe it was a sexual thing for Phillip, she thought,
like *Lady Chatterley's Lover,* but in reverse. She was
the groundskeeper, he was Lady Chatterley…*Lord*
Chatterley. He was drawn to her earthiness, her lush
sensuality. She scratched her arm, lifted her shirt to

check an itchy patch below her left breast. In the bathroom, she smeared on some cortisone. If she used the medication and didn't get stressed, her skin stayed pretty clear. Which would be good, if he wanted to lower her into a bed of calendulas, rip off her clothes and have his way with her.

What was she thinking?

Okay, where had she put her sandwich? On top of a pile of clothes on the bed. She demolished it. Licked her fingers. Shoved the discarded clothes into the closet.

We go back a long way together, she offered herself as an explanation for Phillip's interest, and now our kids go to the same school. He's just dropping by for old times' sake. Quit making a big deal of everything.

ON SATURDAY AFTERNOON, Phillip drove north to see Zoe McCann. He wasn't familiar with the county's northern inland reaches. Other than passing through the string of suburban communities on his way up to Los Angeles, he couldn't recall ever being north of Seacliff. Having impulsively suggested that he help her in the yard, he now wondered what he'd been thinking. About Molly perhaps, a sense that Zoe might be able to impart some child-rearing wisdom. He conjured Zoe as she'd looked that first day in his office, and then at the farmer's market. Her high, almost feverish coloring, as though, he couldn't help thinking, she'd just engaged in a round of vigorous sex, the wild tangle of curly blond hair. The breasts.

He dismissed the image. He had a vague idea, probably from something he'd read in the *Tribune,* that the area was agricultural—a flower-producing area. Given her occupation, it made sense.

As he pulled onto her street, he glanced at the directions Zoe had given him when he'd called back to confirm the place and time. "Bunch of greenhouses on the left," he'd written. "Couple of small houses, big gray wooden house with a white fence, partly falling down." Presumably the fence, not the house. He passed the greenhouses and saw, at the crest of a small incline, a two-story gray house set roughly in the middle of several acres of scrubby, slightly undulating land. He slowed to a stop under a stand of eucalyptus, opened the driver's window and saw Zoe.

Wearing faded jeans, rubber boots and a red bikini top, she was dragging a length of green garden hose using both hands and the whole weight of her body. Three dogs at her heels jumped and lunged at each other. He checked his first inclination to rush to her assistance. Zoe would not appreciate, and may in fact be insulted, he suspected, by the suggestion that she couldn't accomplish her task alone. It was part of her appeal, he decided, watching her. Feisty, unafraid to tackle whatever obstacle fell across her path—brain surgeons or garden hoses. Bring 'em on. He moved along, down a steeply sloping driveway and parked next to a black pickup truck.

"Hey, there." Zoe had spotted him and, trailed by the dogs, walked over to the car. She smiled at him through the open window. "You came."

"Wasn't that the plan?"

"Yeah, but I couldn't see it. I've been waiting for you to call and say something came up and you couldn't make it."

"I've been looking forward to it," he said. Not strictly the truth until seeing her right now, he realized as he got out of the car.

The dogs—a black Lab, a massive shepherd and a smaller brown one that he had no idea about—all eyed him suspiciously. The Lab gave a low growl, and the other two started barking and circling.

Zoe grabbed at the Lab's collar.

"Hey, be nice." Still holding the collar, she looked up at him. "This is Kenna, Brett's dog. That's Lucy—" she nodded at the shepherd "—and the other one is Domino. He's part wolf."

Phillip stretched out his hand and the dogs inched closer, sniffing at his fingers, then his feet. He watched Zoe watching them. She was smiling, the fond, amused way people did at animals and small children, and she looked relaxed and happy, quite different from the tense and combative woman who'd barged into his office that first day. Sunlight glinted off her face and shoulders. The red bikini top, he noticed on closer inspection, was printed with small white flowers. He wanted to apologize again for once thinking she was a boy.

"Well?" Hands on her hips, Zoe regarded him. "I guess you're dressed for work."

"You *guess?*" He glanced down at his attire, everything respectably worn and workmanly, he'd thought. Faded jeans, an old shirt with the sleeves rolled up. No socks, the old Topsiders. "What's wrong with me?"

"Sorry, I don't feel qualified to answer that," she said, straight-faced.

He laughed and then she did, too. The sun was brighter here, several miles inland, than it was at the coast, and the air smelled floral. Beyond Zoe's shoulder, he could see a pen with goats, a sheep and a cream-colored pony.

"Want the grand tour?" she asked.

"Sure." He followed her down a narrow path that had been partially paved with gray flagstone.

"Watch for loose spots, " she said over her shoulder. "As you can see, it's not finished. I had this elaborate story I was going to tell you about how the landscaping firm I use had ran out of the specific kind of stone I need, but…what the hell? I got this first load on sale, then they went off sale and I couldn't afford them, so I'm waiting till they go on sale again or a wealthy uncle dies."

It was exactly this quality in her that intrigued him, Phillip thought. A spontaneous let-it-all-hang-out honesty that was so different from everything he knew. It kept bringing him up short, forcing him to take a closer look at his own life. The fact that he'd been unable to find a house he wanted to buy in Seacliff, for instance. Of late, Seacliff had felt confining and insular, too aware of its own perfection. But as Deanna would say, "Where else would you live but Seacliff?"

They continued down the pathway to a pen where he could see goats staring curiously in his direction. Beyond the pen, there were rows of tomato cages, beans climbing up an arrangement of wires and posts. Closer in, roses bloomed in an enclosed garden.

"I love old roses." Zoe had followed his glance. "The garden's kind of overgrown, but I like it that way. I hate manicured perfection."

Phillip recalled Deanna's insistence on just that and her frustration with the gardener for not deadheading roses the minute the blooms faded.

Zoe threw a handful of something—straw, hay, he had no idea what goats ate—into the pen and they resumed the walk; through a tall rusted gate that opened to a wooden arbor covered in grapes, down some brick steps to a deck that overlooked more land, this covered with rows of purple flowers that he could smell from where they stood.

"Lavender," she said.

"It reminds me of the way my grandmother's bedroom smelled."

"She probably had sachets of it, it's kind of an old-fashioned scent, except it's staged a comeback, aromatherapy, that sort of thing. It's supposed to make you feel relaxed and tranquil."

He grinned.

Zoe shot him a sideways look. "And you're thinking, *Gee she's got fields of it and she's about as tranquil as a tornado.*"

"I wasn't thinking that at all," he said. They were

standing at the deck's wooden rail looking out over the lavender to the hills beyond. "I was thinking that it must be very nice to come home to all this."

"It is. I couldn't imagine living anywhere else."

"Must be a lot of work though."

"It's work, but it isn't, if you know what I mean." She turned her head to look at him, as though to make sure he understood. A strand of curly blond hair hung over her shoulder and she flicked it back with her finger. "I'm tired at the end of the day, but it's a good tired. Happy tired."

"You have people helping you, I imagine."

"Nope. Well, Brett sometimes, but only under duress."

One of the dogs had followed them and Phillip bent to scratch its head.

"I'd have someone if I could afford it," Zoe said, "But, to be honest, I just about squeak by as it is. My family's always telling me I should sell and buy a condo or something. I'd die first."

"What happened after you moved out of the cottage?" he asked. "Where did you go?"

"My mom got her real estate license and we all moved up to this area. She rented a house for a while, then she started making some money and she bought the house. Courtney and I went to school at Buena Vista High. Courtney graduated from San Diego State. She got a degree in—"

"What about you?"

"I met this guy, Brett's father. Got pregnant, dropped out of school, I was going to State, too, but

I got married, then got divorced a couple of years later. I ended up with the house and property and decided I might as well put the land to good use, so I started growing vegetables. That's pretty much the story."

"And this is what you want to go on doing?"

"Growing vegetables?" She nodded. "I'm not overburdened with ambition. It drives my mom mad. She and Courtney both live in Seacliff now. I think it truly embarrasses her that I'm still up here."

"I don't know why it would," he said. "This is very impressive, especially that you do all the work yourself. I would think they'd be proud of you."

"Yeah, well." She shrugged. "You know how families are. What about you?"

"What about me?"

"Tell me stuff. What do you do when you're not taking out brains?"

He laughed. Zoe made him laugh. His grandmother used to describe people she liked as "a real tonic." "Means they make me feel like the world's not such a bad old place after all," she explained once when he'd asked what she meant. Zoe made him feel that way.

"Well?"

"What do I do when I'm not working." He thought for a moment. "Work very hard at relaxing, you might say. The last time I took any time off, I flew up to Vail. Skied from dawn to dusk for four days straight, flew home and wondered why the hell I was exhausted."

"Ah, the privileged life. My heart bleeds for you."

"I wasn't looking for sympathy," he said.

"Good. I wasn't about to give you any. Ready to work?"

"I'm all yours."

Her face flushed. She jabbed a finger at his arm. "The way you talk."

CHAPTER ELEVEN

"I CAN'T BELIEVE IT," Janna was saying. "If someone had offered me a million dollars to guess who I'd find digging weeds in Zoe's garden, I never, ever would have expected to find you here, Phillip."

"I know," Courtney chimed in. "It totally blew me away, too."

Me, too, Zoe thought. Their voices carried in through the open window to the kitchen where she was whipping up snacks. Quesadilla wedges with melted Monterey Jack and green chili peppers, and a short-cut version of guacamole, made with salsa instead of chopped tomatoes and onions because she hadn't planned on doing this and she even more hadn't planned on her mother and Courtney dropping by.

What she'd wanted to say to them when she saw Janna's Mercedes cruise down the driveway was get the hell out, but then her mother was out of the car and hugging Phillip like a long-lost son, and after an hour or so, Courtney started making noises about cold drinks and food while they all caught up with each other's lives and the next thing Zoe knew, she was grating cheese.

She put a piece in her mouth, tore off a piece of tortilla. Ate another piece of cheese. She felt unglued by Phillip. The way he'd seemed not just interested in what she'd done with the place, but impressed, too. He admired her, he'd said, and she'd seen it in his eyes. They'd hammered boards together for three new raised beds, dug in bags of soil amendment. As they were planting some tomato seeds, she'd glanced over at his hands. Long, slender fingers that worked inside the brain. And here he was, carefully sprinkling seeds into the lengthy furrows he'd dug in the soft, loamy dirt.

They'd been working shoulder to shoulder and her eyes had gone from his hands to her own. Her nails were chipped and black rimmed, the roughness of her skin testament to a nonchalance about hand creams and other emollients. Mostly, she only remembered her hands when she was forced into a comparison.

"You should wear gardening gloves," Janna was always telling her, but Janna didn't understand her need to actually feel the soil between her fingers. She carried the plate of tortilla wedges to the stove, heated up oil in the pan. Outside, she heard Phillip laugh. Damn her mother and Courtney. Now there would be endless interrogation, diminishing the secret little thrill of Phillip Barry coming to see her.

"You were always smart," Janna was saying now, presumably to Phillip. "I remember one day you were doing this jigsaw. I was trying to dust the table and you had the pieces spread out all over the place...it's okay if I call you Phillip, isn't it?"

Zoe groaned. God, Mom, why don't you just kiss his ring, and get it over with? She looked at the tortillas slowly turning color. I should tell her and Courtney to get in here and help, she thought. Too much trouble, she decided. They'd both stand around as if they'd never seen a kitchen before, waiting for her to give them orders. Plus a part of her wanted to do this, to dazzle Phillip with her culinary skills. Well, not dazzle exactly, these were quesadillas, for God's sake. But she *wanted* to feed him. The hell with being politically correct. Cooking didn't make her feel subservient, she loved to do it. Already she'd envisioned a dinner she would cook for him—well, she'd designed the vegetable part, braised leeks with melted goat cheese. Okay, she was getting ahead of herself. After today, she might never see him again.

Outside, Janna was still holding forth.

"…but that's my memory of you. This jigsaw, all squiggles and lines, I couldn't make head or tails of it but—"

"I remember it," Phillip said. "Actually, it was a close-up picture of a brain."

"A brain." Janna laughed. "See, even then you knew what you wanted to do, didn't you? I used to tell the girls that they needed to follow your example if they wanted to amount to anything, but—"

"Hey," Courtney broke in. "*I* listened."

"I know *you* did, sweetheart," Janna said. "Courtney's a travel agent, Phillip—"

"Here's my card," Courtney said. "Give me a call

the next time you're planning a trip. I'll get a good deal for you. My office is in Seacliff."

"Small world," Janna chuckled. "My fiancé's place is just a stone's throw away from your parents' house."

Oh, *puhleeeese*. Zoe stuck the spatula under a wedge of tortilla. *Stone's throw*. Arnie's condo was in Seacliff Heights, on the other side of the freeway from Seacliff. His home looked out over a golf course, rather than the ocean view the Barry estate commanded. She wanted to go out there and provide some sort of antidote to all the pretentious crap they'd been feeding Phillip. Muck out the animal pen maybe, or bring out the bag of shirts and sweaters she'd just picked up from Goodwill.

"This place is really something, isn't it?" Phillip said. "You must be very proud of all the work Zoe's done."

At the stove, Zoe did a little dance. *I love you, Phillip Barry. You are my hero.* Grinning like an idiot prom queen, she arranged the quesadillas on a platter, decided something else was needed, another dipping sauce maybe. She stuck the plate in the oven to keep warm, opened the refrigerator and checked around for possibilities. Mango chutney? Maybe. She opened the vegetable drawer. An avocado and a couple of oranges.

Outside the voices were distant. They'd gone down to look at the animals, Zoe figured. If Phillip approved, maybe Janna would be thinking that there was more to Zoe's "little vegetable-growing thing" than she'd realized. Okay, enough with the stupid grin, Zoe told herself. An idea struck her: a little tomato chutney. She could whip it up in a minute and it would go great with the quesadillas.

She gathered all the ingredients from the freezer—chopped onions and tomatoes, basil, all harvested and put away for times like this—and started melting the butter. *Phillip Barry. Dr. Phillip Barry.* She couldn't take the damn grin off her face. She imagined telling Roz and Sandy about everything. "But you hated him," Roz would say. "What happened to that stuff about Dr. God?" "I've just seen another side to him, that's all," she would reply. "And I like it."

The aroma of melting butter filled her head. A golden summer afternoon kind of smell. She added the onions and watched them grow translucent, the color of old silk.

As she tasted the sauce, she felt rather than saw Phillip come up behind her. A dash of cinnamon, she decided. She didn't turn around, pretending that she hadn't sensed him there. Silence swelled up in her— panicked suddenly, she couldn't think of anything to say. At the stove she stood mindlessly stirring the onions around and around, watching them darken to gold.

And then his finger brushed the back of her neck.

The faintest whisper of a touch, but it electrified her. The spatula froze in her hand, her body temperature rose to feverish and the kitchen suddenly felt stifling. She made herself turn around.

"I should go, Zoe," he said.

She stared at him. He looked exactly the same, but not. His face was unreadable, pleasant, smiling politely. Gorgeous. Had she just imagined something?

"You don't want to stay to eat?"

"Thanks, but I've got some work to catch up on."

"Oh." Disappointment flooded her, but she forced a smile. "You don't know what you're missing."

"I'm sure it will be terrific."

"Maybe some other time," she said, and immediately wished she hadn't.

"I'm really glad I came," he said quietly.

"Me, too."

"I've said my goodbyes to your mother and sister." He caught her hand briefly. "Take care."

A WEEK LATER, Phillip called to invite her to dinner. They went to Las Brisas, which he said was his favorite restaurant in Seacliff. "It's probably the last place in California that still does lobster thermidor," he'd told her as he handed over the Jaguar's keys to the valet parking attendant. "One of those things like pasta Alfredo, what do they call it? A heart attack on a plate."

Zoe looked at the menu. The cheapest entrée was more than twice what she was willing to fork up on the few occasions she took Brett to dinner. A salad with artichoke hearts and goat cheese went for thirteen dollars. She was estimating the cost of making a similar salad at home when she felt Phillip looking at her.

"What?"

"You're very nice to look at."

Disarmed, she felt her face go hot. "And that's before the wine."

He smiled.

"Sorry. I'm not good with compliments."

"Too bad. I had a few more."

She put her elbows on the table, propped her chin on her hands, then remembered something about elbows on the table being an etiquette no-no, so she folded her hands in her lap. The candlelit tables all around were filled with expensively dressed Seacliff types, a smattering of local celebrities—a TV anchor she recognized—the see-and-be-seen crowd. She'd worn a red faux-silk dress with a neckline that now seemed too plunging. If she lowered her head slightly, her breasts looked on the verge of escape. The dress felt tight under her arms. A deep breath could pop the seams. The question of what to wear had sent her into such a major panic that, thirty minutes before Phillip was supposed to pick her up, she'd almost called to tell him she was sick. Now she wished she had. Las Brisas wasn't her kind of place.

A waiter in a white jacket approached the table and she realized she hadn't decided. She picked up the menu again and quickly chose broiled chicken, the cheapest thing on the menu.

Phillip glanced at her. "The scampi is very good."

She smiled. "The chicken's fine, thanks."

"Lobster? Salmon? A steak?"

"I have peasant tastes," she said. "I'm happy with chicken."

Phillip ordered the thermidor, then spent some time with the wine list before settling on something with a French name. At least it sounded like a French name. A basket of bread was brought to the table. Phillip ignored it. She wanted to stuff her mouth with it. As though he'd read her mind, Phillip offered the basket. The cuffs of his shirt were just so. His nails looked so perfect they might be manicured, but she hoped they weren't.

She declined the bread. She was starving but she might just make it through the evening if she didn't have to sit there worried about food in her teeth. Which meant no rolls with little brown seeds. Weird how she could ask him about food in her teeth in the market but not here in Las Brisas. Now she needed to pee, but the dress was tight around her rear end, so if she got up Phillip would watch her walk across the room, past all the sophisticated diners, and wonder what the hell had made him bring her here.

When they had walked in, she'd been wearing a fringed shawl over her shoulders that she'd meant to keep on all evening, but she'd got flustered when Phillip pulled out her chair and the shawl had slipped down her arms and fallen off. Now she was sitting on it. It would be all wrinkled, but if she could gracefully slip it back on, it would cover her rear on her way to the rest room.

"You're very quiet this evening," Phillip said.

"Oh." Her wisecracking side, always there in difficult moments, had deserted her completely. She felt as tongue-tied as a shy child in a roomful of elders. "I have my quiet moments," she finally managed. Did that sound lame, or what? Sure, pick dinner in an expensive restaurant for one of her rare quiet moments. She *really* had to pee.

The waiter brought salads.

"Black pepper?" He held a huge chrome mill above her salad.

"Please," she said. *Black pepper in her teeth.* "Stop." She nearly knocked it out of his hand. Both the waiter and Phillip looked at her. "I mean that's enough, thank you." She glanced at her plate, not even a speck of pepper.

Okay. Eat the salad. Think of *something* to say. Polite conversation, it's called. Forget about leaning seductively across the table, exchanging meaningful glances over the candles, the sensuous dessert— that's all part of an advanced course. This was just the basics: eat the damn food, don't drink too much wine, pass on dessert—remember the hips—and just get through the evening.

All week she'd been waiting for him to call. When she'd picked up the phone and heard his voice, she'd felt almost giddy. Now she wanted to be at home, slopping around in sweats, cooking up something for her and Brett. The silenced lengthened. Maybe Phillip was waiting for her to say something. She took a deep breath, held her palms together under the table, pushed tight and relaxed, then slowly forced herself to meet his eyes again.

"How's Molly doing?" It was all she could come up with.

"I haven't seen her for a week or so. I think I told you, she's staying in Los Angeles with her mother. I spoke to her last night and she seemed…" He hesitated. "Okay, I guess. Not happy to be there, but right now we feel it's more important to get her back on track."

"Do you miss her?"

He frowned. "Sometimes, but…this might sound harsh, but missing her isn't as difficult for me as having her live with me often was. Molly requires a lot more in terms of time than either her mother or I can provide."

Zoe pushed her salad plate aside. "But she's your daughter." She heard the disapproval in her voice but couldn't shut up. "How could you *not* give her all the time she needs? What else could be more important?"

A sommelier—she only knew the word because she'd read it in a food magazine—arrived with the wine Phillip had ordered to go with the main course, and went through the whole performance of pulling out the cork, handing it to Phillip to sniff. Good choice of things to talk about, she told herself. Way to go, Zoe. Nothing like a little parental criticism to set the mood. She eyed her glass, debating whether to drink the wine. On the one hand, it might relax her, on the other she already needed to pee. As a first date, this was turning out to be a real stinker.

"YOU WEREN'T YOURSELF tonight," Phillip observed later as he drove her home. "Are you not feeling well?"

She didn't answer right away. He'd taken the coast road and she could see the lights of the pier off in the distance, a sparkling string against the black sea and sky. In her peripheral vision, she noted Phillip's hand on the steering wheel. The inch or so of white shirt cuff beneath his suit jacket. What would you buy him for Christmas, say, or his birthday? The thought came out of nowhere.

Phillip turned to look at her. "Zoe?"

"What?"

"Tell me what's wrong?"

"Nothing."

"Oh, come on. One of the things I like most about you is the way you just say whatever's on your mind. Don't let me down."

She took a breath. "Okay, you asked for it. You just blew a gazillion bucks on an elegant dinner, we're zipping along in a Jaguar that probably cost more than I'll make in five years, not that I'd want one, because somehow I can't see it hauling flats of begonias."

"And…" He nodded. "Go on."

"Well, that just isn't me. That restaurant—thirty-dollar entrées, valet parking. I mean, I probably sound like an ingrate or something, but I hate that kind of thing. I can't see the point of paying that much for a meal when there are kids who go to bed hungry and, well, my mom and sister think I have this hang-up and maybe I do, but your world is a whole lot different from mine. I'm happy in my world, don't get me wrong, and I'm sure you feel the same way about yours, but maybe some things just don't mix, I don't know. Or maybe it's the whole housekeeper's cottage thing and my mom's pretensions. I mean I am who I am and you're who you are and, I don't know…"

She'd run out of steam just as he was maneuvering the car down her driveway. "Watch the pickup truck," she said, wise guy wresting control again. "Don't dent the paintwork with this damn Jaguar of yours."

He switched off the ignition. Turned in the seat to look at her.

"Want to come in?" she said, quite sure he'd never want to see her again after that little speech. "I could probably rustle up a spare bottle of Dom Perignon."

"Your mother's right. You do have a hang-up."

She shrugged. Her arm was itching like crazy, her back, too. Any minute now, she was going to give in to the urge. Might as well destroy all illusions in one fell swoop.

"What if you'd picked something to do tonight?" he asked.

"Where would we go, you mean?" This was a novel approach. She'd expected a defense of his lifestyle. She thought for a moment. "There's a couple of Mexican places I like. One has killer carnitas. They taste best if you walk down the road a bit and eat them on the edge of the cliff, watching the water."

"Let's do that, next time," he said.

"YOU'RE RIGHT, these are fantastic." Phillip unwrapped wax paper from the lower third of his burrito, and consumed the rest of the meal in a couple of bites. "I can't believe I've never had one before."

Zoe licked her fingers. "You just gotta know how to live."

They were, as Zoe had proposed, sitting on the edge of the cliff watching the sun dissolve into the ocean. Since the unfortunate dinner at Las Brisas almost three weeks ago, Zoe had taken over the social agenda. "When was the last time you went to the movies?" she'd called to ask one night.

"No idea," he'd told her. "Years ago, probably."

She'd taken him once to see a Russian film, another time a thriller set in the south of France, and afterward they'd discussed the films over little cups of espresso. One evening, they'd walked through a downpour to a jazz performance at a coffee place in Pacific Beach that was smaller than his living room. Zoe had led him by the hand to a table up front where it seemed the music was being performed just for them.

All his life, he'd been immersed in science, in understanding how things worked. At university and then medical school, where he'd absorbed volumes of technical and scientific information, he'd learned to master the vital skills of focus and total concentration. Nothing mattered when you made that first cut, except the three pounds or so of exposed grayish brain tissue that was someone's son or mother or grandfather. Forget everything else, even the limits of your own endurance. No room for error, no room for faltering attention, no room for doubt, no room for anything but complete dedication.

He'd mastered it well. "Maybe if I covered myself with a sheet like one of your damn patients, you'd pay attention to me," Deanna and then Molly had both screamed at him.

And then along came Zoe.

Earthy, quirky, sensual Zoe with her offbeat comments and throaty cackle of a laugh. Zoe, who made him wish he'd remembered some of the nonscientific courses he'd been forced to take. Literature and poetry might contain more imaginative ways to describe the way in which she'd opened his eyes to a world he hadn't known existed. *A world of the senses.* The term still struck him as overblown and melodramatic; before Zoe, it wouldn't even have occurred to him.

Zoe, sitting beside him now with her wild blond-on-brown-streaked curls blowing about her face, catching in the fringed shawl she wore around her shoulders. Barefoot, in a long red gypsy dress, her neck smelling of lavender soap. Before Zoe, he couldn't have identified lavender soap if his life depended on it.

Zoe, who had taken him to a street market close to the Mexican border.

Walking beside him through the narrow, push-cart-jammed streets, a straw shopping bag on her arm, opening his eyes to everything around. Fish, eels, cod and halibut arranged like a rainbow on a bed of ice, brown feathered chickens hanging upside down, next to gray pigeons. "Not that I could actually take them home and pluck them," she'd said, "But I like the realness of it. Seacliff's market is fine, but it's kind of antiseptic compared to this." A moment later, he'd turned to see her eyes brimming with tears. "It's just kind of sad to see them—the chickens, with their feathers and those sad little pink feet. When you buy some neat, plastic-wrapped package in the market, you forget what you're buying used to be this living, breathing thing."

She'd fed him strawberries as they strolled in the hot sunshine and then, on the way home, suggested a detour to a bakery tucked away in a maze of dark streets where they'd bought hot bread, demolishing most of it before they found the freeway again.

"Does it bother you eating this?" He nodded now at the discarded carnitas wrappers in the paper bag between them. "I was thinking about how the chickens at the market upset you," he elaborated.

Her brow furrowed, she bent her head to one side, considering. "Thank you for waiting until after I finished devouring this to ask me."

"I'm sorry, I just—"

"No, no it's fine. I wanted to eat it, but if I'd had to stop to think about what I was eating, I don't think I could have finished. It's like I'm *this close*—" she held up a hand, first two fingers pressed close together "—to not eating meat at all, but I don't want to declare myself as a vegetarian because sometimes

I just want to taste something. Senses are a really big deal to me—taste, texture, smell, all that stuff." She laughed and pinched the flesh at her waist. "As you can tell."

Phillip put his arm around her. "You're perfect."

She snorted. "You're blind."

"Let's go somewhere together."

She leaned her head into his shoulder. "Where?"

He laughed. "Oh, no, I'm not about to fall into that trap. You're just waiting for me to suggest the Four Seasons or the Ritz-Carlton so that you can lecture me on ostentatious consumption."

"Conspicuous consumption."

She caught his free hand, brought it up to her mouth, kissing it gently, but with such promise that it was all he could do to concentrate on her words.

"I've had a lot of guilty thoughts about Las Brisas. Like it was your favorite place and everything and all I did was complain."

"But you were quite right," he said, and he meant it. He squeezed her shoulder. "You opened my eyes to the fact that it was pretentious and overpriced. I will never walk through those doors again. Tomorrow, I'm placing an ad for the Jaguar. I've decided I'll ride a bike to work."

"Jerk. Just when I was starting to like you."

"No, you've changed my thoughts about a lot of things. In a good way. I'll probably never be able to order a thirty-dollar entrée without thinking of you."

"Actually, I *was* going to congratulate you. You're a whole lot less uptight these days."

"Molly once teased me for walking on the beach with my shoes on."

"And look at you now." She ran her toes along the top of his bare foot.

"So? What would be a Zoe McCann approved destination for an illicit weekend?"

"Um…I'm thinking."

"Does it hurt?"

She smacked him.

"Come on, how difficult could it be? Where did you take the last unsuspecting guy?"

Zoe chewed her thumbnail. "There was no last guy, unsuspecting or otherwise. And don't start asking questions about how I meet my physical needs or—"

Phillip burst out laughing.

"What?"

"You're just so…whatever comes into your head. I wasn't even thinking of asking you that."

"But now that I mention it," Zoe said teasingly.

"Forget it." He shook his head. "I'm quite happy to believe that sex didn't even rear its ugly head until I came along. But I've proved to be so irresistible, of course, that now you're forced to deal with it. Where oh where can I take this hunk of a man—"

Zoe jabbed her elbow into his side. "Dream on, buddy."

"So would you like to go away somewhere?"

"Yeah. It's Brett, though. I guess we could pick a weekend when he goes to his father's, but…"

"But?"

"You're going to think I'm weird."

"I already think you're weird." He turned to kiss her, his chest flattening against her, pressing her back into the rough grass. She locked her arms around his neck and he felt her mouth soften and open under his, inviting and so intimate that it took his breath away. They'd been taking things slowly, an unspoken agreement to put their children first, but he knew the tension was building for her as well as for him. When she pushed him away a few minutes later, her eyes were heavy, her mouth wet from his, and he couldn't help but feel a stab of pure male pride that he could create this reaction in her.

"I was trying to answer your question." She raised her knees, wrapped her arms around them. "When you rudely interrupted me."

"My apologies." He wasn't sorry at all, and he knew that she knew it.

"What I was going to say was…" She sighed. "God, I don't know, Phillip. I guess…okay." Inching away from him a little, she held her palms a few inches apart to describe a rough circle. "Okay, pretend this is a bowl. Right now it's full of all the things I do for Brett. The things that will make him happy, his needs, his wants, whatever."

Phillip watched her face. Set in concentration, her eyes fixed on the imaginary bowl, lower lip caught between her teeth as though she were wrestling with a huge problem, which he supposed she was.

"All right, so this bowl contains everything that

makes me a good mother. I mean, that probably sounds conceited, I just mean—"

"I know what you mean. Go on."

"This is the weird part. I feel that if I dip into that bowl for something *I* personally need, Brett will lose out because of it."

Phillip waited a minute, choosing his words carefully. "You know, intellectually, that's not true? You have a right to your own happiness, which isn't mutually exclusive to being a good mother."

She nodded. "I do know that. But when I was growing up, my mom always seemed more interested in who was taking her out to dinner, or whisking her off somewhere fabulous. I couldn't help it, I just thought she cared a whole lot more about that sort of thing than she did about me and Courtney."

"Does Courtney feel the same way?"

"We never really talk about it, but I don't think so. Courtney is much more like my mother than I am. I don't think she'd understand. Plus, I had the skin thing." She tapped a finger against her right arm, which bore the faint redness of a rash inside her elbow. "I never felt too lovable."

"Come here." He caught her in the crook of his arm. "How about if I just slice off the top of your head and look for the part of your brain that's storing all this bull and whip it out?"

"Could you?"

"No. But I can honestly assure you that if we spent the weekend together, there would still be plenty of room in that bowl for all of Brett's needs."

CHAPTER TWELVE

"ZOE IS GETTING on my nerves." Sandy broke off a piece of pumpernickel bagel and dipped it into a little cup of cream cheese. It was Wednesday, just before the market, and she and Roz and Zoe and Rhea were having coffee at a place over on the next street. "She's too damn happy for her own good. Call me selfish, but it drives me nuts, that smug little smile of hers."

"Tell me about it," Roz said. "It's sickening. If anyone's going to be in love, it should be me."

"I'm not in love," Zoe protested. "I'm…in like." The others all groaned and shook their heads.

"Where did you go last night?" Sandy asked.

"Phillip helped me plant some calendulas…shut up." Even without looking, she sensed the knowing grins around the table. She tossed a packet of sweetener at Sandy. "He's very sweet," she said sedately, staring into her coffee. Her mouth curled involuntarily into a smile she could feel spreading across her face. Last night Phillip had told her that she'd changed his life. On his next free weekend, they'd decided, they would drive down to Mexico. She'd told him about the lobster dinners in Puerta Nuevo. Hadn't mentioned, but had thought a lot about being naked together in the double bed of a hotel over-looking the Pacific.

"Oh God, look at her," Roz said. "Cover her head with a napkin, before I throw up."

"How does Brett get along with him?" Rhea asked.

Zoe looked at Rhea, sitting beside her, and felt the mood of lighthearted teasing suddenly evaporate. *God, I'm an insensitive idiot.* Shame, embarrass-ment, a whole stew of churning feelings, burned her face. The companionable closeness of the booth sud-denly felt suffocating. She drank some water, ice melting as it slid down her throat. Phillip had come into her life again, because of Jenny. Rhea had never blamed Phillip for Jenny's death; she herself had. But what if the tables were turned? What if it hadn't been Jenny, but Brett…no, she couldn't even go there.

"Rhea, I'm so sorry…" she started and then, the words clogging in her throat, she just shook her head.

"Hey." Rhea put her arm around Zoe. "It was a simple question."

Roz shook her head. "There are no simple ques-tions when it comes to Zoe and her kid. It's like sep-arating out one strand of spaghetti from the pot. You pull up this mess of melted cheese and sauce and clumps of noodles, and even if you get it separate from the rest, it's still going to have bits of sauce."

Zoe, laughing through tears, drank some more water and choked. Soon Sandy and Rhea were laughing, too, and then Roz joined in although her puzzled expression said she wasn't sure what was so funny.

"Trust one of us to bring any subject back to food," Rhea said.

"But you get my point, right?" Roz was leaning across the table. "Zoe's got so much of her own baggage that somehow it all gets dumped on Brett."

"If you'll excuse a mixed metaphor," Zoe said, vaguely irritated and not quite sure that she had, in fact, got Roz's point. "All you're talking about is interconnectedness. Part of why I am who I am is connected to the way my mom was and it's the same with Brett. He's the way he is because—"

"A little sauce goes a long way," Roz said.

Zoe stared at her.

"Let me give you an example," Rhea said. "Did Brett ever tell you about the girl at school he likes?"

"Molly? He doesn't like her, he feels sorry for her."

"Sophie," Rhea said.

"Sophie?" Zoe turned her head to look at Rhea. "I don't…"

"I know. "

Zoe put her elbows on the table, held her head.

"He didn't want to mention her to you, he said, because you'd question him and make some great big deal out of it and drive him crazy."

"Did he say that?"

"Pretty much." Rhea grabbed Zoe's left hand. "And quit scratching."

"Poor Zoe," Sandy said. "Come on, you guys, let's talk about something else."

"No. Go on. I need to take my medicine."

"Brett's a kid now," Rhea said, "but he's going to fly the coop pretty soon." She paused. "If you're lucky…"

Zoe flinched. Maybe this whole discussion had gone too far. She'd practically floated into the coffee shop. Now she wanted to go home and bawl her eyes out and she wasn't entirely sure why.

"I loved Jenny with every ounce of my being, Zoe," Rhea was saying now, "but she was growing away from me and I knew it. That's the way life is, the way it should be. I accepted it. With Brett, I honestly don't think you've reached that point."

"WHAT DO I WANT?" Zoe wrinkled her nose. "For Brett to—"

"For yourself," Phillip said. They were standing in Zoe's rose garden. It was dark, a handful of stars visible in the milky navy-blue sky. Darkness, he observed, seemed to leach the color from flowers that were vivid during the day, making them appear to glow with a pale light that was almost eerie. The observation intrigued him, mostly for what it said about Zoe's influence. Before she'd come into his life, he was always thinking, I would never have noticed. "You." He kissed her nose. "What does Zoe McCann want from life, just for herself alone?"

Smiling, she circled her arms around his neck. "A trip to Mexico? A big soft bed. You in the bed."

He kissed her, long and hard. He'd already made hotel reservations at a small hotel on the beach, the place recommended by a colleague. Zoe had handed over the entertainment reins, albeit with obvious misgivings—"You'll book us into a four-star place and we might as well be in Los Angeles or Dallas. I want to *know* I'm in Mexico." At odd hours during the day, he'd find himself, like a kid, counting the hours to their time alone together, even though it was still a couple of weeks off.

Thinking, even as they kissed, of something he wanted to tell her, he moved to pull away, but Zoe's arms tightened around him and she kissed him harder, her tongue inside his mouth.

"Phillip, I want you so much," she murmured as they finally pulled apart. "I feel like I'm sixteen, kissing through five songs on the radio." She stood back to see his face. "Remember dances? Those spangly things on the ceiling that threw bits of light all over everything?"

"No."

"No?"

"I never went to dances," he admitted.

"Huh?" She studied his face. "Oh, you always had your nose in a book?"

"Most of the time."

"Not me."

"I bet."

"What's that supposed to mean?"

"Just, I bet. Too bad I lost touch with you after you stopped being a boy. I bet you were a knockout."

"A knocked-up knockout."

"Really?"

"Yeah. I mean we were planning to get married, but…" She bit her lip. "Could we pretend I didn't say that? It sounds like Brett was accidental or something and that's not the way it was."

"What *were* you planning to do?" he asked after a moment.

"If I hadn't got pregnant? Don't laugh. I wanted to be a doctor."

"Why would I laugh?"

"I don't know…Zany Zoe, the madcap gardener. Actually, I wanted to be a dermatologist. Come up with a cure for eczema. I figured I had enough personal experience with it."

"You could have done it anyway."

"I know, but after Brett was born, I sort of stopped thinking about it. Now I'm totally focused on him…"

"On him—"

"Becoming a doctor." She put her hands on his shoulders. "You're giving me a weird look. I know what you're thinking, that I'm sublimating or something."

"What I was really thinking about was kissing you again."

She grinned. "Well, quit thinking and get on with it."

BRETT STOOD at his bedroom window, listening to Weird Molly babble on the phone and, get this, watching his mom kiss Molly Barry's dad. *Yech.* It wasn't something you'd want to spend a whole lotta time looking at, your mom making out, for God's sake, so he moved away and sat down on the bed.

"You know what?" he said to Molly. "I don't give a shit. Kill your stupid self, I don't care."

"Thanks a lot."

"You're welcome."

"You don't think I would, do you?"

"Read my lips," he said, which was kind of dumb since they were on the phone, but he was in a bad mood. Ever since Dr. Barry started coming to see his mom, she'd been ditzier than hell. Dragging stuff out of her closet, bitching about her weight, jumping up every time the phone rang. In one way, it was cool because she wasn't on his case so much, but it also kind of freaked him to see her, like she'd turned into someone else or something. One day, he asked what was for dinner and she told him to defrost something because she was going to this play with Dr. Barry. *Defrost something.* That was a first.

"Want me to tell your dad you're gonna kill yourself?"

"My dad?"

"He's out in the backyard with my mom."

"What?" Now she sounded, like, totally freaked. "Are you serious?"

"They're making out."

"Liar."

"He's kissing her face off. Swear on a stack of Bibles."

Molly started crying. Big, gulping sobs.

"So what's the big deal? He's not allowed to kiss?"

"Go to hell," she said, and hung up.

One truly weird chick. He flipped on the TV, watched a video until he heard the front door slam, then went downstairs, quietly, in case that wasn't Dr. Barry leaving. In the hallway, he glanced through the pane of glass at the top of the door and, sure enough, Dr. Barry's car was still parked in the driveway. It was this really cool black Jaguar and his mom was leaning against the driver's door and Dr. Barry had his hands on either side of her head and they were going at it again. There was this girl at school, Sophie, who he liked a whole lot. If Sophie would kiss him like Dr. Barry was kissing his mom, he would be one happy dude.

He went into the kitchen, opened the freezer and took out the last frozen burrito in his stash. Good thing he was staying with his dad this weekend. Pam would give him another supply. He was nuking it in the microwave when his mom came in with this kind of sneaky look on her face like she'd just done something she didn't think anyone saw. Ha-ha, Mom. Fooled *you*.

"Hi, honey." She looked in this little mirror she kept on the wall by the window and started patting her hair and stuff. "Wow, look at the time. Why aren't you in bed? What's that you're eating? Oh God, Brett, where do you get that junk. Let me make you something. The movie got out later than we thought, I…is something wrong sweetie?"

"No." He licked some melted cheese off his fingers. "Why would something be wrong?"

"No reason, I just thought…oh, never mind. Did you get your science project finished?"

"That was last week, Mom. I told you twice."

She bit her lip like she was trying to think. "Oh, right, you did."

He thought about shaking her up some and asking why Dr. Barry didn't do something about his weird daughter, but she had this kind of dazed, happy look on her face and he didn't want to be mean or anything, plus right now was a good time to ask her about going away with his dad and Pam for a week at Thanksgiving. It was still months away, but he needed time to get her ready for the idea. Give her time to chill out from the fit he knew she'd throw. *"Thanksgiving?"* He could already see the hurt look she'd get on her face. *"A whole week? But Brett, you spent last Thanksgiving with your father."*

His mom was making tea now, humming to herself as she moved around the kitchen. He'd left this surfing magazine on the table and he sat down and started to flip through it. Every few minutes, he could feel her look at him as though she wanted to say something.

"Sweetheart." She poured boiling water into mug. "You haven't *properly* met Phillip…Dr. Barry. I guess it would be okay if you called him Phillip. What would feel most comfortable for you, Phill—"

"Jeez, Mom." He couldn't help it, he started laughing. His mom was a freakin' genius at turning everything into a federal case. "How about I call him…Zippy Cone Head?"

His mom looked at him, slightly puzzled, as though she might be thinking it over. "Zippy—"

"It's a joke, Mom." He went back to the magazine. "Jeez."

"Would you like to meet him?"

"Can I meet Angelina Jolie instead?"

"I'm serious, Brett."

"So am I."

She brought her tea over to the table and sat down. "Do you have a problem or anything with…" Her face went red and she blew at her tea, then set the mug down. "With, uh, well, I've made it a point not to…I've never gone out on dates or anything. I mean, I remember I hated it when Granny Janny went on dates—"

"Granny Janny?" He started laughing again. This was the freakiest conversation. "Did she make out in the backyard?"

"Huh?"

"Nothing."

"Tell me."

"Tell you what?"

"You're mad at me about something, aren't you? Just tell me. We need to talk openly about this sort of thing."

"Yeah, Mom." He folded his arms across his chest, put this real serious look on his face. "Now that you asked me, I am kind of…"

"Well, let's talk about it then."

"I don't think I can."

"Is it…embarrassing for you?"

"Yeah, kind of."

"Come on, honey. It's just me. What's the problem, just tell me."

He chewed his thumbnail. "Okay...well, see we're out of frozen burritos and I really, really like them."

"WHAT EXACTLY ARE YOU looking for?" the saleswoman in Second Time Around asked Zoe some fifteen minutes after Zoe had rejected her offer of assistance but was still sliding hangers and poking through dress racks. "A special-occasion dress? Something for a wedding? We have a couple of really darling mother-of-the bride dresses...or mother of the bridegroom," she added with a laugh. "Funny how we always think mother of the bride as though the groom doesn't have a mother. I know when my son got married last year, I spent six months, *six months,* I kid you not, looking for something. What size are you? Twelve? Fourteen?"

One more word from you, lady, and I'm going to slap you silly. As she briefly eyed a gauzy peach number, Zoe could feel the woman hovering behind her, sizing up her hips and rear end. *Fourteen.* Is that what she looked like? A fourteen? No more food. Nothing but water until Phillip's damn medical association dinner. If she didn't lose ten pounds, she wasn't going. Ten pounds by Saturday. Today was Wednesday. She felt sweat popping out across her forehead. *Ask me if I'm having a hot flash, lady, and I'll belt you.*

He'd called to ask her about two weeks ago and at first she'd been all excited because this had to mean something, right? Phillip taking her to a fancy event where they'd be around other doctors and people he knew? Didn't it have to mean that maybe he liked her...just a *leetle* bit? Okay, that was dumb, he did like her, maybe even as much as she liked him. But this was bumping things up another notch, right? Which had made her heart do this little leap. Kind of scary but terrific at the same time. So of course she said she'd go, but the minute they hung up she'd started panicking about not having anything to wear and things kind of went downhill from there. This morning, stress alone had made her finish the pancakes Brett had left on his plate. Syrup, slimy bits of pancake, and she'd stood at the sink trying to make herself stick them down the garbage disposal, or at least run water on them so they wouldn't be so tempting. But no, she'd gobbled them down as if she hadn't eaten for six weeks.

"Black's always slimming." The woman held out a short, strapless cocktail dress. She had long red fingernails and a massive diamond ring that glinted under the store's dim overhead lights. "This is darling...if you think you could squeeze into a—"

"I don't like black." Zoe decided she'd try the mall. She hated malls, almost as much as she hated pushy sales assistants who were too stupid to know when to keep a discreet distance. *And you don't fool me with that rock. It's a cubic zirconia, if I ever saw one.* "Thanks anyway." She slid her purse strap up her shoulder, deliberately averting her eyes from the full-length mirror as she headed for the exit. Maybe a juice fast would be more effective than all water, something about the laxative effect.

"I DON'T *KNOW,* Grandma." Brett was in the kitchen, trying to fix himself a peanut-butter-and-jelly sandwich, which wasn't exactly brain surgery, but his grandma was standing so close he could smell her perfume and asking him stuff in this whispery voice that was starting to get on his nerves. If she wanted to know so badly, for cripes' sake, why didn't she just ask his mom? Except he knew the answer to that. One more question about Dr. Barry taking his mom to this big fancy mucky-muck thing at the country club, or wherever it was and his mom would bite his grandma's head off.

"I don't understand your mother, honey, that's all I can say," Granny Janny was whispering. "She's acting like it's something to be ashamed of. I think it's wonderful that Phillip obviously thinks enough of her that he wants to be seen in public with…oh, shoot!" She gave this embarrassed laugh. "That didn't sound right, did it?"

"That's okay, Grandma." He screwed the lid back on the peanut butter jar. "I know what you meant."

She peered at him. "Do you, honey? Your mom can be so prickly about these things. I tell you, I've been tickled to death since she started seeing Phillip, but God forbid that I ask her one question." She leaned so close her nose almost touched against his. "Did she get a dress yet?"

"A dress?"

"For the big event?"

"I dunno." Brett took a bite of his sandwich. "Hey, Grandma, I've gotta go feed the animals, okay?"

"Sure, sure, honey, but just humor your old granny." Her voice dropped, like someone had just turned the volume way low. "Has she even looked?"

"Looked for what?"

Granny Janny sighed. "Go feed the goats, honey."

"I'VE THOUGHT about it and thought about it and I've decided I'm not going to go," Zoe told Rhea as they sat on Rhea's back porch shelling peas. It was Friday, and Phillip's shindig was the next night. She hadn't found anything to wear, her arms and back were all broken out from the stress of not finding anything to wear, her hair was going through this impossible stage and she'd gained two pounds. On her lap was a yellow enamel bowl full of shelled green peas. She was looking at the peas thinking about how the pale green looked so pretty against the yellow when her eyes just filled up with tears and suddenly she was bawling like a baby.

Rhea put her arm around Zoe's shoulder and they sat there, not talking, while Zoe sniffed and gulped.

"I wanted to look…I don't know, all elegant and sophisticated," she finally said, "and everything makes me look like some stuffed sausage, not to mention that I can't afford elegant and sophisticated, so I'm running around to all these secondhand-rose places and, oh God, Rhea, it's not just that…me and

Phillip, or Phillip and I...hold on." Wiping her eyes with the back of her hand, she got up, grabbed a length of paper towels from the roll in the kitchen, blew her nose, then came back outside again. She sat down on the steps. "It's not going to work."

"I thought it was working just great."

"Well, it was." She scratched her arm. "Is. But I think this is a sign that there's trouble down the road."

"Zoe." Rhea grabbed her hand. "Quit scratching. Go run some cold water on your arms."

Zoe sat on her hands to stop them attacking her arms. "I'm not a happy camper, Ree."

"I can tell. But..." She slid her thumbnail along a row of peas. "I mean, what if you'd found the perfect dress?"

"I don't know. Maybe that's what I mean by a sign. If things were meant to work out with Phillip, I'd have found a dress. But I didn't."

"You're going to tell him you're breaking up with him because you can't find a dress?"

"No. I'm not saying that, I'll just...I don't know, maybe I'll tell him I have an incurable disease, or something."

Rhea laughed and then Zoe did, too. But it wasn't really funny. Deep inside, as much as she liked Phillip, there was always this kind of feeling that they were mismatched...like Gucci luggage and the battered flea-market suitcase she'd hauled out when she took Brett to Catalina last year. She tried to explain to Rhea.

"I mean, he's a great guy and it's fine if we're on my territory, but that's not his world and I just think it's better if we end things now before…"

"Before?"

Zoe sighed. "Before someone gets hurt, I guess."

"That someone being you?"

"*Duh*," Zoe said. "Like *I'm* going to break Phillip's heart?"

PHILLIP WAS ATTEMPTING to revive a moribund head of lettuce by submerging it in ice water when his doorbell rang. He glanced at the microwave clock— 9:09 p.m. The bell rang again. He wiped his palms down the sides of his jeans and padded, barefoot, through the quiet house. Before Zoe, he'd never really thought about silence—no radio, or TV, he'd never been into music. Except for when Molly was over, the only noise was of his own making. The turn of a journal page, a cough or sigh. The way he preferred it, he'd always thought. But with Zoe's vibrant hum filling his head, the silence had started to feel oppressive. He opened the door.

"Hey." Zoe, in a filmy blue skirt, a cardigan over her shoulders. "Were you in bed?"

"No." He grinned at her. "But it's not a bad idea."

She pushed his chest. "Animal."

He growled.

"Phillip."

"What?" She looked unusually solemn. "Is something wrong?"

"I don't know. Maybe. Can I come in?"

He motioned her inside and she followed him through the house and into the kitchen. At the sink, she lifted the submerged lettuce between thumb and forefinger and shot him a reproving look.

"I know," he said. "I didn't feel like shopping for anything."

"So, is this dinner?"

He shrugged. "Unless someone takes pity on me."

Shaking her head, she pulled open the refrigerator door. "And you've probably got zip in here. Jeez, Phillip, no eggs, no cheese." She turned to look at him. "Hopeless."

"Want to go out?"

"No." Arms folded across her chest, she appeared to be studying the floor tiles. "We need to talk."

A sudden awareness that he was in fact hungry and could demolish a pizza gave way to the growing suspicion that whatever she'd come to talk to him about wouldn't be something he wanted to hear.

"Are you starving?" she asked.

"I'm fine." They stood in the middle of the kitchen, arms folded in almost identical positions. "What's up?"

"I can't go to your thing tomorrow."

"My thing. You mean the association dinner? How come?"

"I just can't." She unfolded her arms, raked back her hair. Looked at him, looked away again. "It's just…remember how you wouldn't let me get in the cannibal pot?"

He scratched his head. "It's been a long day, Zoe."

"When we were kids. You let Courtney get in, but you wouldn't let me...because of my rash. You said you didn't want to get cooties."

He stared at her. Zoe's frequently convoluted train of thought was part of her charm, he enjoyed the challenge of trying to follow it. This one had him stumped. *Cannibal pot,* he was saying to himself, *cooties.* Huh? Then as he stirred through the stew of ancient memories, he recalled Joe mentioning something about a game. "That wasn't me," he said, eager to redeem himself. "My brother told me that story just the other day. He was the one who wouldn't let you in."

Zoe looked momentarily taken aback and then a smile slowly spread across her face. "Oh, sure, blame your brother."

"I'm serious."

The smile faded. "Well good," she said. "I didn't want you to think you'd do something like that."

"So?" He felt a wash of relief. "The dinner's on again?"

She shook her head. "No. It doesn't really change things that much."

"Zoe, my sweet." He put his hands on her shoulders, looked into her eyes. "I know if I weren't on the verge of starvation, I'd be able to put it all together, but right now, I have to say I don't have the foggiest idea what you're talking about."

She pulled away and leaned back against the counter. Her forehead creased in concentration, she studied the tiles some more. "I can't see you anymore, Phillip," she said slowly. "The dinner thing just made me realize all the reasons why this isn't working. I mean, it's pretty obvious how different we are and eventually, those differences are just going to clash. Either that or I'll start trying to be something I'm not and that won't work, either, so I think it's best if we just end it now."

He swallowed, stumped momentarily for something to say. "Look, it's late," he finally managed. "I'm exhausted and you look pretty wiped out yourself. Let's not make any decisions tonight."

"I've thought about it," Zoe said. "And I think it's best this way." She stood on tiptoe to deliver a quick kiss on the lips, then she fluttered her fingers at him and left.

When the phone rang thirty minutes later, he had no doubt that it was Zoe calling to say she'd changed her mind. He'd felt the smile form on his lips as he picked up the receiver, but it wasn't Zoe.

While Deanna was out for the evening, Molly had jumped from the second-floor balcony of her mother's apartment.

CHAPTER THIRTEEN

FOUR WEEKS LATER as he jogged along the Malibu beach, a mile or so away from the private clinic where Molly had been hospitalized, Phillip was thinking about *Zoe*. Even saying her name felt liberating somehow. He thought about her constantly, imagining her as an open window on the closed and claustrophobic room of his world and then, despite everything, finding amusement in the fanciful train of thought, which, he recognized, was pure Zoe.

He hadn't seen or spoken to her since she'd left his apartment that night.

He sidestepped a dog digging furiously with its forepaws, sending sprays of sand airborne. How much easier it would be now, if, when he'd first met Zoe, he'd leveled with her about Molly's illness. Back then though, he'd barely been able to level with himself, much less a woman he hardly knew. Teenage problems, both he and Deanna had wanted to believe. He'd even been willing to concede that Molly's problems were a little more severe than most, but he'd drawn the line at mental illness.

The blinders were off now.

According to Molly, she'd been watching TV and the guy giving the weather had sent a message directly to her. By throwing herself off the balcony, he'd assured her, she would end world hunger and save the world from domination by evil forces.

Shrubbery beneath the balcony had cushioned her from physical injury, but later, after she'd swallowed a handful of prescription tranquilizers, she was found wandering, incoherent and distraught, along Hollywood Boulevard.

They'd admitted her to a hospital close to Deanna's apartment. Weekends began to take on a pattern. His partner Stu and Malcolm Thomasson had taken over all of his on-call responsibilities. Days and weeks passed in a blur. Late at night, or while driving up to Los Angeles, he'd think about Zoe and want to call her, then decide against it. His life felt like an overpacked suitcase, straining to contain what it already held. Perhaps even more than that though, he couldn't avoid the sense that Molly's illness was somehow caused by his failure as a parent.

With benefit of hindsight, he could now see certain barometers to Molly's state of mind. The breathless, seemingly uncensored stream of words rushing forth in her light, childlike voice, the peals of laughter, *ha-ha-ha-ha-ha,* the exaggerated body language—hands cupped to her chest, arms flailing to indicate circles. None of which—it now seemed incredible—he'd recognized.

Time after time, as he'd picture himself describing it all to Zoe, he would see as clearly as if she were in the room, her look of incredulity. "Two suicide attempts and you didn't think she had a *real* problem?" And, in his defense, he'd say that it was really a case of not *wanting* to believe. He was at the top of his field, on the receiving end of invitations from all over the world to lecture on the brain and its complexities. Difficult cases beyond the scope of other highly competent physicians were referred to him. How could *his* daughter be mentally ill? And he'd see the expression on Zoe's face as he unburdened himself and decide that he couldn't, as much as he wanted to, bring himself to call her.

ZOE WAS THINKING about Phillip as she looked through the refrigerator. Her head ached and she felt strung out, every muscle taut. The phone was about to do her in. Every time it rang, she'd jump as though she'd been shot. She opened the vegetable bin: some graying carrots, a Jerusalem artichoke that she'd meant to do something with but now couldn't remember what, two pears and a plastic bag of dried apricots.

Exactly five weeks now since she'd told him they were through and the hollow, sick feeling in her stomach was just as bad as the night she'd left his apartment.

She stared at the shelves. An opened bag of tortillas, a plastic tub of mango salsa. A gallon of milk, a diet soda. She popped the top of the soda and drank some. Call him. Just pick up the phone. Flip, casual. "Hey, it's a woman's prerogative to change her mind right? Guess, what? I'm changing mine. Can we pretend I never said we were through?"

She shut the refrigerator door. On the counter, half an English muffin left from Brett's breakfast, a loaf of raisin bread, a jar of boysenberry jam with a spoon in it. She removed the spoon, licked off the jam and dropped the spoon into the sink. She stared at the coffee mug and glasses in the sink. Load them in the dishwasher, she thought. Go water the seedlings. Feed the animals. Pick up your keys and drive someplace where you can't hear the phone ring.

Five weeks now since she'd told him they were through.

Not that she was obsessing or anything. She sat on the edge of the cliff—practically the same spot where she and Phillip had sat—eating a Juanita's carnitas burrito, just as they had done, watching the waves, just as they had done and playing everything over in her brain. Why, why, *why* had she made such a big deal about the damn medical dinner? So what if she didn't have the perfect dress? Maybe that's exactly why he liked her, because she wasn't perfect.

She picked a shred of burrito off the leg of her knee.

Has he called you though?

She crumpled the food wrapper in her fingers, her mood suddenly taking a dive. Grease glistened on her fingers. *Pig.* Her thighs looked like tree trunks. Waiting around for the phone to ring required emotionally soothing and frequent trips to the refrigerator. Last night, after she'd hung up on a telephone marketer who she knew, just knew, was Phillip calling, she'd removed a gallon of Rocky Road, a flavor she didn't even like that much and stood at the open freezer door eating the soft melty stuff around the edges of the carton. When that was gone, she moved into the harder stuff near the middle. By the time she was through, there was this ice cream pinnacle surrounded by a deep moat. If Phillip ever did get around to calling her, she'd be twice the woman he'd once known.

Damn, crap, phooey. She stretched her legs out and felt the breeze beneath the hem of her long cotton skirt. Her life, which had been merrily humming along, seemed to have gone decidedly south. It wasn't just Phillip. Fights with Brett seemed to happen almost every day lately. She couldn't say anything to him without making him mad. When she tried to find a reason, she always traced the start of it all to Phillip coming into her life. Except that now she and Brett were still fighting and she hadn't even had a phone call from Phillip.

Which was good or bad news depending on how you looked at it, she guessed. The good news was that if Phillip had figured she'd done him a favor by breaking things off, she could go back to being Brett's mother. Insert the words *responsible* and *conscientious* between Brett and mother. While she and Phillip were doing their thing, she'd been neither responsible nor conscientious…except that, when she thought about it, she couldn't come up with any blatant instances of her irresponsibility. Except for maybe serving Brett a defrosted dinner or two on nights when she and Phillip went out.

And Brett hadn't complained. The opposite, in fact.

"Hey, it's cool, Mom," he'd said a couple of times. "How long have I been saying you should get a boyfriend?"

Still, as much as she'd enjoyed herself with Phillip, she'd always had this niggling fear that it was somehow at the expense of her son and, ultimately, she would pay the price. She and Courtney had talked about it on side-by-side elliptical machines at the gym. Courtney had been trying forever to get her to join so they could work out together. A fifty-percent-off membership drive and the refrigerator dependence had finally convinced her.

"Brett would never come right out and say it, but I think maybe Phillip made him feel kind of insecure," she'd told Courtney. "The last time Phillip was over, Brett was obviously upset about something."

"How could you tell?"

"Oh, he was just kind of a wiseass. That usually means he's hiding what he really feels."

"Wonder where he gets that from?"

"Shut up."

"Zoe, if you want my opinion, here it is. Go for it. How long have we all been telling you to get a life? Enjoy it. Brett will be just fine."

But Phillip didn't call.

She watched a seagull hopping around a few yards from where she sat. Hoping for a tidbit of left-over carnitas. She watched the waves and practiced breathing. *Everrrrr. Sooooo. Slowleeeeeeee.* You're feeling calmer, an Indian-accented voice in her head intoned. "The waves are carrying your anger out to sea, washing all stress awaaaaaaaaay."

Okay, deep breathing wasn't working either. Eating, watching the water—her two most reliable mood elevators—and she still felt blue and restless. She carried the detritus of her lunch back to the truck, tossed it into the back seat amidst the clutter of gym shoes, old newspapers and an assortment of never-used umbrellas. If the Southern California coast should ever experience a sudden and violent downpour, she'd be prepared. She snapped on the radio.

"...and I know he runs around on me," a woman was telling a radio psychologist. "But I love him. I don't know what's wrong with me, but—"

"You're an idiot." Zoe changed the station while easing the truck onto the Coast Highway. "Free diagnosis. Next?"

"WHAT'S STOPPING YOU from calling him?" Sandy asked the following Wednesday. They were all sitting around The Daily Grind, setting the world straight. Zoe, moping silently while the others talked, had finally admitted that she was bummed about the way Phillip just seemed to have dropped out of her life. "Why don't you?"

"I don't know," Zoe replied truthfully. "I've

picked up the phone a few times, but maybe I just don't want to hear him make some lame excuse, like he'd lost my number or something."

"Or maybe he just wasn't your type," Roz said. "Maybe it was the novelty of meeting up with someone from your past. It's like one of those cute meets, the rich guy and the housekeeper's daughter who meet again in another life and it's instant attraction."

"Yeah, maybe," Zoe said.

Still she couldn't stop thinking about him. But the day she found herself consulting the daily horoscope for clues about whether this would be the day Phillip finally called, Zoe decided she'd truly lost it. I have mentally washed my hands of him, she told herself. It is over, *finis*. I have absolutely no interest in him.

The phone rang.

Once. Twice. Her heart was going nuts. *Please.* Her eyes screwed shut, she picked it up just as the third ring started.

"I have a great idea for Mom's birthday," Courtney said.

For a long moment, Zoe couldn't speak. Tears stung her nose. "Uh, can we talk about this some other time?"

"Are you sick or something?"

"I'm working, Courtney."

"Sorry." Courtney sounded offended, but kept talking anyway.

The phone at her ear, Zoe wandered back into the kitchen and opened the refrigerator. Tucked into one of the door shelves was a bag of chocolate chips

she'd bought for cookies and forgotten all about.
She ripped the top with her teeth, tipped her head
back and emptied part of the bag into her mouth. The
chocolate melted slowly, rich and dark and sweet. It
was good, but she knew enough to realize that the
comfort of chocolate wasn't what she really craved.
She put the bag back. Phillip was what she wanted.

Phillip. She missed him so thoroughly it was as
if he were always just about to walk through the
door, or wave to her from across the street. She could
see him that clearly—in his hospital scrubs, arms
folded across his chest the way he'd been that day
she'd gone to the hospital. Or in the blue shirt that
matched his eyes. Or with his arm around her as
they sat on the cliffs. He sometimes had this absent-
minded look, as though he were mentally somewhere
else. Which he probably was a lot of time. But not
with her. "You're teaching me to have fun," he'd told
her once. "To be in the moment." And now that moment didn't include her.

"Do you want to hear my idea?" Courtney said.

"I'm holding my breath in anticipation."

"I'll call you when you're in a better mood."

"Fine."

Courtney sighed. "Zoe, come on, can't you just
work with me on this? Okay, I'm going to tell you
anyway. We charter a sailboat for a sunset champagne cruise. Everyone wears dressy casual, white
pants for the men, maybe little cocktail dresses—"

"For the men?"

"As the sun goes down," Courtney went on, "We

all raise glasses in a toast to the birthday girl. And then Arnie appears with the birthday cake, candles twinkling in the evening light. Can't you just see it?"

"Who's paying for this shindig?"

"Well, I thought we could share the expense. It sounds extravagant—"

"It *is* extravagant."

"So…" Courtney's voice was elaborately casual. "Still nothing from Phillip?"

CHAPTER FOURTEEN

IF GIVING UP ON EVER HEARING from Phillip again was a hard thing for her to do, Zoe would reflect at times, it was practically impossible for her mother. Janna was still acting as though her youngest daughter had gone and lost a winning lottery ticket.

The topic came up all the time, like right now at the gym where Janna had gone to work out with her two daughters.

Zoe was sitting on a bench, tying her sneakers. The air smelled of steam and fruit-flavored shampoo; women wafted around in various stages of undress. One palm on a locker front, arm stiff, Janna began some preliminary warm-ups.

"Nothing from Phillip, I guess?"

"Yeah, Mom, last week he sent this humongous care package. Canned food, blankets, sacks of rice and sugar...that's what you meant, right?"

"Well, right there you have one reason he hasn't called," Courtney said. "Who the hell wants to hear smart-ass comments all the time?"

Zoe twirled a strand of hair. She was always coming up with elaborate reasons, kept strictly to herself, to explain why Phillip couldn't even pick up the phone to call. The famous actress with a malignant brain tumor, for example, who, swearing Phillip to secrecy, had whisked him off to a distant and undisclosed location to operate on the tumor.

"But he was there in Zoe's house," Janna was saying. "No one's going to tell me that a man like Phillip Barry, a brain surgeon, for God's sake, would have come over to do yard work if he hadn't been interested."

"Maybe he only liked me for my tomatoes, Mom," Zoe said. "I find that happens with a lot of the guys I meet."

Courtney rolled her eyes. Her contention was that Zoe might have stood a chance with Phillip Barry—weirder things had happened—but she'd probably blown it by not fixing herself up. "You only have to look at Deanna Barry to know the kind of woman he's attracted to," Courtney said. "It's the little things, Zoe. A manicure, a decent haircut."

"I'll make a note of that, Courtney," Zoe said.

MOLLY'S TREATMENT was helping, Phillip decided. She seemed calmer and more in control. Less blue and weepy than she'd been before. She'd been released from the hospital and, although she wanted to return to Seacliff, it made more sense that she continue to stay with Deanna where she could be close to her doctor.

One day, he found himself strolling through the Seacliff farmer's market, pretending to himself that he wasn't really headed over to Zoe's stall, but was just there to pick up something for lunch. One of the nurses had made a disparaging remark about his dietary regimen of bagels and bananas. "Quick and easy," he'd replied. "Don't have time for anything more."

If it was incredible that he'd walked out of the hospital in the middle of a typically hectic day to seek out a woman, the fact that the woman was a hippy, flower child—how would you describe Zoe's look?—vegetable seller with a son on scholarship and more beads and bracelets than he could count—made him wonder if maybe he'd developed some sort of mental short circuit of his own.

Here he was, picking up frilly green things—lettuce, he mused, although it didn't look quite how he thought lettuce should—and sniffing at flowers and pretending to listen to a recipe that an elderly woman in a straw hat was trying to give him.

"Lots of grated cheese," she said. "Remember that."

"I will," Phillip said, having no idea what she was talking about.

"And a beaten egg."

"Got it." He thought he could see the top of Zoe's stall three aisles over. He narrowed his eyes, trying to spot Zoe herself.

"A pound be enough?" the old woman asked.

"A pound." He gave her a blank look. "Yeah, fine, uh…"

Minutes later he walked off with a bulging brown paper bag of something he couldn't identify. He slowly strolled the perimeter, marking time before he would meander over and casually greet Zoe as though bumping into her were just a coincidence.

Coinkadink, as Molly would say. Molly, who according to Deanna, appeared to be "chugging along well enough. God, her timing stinks though," Deanna constantly complained. "I can just see some damn interviewer finding out about the latest problems. 'Now, your book, *My Daughter, My Best Friend,*'" she'd imitated an announcer's measured tones. "'Would you say that describes the relationship with your own daughter?' Hell no. Not that it's my fault. If she were a normal girl…"

Phillip stopped now to look at a stall of odd-shaped vegetables. Tall green stalks, maybe fifteen inches long, clustered with what looked like miniature cabbages. He picked up a piece, examined the small green balls of tightly packed leaves.

"Brussels sprouts," the stall owner said.

"Really?" Phillip set the stalk down. "This is how they grow?"

The guy gave Phillip a look that said there's an idiot around every corner and moved away to serve another customer. Phillip glanced down at the bag in his hand and then headed in the direction of Zoe's stall.

No Zoe.

"She had to leave for a while," the woman in an adjacent stall told him. "But she should be back in thirty minutes or so. Can I give her a message when I see her?"

He hesitated. On the heels of disappointment, he recognized a definite sense of relief. No child of Zoe McCann's, he was quite sure, would make three suicide attempts before her problems were taken seriously. "That's okay," he told the woman.

"YOU MUST BE SO PROUD of him," the guidance counselor said to Zoe. "There's so much in the news these days about problem kids, it gives me hope to work with a kid like Brett. Bright, motivated, conscientious…" She smiled. "An all-around good kid."

Zoe felt her heart swell. The all-around good kid, who of late had been a surly uncommunicative brat at home, had been named to a state-wide honor roll of high-school seniors.

"Yeah." She smiled back at the counselor. "I'm pretty happy with him."

"He tells me he wants to go into the navy," the counselor said.

Zoe stared at her in disbelief. "That's the first I've heard about it," she finally managed to say. "When did he say that?"

"I'd have to look at my notes, but it would have been since school started again. His dad was in the navy, he said. He seems very close to his father."

Zoe shifted her bag to the other shoulder. The counselor had sensed something amiss. Her smiled had turned quizzical. She wore glasses with blue plastic rims; light glinted off the lenses. "Well…"

"Um." Zoe licked her lips. "He hasn't mentioned medical school?"

"Medical school?" The counselor thought for a moment. "No, I don't recall him saying anything recently about medical school."

By the time she got back to the market to close up, the crowd of shoppers had trickled to a few and there were long shadows over the stalls. Her mind on Brett, Zoe piled unsold vegetables into a wooden orange crate that she would drop off at a food bank on the way home. Obviously Brett's idiot jerk of a father had been working on him. *Hey, forget stupid medical school, be a goof-off surfer like me. Dude, we'll have a blast.* Adrenaline-fueled anger pumping through her body, she carried a crate over to the truck. *God, I am so damn mad.* She set the crate in the truck bed, marched back to the stall, her head full of what she would say to Brett and then to his idiot father.

At home, twenty minutes later, she found a knife smeared with peanut butter on the counter she'd left clean that morning.

"Goddamn it." She picked it up, carried it upstairs and rapped on Brett's door.

"Yeah?"

She opened the door, flung the knife on the bed. "The maid quit."

"Huh?" He was standing beside the bed, stuffing T-shirts and underwear into a black backpack. "What's up with you?"

"Since you're going to your dad's, take it there. Let him wash it. Or Miss Bubblegum Brain."

He rolled his eyes. "Jeez, Mom. D'you have a fight with Granny Janny or something?"

"No." She tried to keep her voice even. "I was just kind of surprised to hear your new career plans."

"Huh?" He held up a shirt, examined it for a moment and stuck it in the pack. "What career plans?"

"Good question."

"Hey, Mom, there's no school Monday. Some teacher trainer thing, or something. Is it okay if I stay at Dad's Sunday night, too?"

Zoe folded her arms across her chest. "Oh, sure, Brett. Why not? All you ever want to do anyway is be over at your dad's. Hell, why should I care? I'm just your mother. It's probably stupid of me to have hopes and plans for you. I mean, what's really important in life? Go to your dad's, for God's sake. Go surf your brains out. And, hey, forget medical school. Going into the navy is a great idea. Like father, like son, right?"

CHAPTER FIFTEEN

BRETT SAT ON THE FLOOR of the room he had in his dad's house reading his dad's *Playboy*. That was the cool thing about his dad. He didn't get all bent out of shape about stuff like that. You wanna look at pictures of naked women? Sure, what the hell? Give you some practice for the real thing? His mom now…he didn't even want to think about his mom. Like, he still felt bad about the fight they'd had before his dad came to pick him up. His mom just made such a big deal out of everything. He was seventeen, for cripe's sake. Maybe he wanted to be a doctor, maybe he wanted to go in the navy. Tons of time to figure it all out though, right?

Except for his mom, things were going pretty cool in his life. Especially now that Weird Molly wasn't around to bug him. She still called him all the time, but she hadn't started school this fall at Country Day. That gave him the chance to focus on Sophie, who'd moved to Seacliff from France. He liked the way she sometimes said the words wrong when she talked and she was really cute. The thing is he shouldn't have told Weird Molly about her because now she was like always asking him questions about whether Sophie was his girlfriend.

He flipped the page and his eyes nearly bugged out at this woman with the most bodacious tatas he'd ever seen in his life. He was still, like gaping at them when he heard the phone ring downstairs.

A minute later, his dad called out to him.

"Some girl on the phone for you."

"What's her name?"

"She's got some kind of accent." His dad was at the bedroom door now, holding the phone with his hand over the mouthpiece. "I can't understand what she said her name was, *Zoffeee?* Something like that."

"Cool." Brett grinned at his dad and reached for the phone. "Hi, Sophie," he said. "How's it going?"

"*Iz goeen?* What is *zit goeen?*"

Brett tried to think how to explain. She sounded more French on the phone than she did at school. It sounded kind of cute though. Maybe she'd teach him some French. "It's just something people say, Sophie," he told her. "Like asking 'how are you?'"

"Ah."

He couldn't keep this dumb-ass grin off his face. It was so cute to think of her talking on the phone, saying "Ah" like she understood what he meant.

"*Brit?*"

"Yeah?"

"I am to go to *ze* party. You would like also to go?"

"With you?" *Cool.* He thumped his fist on the bed. "Sure."

"You go?"

"I go. When?"

"Tonight."

"Tonight?" He checked the time. Almost five. His dad had said something about renting movies and ordering in pizza, but it wouldn't be any big deal if he did something else instead. That was the cool thing about his dad. He could pretty much do his own thing. His mom would make some federal case of it and look all hurt. "I gotta ask my dad if I can use his truck," he said. "Where's the party?"

"The party *eet iz* in, how you say? *Mahlayboo?*"

Mahlayboo? Brett tried to think. At school he could understand her pretty good, but her accent sounded way strong on the phone. Mahlayboo. He said it in his head a couple of times. "You mean Malibu?" he asked.

"*Mahlayboo,* yes *zat* is right. My *coohzahn,* she is very famous movie star, we go to party at 'er 'ouse on *ze* beach."

Malibu. Jeez, that was like near L.A., maybe a hundred miles north. Even his dad might have problems with that. But a party at a famous movie star's beach house. Cool. With Sophie. Way cool.

"You want me to pick you up?"

"Already I am in *ze* house on *ze* beach."

"You're in Malibu now?"

"With my *coohzahn.* We wear *beekeenee* and frolic in *ze watair.*"

Yowzers. "Hey, listen Sophie, it's gonna be late when I get there. And I'm gonna need directions."

In the living room, he saw his dad and Pam all co-zied up together on the couch drinking beer and watching TV. Pam had on this silver halter top and her boobs were practically falling out. He figured if he wasn't there his dad wouldn't miss him a whole lot. Too bad his mom wasn't going with Dr. Barry anymore. He'd had a whole lot more freedom then, that was for sure. Plus she wasn't always mad at everything.

"Hey," he said, and they both smiled at him.

"That wasn't the weird girl, was it?" his dad asked.

"No way." Brett flopped onto the other end of the couch. He'd meant to ask Sophie how she got his number, because he hadn't given it to her. Oh, well, if she'd had to go around asking people for it, it kinda sounded like she really liked him. Cool. "Hey, Dad, can I use the truck?"

His dad was back to watching the TV again. *Cops.* His dad and Pam were these huge *Cops* freaks. Some nights all they watched were reruns, and they'd seen every show so many times they knew what the bad guy was going to do and they'd be saying stuff like, *Watch this part. Look. The bad guy's gonna jump the fence. Okay, here comes the cop. He's gonna shoot him.*

"Omigod, I hate this one." Pam buried her face in his dad's neck. "That little dog runs out in the street right in front of the cop car. I can't look."

"Turn it off," Brett suggested. "Then you won't know."

Brett's father shook his head like he couldn't believe how dumb she was sometimes. "Jeez, Pam, you know the cop stops in time. Remember he wraps the dog in a blanket? How come you need the truck?" he asked without taking his eyes from the TV.

"That girl who called?"

"Yeah." His dad grinned. "Hot?"

"Kinda," Brett said, like he knew. "So anyway, she like, wants to go hang out at the mall—"

"What mall?" Pam asked. "If it's Horton Plaza, I'd have you pick up some Clinique from Nordstrom's. They've got a free gift deal going and today's the last day."

"It's not Horton Plaza," Brett said, thinking about how the expression *free gift* drove his mom crazy. "If it's a gift, of course it's free," she'd say. Brett looked at Pam. "It's some other one. I'm gonna pick her up at her house and then we're gonna go to the mall."

"Where does she live?" his dad asked. "Okay, okay, the bad guy's hiding under the bed," he added in a low voice like the bad guy could hear. "Okay, watch this…*pow*. The cop takes him out."

"Chula Vista. That's where she lives."

"Chula Vista. She Mexican?"

"French."

"I thought she didn't sound Mexican."

"Can I use the truck?"

"The keys are on the kitchen counter." His father set his beer can down. "Call if you're gonna be late, okay?"

"Like how late?"

"I dunno." His dad looked at Pam. "Midnight?"

"Midnight." Pam rolled her eyes. "That's when the fun's just getting started. Brett's a big boy. He'll come home when he's ready to come home, right Brett?"

"Right." He went to get the keys. His dad and Pam were so cool, he was kinda sorry he hadn't told them about Malibu. Pam would have got a kick out of the famous movie-star house bit. But Malibu was kinda far, even for his dad. His mom would totally freak out if she knew half the things he got to do at his dad's. That was the deal, though. If neither of them told her anything, she couldn't give them a bad time. His dad's key ring had this big pink plastic heart with Pam written on it in sparkly letters.

"Hey, Brett, you're gonna need gas." His dad came into the kitchen and held out two twenties and a ten. "Have fun. And take it easy, okay. Don't forget what I told you about the condoms."

WHAT IS HE THINKING When He Sees You Naked For The First Time? Zoe was waiting in the checkout line at the market, reading headlines about the Hollywood crowd—their plastic surgery, their affairs, their substance abuse. Not that she'd ever buy something like the *National Enquirer,* but she kind of liked hearing that the rich and famous had problems, too. She set a carton of cottage cheese and a bunch of celery on the counter. This week she was taking control of the *avoirdupois*. As she continued to unload her groceries her attention kept going back to the "naked for the first time" headline.

Phillip had never seen her naked.

He'd taken a powder before they'd had the chance. Which was maybe a good thing. Phillip was lean and in shape. She wasn't. She pushed a carton of fat-free frozen yogurt down the counter toward the cash register. Chocolate caramel crunch. How could that *not* be sinful?

Roz said she ate junk food when she was truly horny and there was no guy on the horizon. Fat-free frozen éclairs were placed next to the yogurt. If she'd had wild and crazy sex with Phillip, would she stop craving sweet, gooey desserts?

What is he thinking when he sees you naked for the first time?

She unloaded the rest of her cart. Opportunity would be a fine thing.

Naked.

She reached for the magazine, flipped through the pages as her groceries were rung up.

Naked.

Weird the way a particular word would play over and over in her head, just like irritating tunes. She ran her ATM card through the machine on the counter, punched in her code. Naked was making her feel hot. Feeling hot made her think about Phillip Barry.

If she did say so herself, she'd done a pretty good job of not thinking about Phillip Barry. Sometimes though, he'd barge into her brain anyway. Like she couldn't deliver fruit to this little gourmet market in Seacliff without thinking about him, mostly because it was the kind of exclusive place she imagined him shopping in.

At odd moments, she'd find herself comparing whatever she might be doing at that particular moment to what she imagined Phillip might be doing. Dumping a five-pound roll of ground beef into her cart at the market for example, she'd picture Phillip at one of those small expensive gourmet places, trying to decide whether he was more in the mood for the ten-dollar-a-pound filet mignon, or the sixteen-dollar-a-pound giant scampi. And while she picked up cans of store-brand fruit juice, he'd be over in the wine section, comparing the merits of two very good merlots.

As she wheeled her cart out into the parking lot, she began to feel vaguely sorry for herself. Saturday night and Brett was at his father's; Sandy and Roz both had plans. All she had was a long evening at home with a box of frozen éclairs.

Naked.

Outside the market there was a phone booth. She unloaded the groceries into the truck, and then walked back across the lot to the phone. Did she even have quarters? His machine might be on. Would she leave a message? Better if he answered. She conjured his voice. Her own. "Hi, remember me?" Casual, no pressure. What if a woman answered? That would be bad. Better to imagine Phillip thinking longingly of her but, for whatever reason, unable to call her.

Naked. She could go home and fill her mouth with frozen éclairs, or take the éclairs over to Phillip's, just like it was the most normal thing in the

world to drop in on a guy you hadn't seen in months.
"Hi. I brought you some éclairs." And then...

A kid came up.

"Ma'am. Are you waiting for a call?"

"No." Zoe shook her head. *Ma'am*. As if she
didn't feel yukky enough. But the kid had saved her
from making an idiot of herself. Actually, she didn't
even have Phillip's home number anymore. One day,
during the time she'd been hanging around the
phone, willing him to call, she'd ground the slip of
paper with his number on it down the garbage disposal to stop herself from calling him. For a while,
even that wasn't sufficient insurance because she'd
memorized his number. Over time though, she'd
trained herself to forget it.

But she could page him at the hospital!

The thought had just popped into her head. Fortunately, the kid had come along just in time prevent
her from making an idiot of herself.

She drove slowly north on Pacific Coast Highway.
The truck needed gas. She got out, used her ATM
card again and started to fill the tank. The sidewalk
was wet and reflective. The pay phone by the door
to the gas station seemed to wink at her. The quarters jiggled in her pocket. Why call him here though?
Why not wait and call him from home? She watched
the numbers on the gas pump flip over. If she waited
till she got home, she knew she wouldn't call. No
reason. It was either give in to this impulse to call
him on a pay phone, or not call at all. She tried to
think about something else. Like, Denny had inad-

vertently let it slip that he'd once let Brett stay out after midnight. They'd had a huge fight about it and then she and Brett had had yet another huge fight. This one had ended with Brett telling her he wanted to go live with his dad.

The pump clicked off. She replaced the nozzle, screwed on the gas cap and got back in the truck. Through the rearview mirror, she saw the phone again. There was some reason she was thinking about Phillip at exactly this moment. Sandy was big on synchronicity and nothing being a coincidence. Her hand on the keys in the ignition, she thought about calling Sandy to see if she should call Phillip, because maybe this weird fixation with pay phones was some kind of sign.

She started the truck, steered out of the lot and back onto the highway. Her mind ran through the various gas stations and convenience stores she would pass on the way home. Proximity was a factor. The closer to home she got, the farther away she would be from Phillip's home. Too far and she wouldn't call. *Naked.* She squeezed her knees together. Okay, the next phone booth she came to. If no one was using it, she'd call. If it was in use, she'd drive on home and fall asleep watching TV.

Plus there were the éclairs.

PHILLIP SAT on the balcony of his apartment staring out at the dark expanse of ocean and listening to Molly's voice on the phone for signs that she was, as she kept insisting, peachy keen. *Peachy keen.* Where had that come from?

"Well listen, sweetheart," he said after they'd talked for thirty minutes or so. "Let me talk to your mother for a few minutes."

"Um, she's not here right now."

Phillip silently cursed his ex-wife. "I want her with me," Deanna had insisted when he'd mentioned having Molly come back to Seacliff. "You're too preoccupied with work to pay her the kind of attention she needs."

"Where is she?"

"She had to go to a meeting."

"What time will she be home?"

Molly sighed. "I hate this, Dad. You make me feel like a baby. Like I can't stay home by myself. What if I told you she wouldn't be home till tomorrow?"

"Is that true?"

"No. You just get so uptight."

"It's not a matter of being uptight, Moll. I love you, I care about you. Maybe I haven't always done the best job of demonstrating that—"

"I'm sorry," she said, sounding contrite now. " I didn't mean to make you feel bad. Look, don't worry, okay? You can call me if you want."

They talked a little longer, then he hung up.

The phone rang again almost immediately. The answering service had a message for him from Zoe McCann.

"Want me to read it to you?" the woman from the answering service asked.

"Sure."

"Okay, here goes. 'Are you lonely tonight?'"

Phillip smiled. "That's it?"

"That's it. Here's the number."

He carried the phone inside, grabbed a piece of paper and wrote down a number that he didn't recognize. He hung up, and set the phone down on the table. In the kitchen, he made himself a gin and tonic. He tasted the drink, set the glass down and went to the refrigerator. In the vegetable drawer, he found a lime. Shriveled. He cut it in half, then quarters, squeezed a piece into his drink.

Zoe.

He took the drink out onto the balcony. In one direction, he could see the lights of Seacliff Pier. In the other, the dark mass of the headlands. Straight ahead, a pinpoint of light from a boat on the horizon.

Are you lonely tonight?

He went back inside, set his glass down and called the number.

"Well?" Zoe's voice asked. No preamble, typical Zoe.

"Yes."

"Good. Me, too."

"I can hear you smiling," he said.

"I can hear you, too. I...um, I've wanted to call you so many times. But I found that if I waited long enough, the feeling went away. Tonight that didn't happen. I was coming home and I kept noticing phone booths for some reason. I made a deal with myself, if the next phone booth I came to was empty, I'd call you and wait for exactly twenty minutes for you to call back."

"Where are you?"

"About fifteen minutes north of Seacliff."

"Come over," he said.

"Now?"

"No, Zoe, two weeks from tomorrow."

"Hey! *I* do the wiseass stuff."

"Your influence rubs off," he said.

"Yeah?"

"Yeah."

"I'm on my way."

"Hurry."

"I will."

"Zoe."

"What?"

"I've missed you."

CHAPTER SIXTEEN

BRETT GLANCED at the clock on the dashboard.

Eleven fifty-two.

Crap. By the time he got to freakin' Malibu, he'd have missed half the party. It was taking way more time than he figured it would, mostly because he kept getting lost. Now the traffic was bunching up. He could see red lights up ahead. Great, just what he needed. If Sophie wasn't such a fox, this wouldn't be worth it. Now he was tired and hungry and he felt kinda guilty for lying to his dad about where he was going. Seemed like he spent his whole life feeling bad about something or other. Mostly his mom, because they hadn't been getting along so good lately, but like his dad was always saying, his mom was her own worst enemy.

But whenever he said something like maybe he'd kinda like to go live with his dad, because sometimes he really wanted to, especially when she started getting on his case for every little thing, she'd get this hurt look on her face and go all quiet. Like the fight they had last week. He couldn't even remember what it was about now, but they'd yelled at each other and she walked off and started doing stuff in the kitchen. He'd heard her clattering around out there. The thing was, he knew if he didn't go tell her he was sorry for hurting her feelings, that's how it would be for the rest of the night. Her walking around all sad and injured. It wasn't that she was a bad mom, or anything. It was just the opposite, in fact. She was too good. That might sound great, but mostly it felt like this big weight on his back.

Cool. Up ahead he could see the sign for Topanga Canyon Road, which Sophie said he should look for, except the way her accent was he could hardly understand what she was saying. He took the exit. Here I come, Sophie, darlin'. *This better be worth it.*

Fifteen minutes later, he rang the buzzer for her front door.

The door opened.

"*Allo Brit, eez* so *fantasteek* you 'ave come all *zees* way to see me."

"*Molly.*"

"Tricked you!"

"I WAS IN THE MARKET, looking at those junk magazines they have by the cash register," Zoe said through the open door of Phillip's bathroom. "And I saw this article…" She stepped out of her skirt, reached for her underpants, pulled them down to her ankles. Goose bumps had broken out along her arms. From the bedroom, she could see the flicker of light from the candle Phillip had set on the dresser. Her teeth chattering, she unbuttoned her cotton sweater.

When she'd dressed that morning, seduction had been the furthest thing from her mind.

"And…" Phillip's voice from the bedroom. "You saw an article…"

Zoe licked her lips. Wearing only her bra now, she stood on tiptoe to see herself in the mirror over the sink. God, her stomach…her hips. She eyed a towel hanging over the shower stall. "And…um," she unfastened her bra. Naked now, she felt simultaneously turned-on and apprehensive. She grabbed the towel, wrapped it around herself and walked into the bedroom. Phillip was under the covers, his hands clasped behind his head. The flickering candlelight threw shadows across his face.

"So anyway…" Zoe stood a few feet from the bed, holding the towel in place with one hand. "The headline on the article said, 'What is he thinking when he sees you naked for the first time?'"

Phillip smiled.

"And so I started thinking about you. Us…well, not us us, like we're an item or something, but just…you know…and, well, I had this idea that I would just stand before you in all my naked glory and you would tell me that what you're thinking is that I'm gorgeous and magnificent and all that, but then I kind of lost my nerve, so that's why…" An involuntary shiver ran through her. In an instant she was across the room and in the bed beside him, the covers pulled to her chin. "I decided I needed a towel. Hey," she squealed as he pulled the towel away and tossed it to the floor. "Did I say…" But his arms and legs were wrapped around her and he was kissing her and growing hard against her thigh and then she pretty much stopped thinking altogether.

PHILLIP WOKE UP thinking about Molly. He glanced at the clock on the bedside table. Just after two in the morning. Zoe was asleep in the crook of his arm, her hair brushing his chin. He touched his lips to the top of her head, tightened his arm around her.

"Hi," she said in a soft, sleepy voice. "Can't sleep?"

"Just woke up."

"Mmm." She snuggled closer. "This is nice."

"I think so, too." But he couldn't stop thinking about Molly. She had called around eleven. Zoe had been sitting on his lap, feeding him a chocolate éclair. When the phone rang, he'd debated even answering—chocolate was everywhere, his mouth and hands, the tops of Zoe's breasts—but a niggling unease about his daughter had prevailed over his desire to cover Zoe's entire body with chocolate. Molly had sounded agitated but, when questioned, insisted everything was fine. Her mother had called, Molly told him, promised she wouldn't be late. Because of Zoe, he'd allowed himself to be reassured, but now he was wide-awake, his head full of the kind of dire scenarios that sound entirely plausible in the sleepless wee hours of the night, but ridiculous and overwrought by morning light.

Zoe mumbled something and curled up on her side, her back to him.

He closed his eyes and tried to sleep.

"Phillip."

He rubbed the small of her back with his palm. "Zoe?"

"What's going on?"

"I'm not used to sharing my bed with voluptuous women."

"Liar."

"It's true."

"You don't have a bevy of beauties available to fill your every sexual fantasy?"

He laughed.

"Hey, I have a stable of studs."

He pressed his thumb against her spine and moved his hand slowly up her back. "You do?"

"Different one every night. Seriously, if you need to sleep…"

"Not nearly as much as I need you here." He turned on his side, held her body to his.

"Now I'm wide-awake," Zoe said.

"Want to talk?"

"Sure."

His chin was on her shoulder, one arm thrown over her body. "It's Molly. You know a little about her, but I haven't told you everything. She has a severe mental problem. One psychiatrist diagnosed her with a form of schizophrenia. I haven't wanted to believe it myself. I've minimized it in my own mind, pretty much managed to convince myself she was just going through a difficult phase the way teenagers do. When we've talked about our kids, you've told me so much about Brett. I couldn't bring myself to talk about the extent of her problems. I envy the relationship you have with Brett—I admire you for it. You're there for him in a way I haven't been for Molly."

Zoe said nothing, just reached an arm around to stroke his back and he talked and talked, pouring out all the guilt and frustration that until now he'd barely acknowledged, even to himself. As dawn filtered into the room, they made love again and drifted into a deep sleep from which he didn't wake until the phone rang early Sunday morning.

Deanna. Calling from Cedars-Sinai emergency room.

"Someone broke into the house last night and attacked Molly," she said. "The place is a shambles, there's blood everywhere. She's totally out of it. I came home and she was incoherent. Clothes ripped off. I've called the police. You've got to come up here and stay, Phillip. I can't deal with this alone."

He hung up the phone. Zoe was sitting up in bed, the pillow covering her breasts. As he summarized Deanna's call, he heard his voice shaking. "I've got to get up there." He was out of bed, searching the floor for his clothes.

"Do you want me to go with you?" Zoe asked. "Brett's at his dad's. I'll just give him a call and he can stay there for a couple more days."

"Thanks, but, no." He buttoned his shirt. "I'll call you as soon as I know anything." He caught her face in his hands. "I love you," he said.

"I LOVE YOU."

Zoe spent Sunday alternating between replaying the tape of Phillip's voice in her head and waiting for him to call and tell her about Molly. She felt restless, unable to settle down to anything. She wished Brett was home so they could talk about the way things had been between them lately. She wanted to tell him about Phillip. And Phillip's daughter. Molly. They both need our support and understanding, she would say. She felt awful for all the times she'd called Molly weird. She would talk to Brett about that. They would turn over a new leaf. "I'm kind of growing up, too," she would tell him. "News flash, I don't have all the answers."

By four o'clock, she hadn't heard from either Phillip or Brett. The phone rang. Brett's friend Kevin. "He's over at his dad's," she told him. "He should be home soon." By five, she'd worked up a mild anger at Brett. And why hadn't Phillip called? The various scenarios she came up with only served to increase her anxiety.

In the kitchen, she made pesto from the basil she'd picked from the garden, froze it in plastic bags, washed the dishes she'd used, wiped off the counter and reorganized the cabinet where the pans were stored. She thought about the way she'd felt driving over to Phillip's house last night. Kind of charged and excited—the way she'd decided out of the blue to call him, his voice when he answered. He'd sounded really pleased to hear from her. And he'd been waiting outside when she drove up, looking pretty happy to see her, too.

But then, inside the house, she'd followed him into the kitchen and they'd stood looking at each other and her head was so full of things she wanted to say that her brain had sort of frozen and all she could come up with were inane formalities—nice place, wow, great view, blah blah blah. Instead of the passionate embrace and knee-weakening kiss she'd been fantasizing on the way over, it was like an invisible curtain had fallen between them, and calling him had seemed like a flaky, impetuous move that she'd started wishing she could take back. And then she'd remembered the chocolate éclairs in the truck, which sort of broke the ice.

Cedars Sinai, Phillip had said. Maybe she should call and leave a message. And that damn Denny. What the hell was wrong with him? She vacuumed the living room, mentally rehearsing what she would say when he finally brought their son home. "Parenting may be all fun and games to you, blah blah blah, but it's not to me. School, mundane stuff like that."

At seven, she called Denny.

"Helloo," he said after she'd vented her anger into his ear for several minutes, "If I can get a word in someplace. He's not back yet."

Zoe drew a breath, tossed the sponge she'd been using in the sink and lowered herself onto one of the counter stools. "Not back from where?"

"Wherever he went last night. Some girl's house."

Zoe blinked. She hadn't heard what she thought she'd just heard. "What?"

"He used the truck last night to go to some girl's house."

"And he's not back?"

"Nope."

"He hasn't called?"

Denny laughed. "He's getting laid. Like he's gonna think about calling home. When he gets back, I'll tell him to call Mommy, okay?"

The phone rang again almost instantly. Zoe grabbed the receiver. "Brett?"

"It's Phillip—"

"Phillip, oh my God…" She tried to rally her thoughts. "Is Molly okay, what's going on?

"No, she's not okay. She's, I can't go into it here, Zoe, I'm at a pay phone in the hospital lobby and there are people waiting—"

"But wait…" Nausea swept over her, her lips felt numb. For an instant her panic over Brett faded. "Just tell me…she's not in any danger, or anything?"

"No, no. It's…" He hesitated. "More of what I told you about last night, look, I've gotta go. I'll call you as soon as I can talk longer. Everything okay with you?"

Zoe swallowed. "Sure, fine." Brett's not home yet, she wanted to say, but his voice sounded weary. "Listen, take care, Phillip." I love you. She heard the click as he disconnected and burst into tears. As though she were someone else, looking down at herself, she could see this solitary figure, curled up into a corner of the couch crying. The image frightened her. Any minute now, the phone would ring and it would be Brett, or the front door would open and she'd hear his voice. So why was she acting like a basket case. What was going on? She got up from the couch, fed the dogs, started dinner. *Act as though everything is normal and it will be.* She looked at the phone on the kitchen wall. Willed it to ring.

She called Denny.

Pam answered. "Oh, hi, Zoe, Brett's still not back but we're—"

"Let me talk to Brett's father, please."

"Who was the girl?" She'd been working around the idea that it was Molly. If it was Molly, she could call Phillip.

"Sophie."

"I've never heard of a Sophie," Zoe said before she realized what the admission revealed, and before she remembered that Rhea had once mentioned the girl's name.

"It's not like it's the first time he's stayed out all night, for God's sake."

By ten, Brett still wasn't home. Itching had broken out all over her back, her legs and arms. She was going insane with it. She dialed Denny's number and got his answering machine. Again.

She started crying again. Picked up the phone to call the police, set it down again. *He's getting laid.* Fine, she didn't care. Last night *she'd* got laid. No, that wasn't the way it had been with Phillip. Not just getting laid. God, she wanted to talk to Phillip again. She picked up the phone, set it down. Phillip had his own troubles. Had she even asked about Molly? Now she couldn't remember. Maybe she hadn't sounded concerned enough. She was, but where was Brett? Again she reached for the phone. No, it would tie up the line if Brett called. Where was he? Why didn't he call? Where was Brett? Just let me hear from you. I don't care what you're doing. Just call.

Eleven.

Twelve.

Twelve forty-five. She called the police. "Yes, well, my son isn't home yet and...he's seventeen. But, see you don't understand, he's not that kind of kid."

One.

Two.

Two-fifteen. The phone rang. Denny.

"There was this message on the phone when we got home from a neighbor's party. Brett's been in some kind of accident. It doesn't look good."

CHAPTER SEVENTEEN

AFTER HER INITIAL emergency-room evaluation, Molly had been transferred to the psychiatric unit for observation. When Phillip arrived at the hospital after a three-hour drive in weekend traffic from Seacliff, he'd had to ring a bell outside a set of locked doors to summon a nurse. She'd let him in and he'd followed her along a bleak corridor with scuffed paintwork and harsh overhead lighting to the visitor's room.

Molly sat on a molded plastic chair, her head bowed, hands folded in her lap. "Hey, Moll." He'd knelt down at her feet, caught her hands in his. "It's Dad." Slowly she'd lifted her head, but her vacant eyes showed no flicker of recognition.

He'd stayed with her until late Sunday night, then checked into a hotel. It was after midnight when he remembered he'd promised to call Zoe again. Too late now. He'd call first thing tomorrow.

PEOPLE KEPT TELLING ZOE she couldn't see her son.

Her son.

She sat in a little room somewhere in the hospital. The overhead lights were very bright. Too bright.

A small squirmy worm of panic slithered up through her chest and into her throat and came out in a little squeak.

If they'd let her see him, she could make him better. She could.

The room was full of people all breathing in the air she needed for herself. Courtney and Janna on either side of her. Denny was there and Pam. Pam was reading out names from an address book. "I got hold of your mom, babe." Pam had her arm around Denny's shoulder. "She's on her way. What about your sister? Want me to call her?"

Zoe stared at Pam. Pam's hair was the color of cream. When she bent her head, long strands hung down on either side of her face like a curtain. Pam had taken command. What did this have to do with Pam?

Go away. Just go away. This is my son.

"He's going to be okay, Zoe." Janna clutched a tissue. "I promise."

"Anyone want some coffee?" Courtney asked.

"You're a doll," Pam said. "Black for both of us. Zoe, is there anyone you want me to call?"

Zoe shook her head. The room felt claustrophobic. She got up, walked out into the corridor and leaned her back against the wall. If she held her breath and stayed very still and quiet Brett would be okay. Any sound or movement would attract the attention of a malevolent presence. Recognizing that she had been unfairly blessed in the first place, it would try to snatch Brett from her.

Stop. That's crazy thinking. He was going to be fine. He would walk out of the room where they wouldn't let her see him, with maybe some bandages, and a sheepish grin and she'd pretend to be mad because he'd scared the hell out of her. "Hey, Mom, I'm hungry," he'd say, and she'd take him to Angelo's for double cheeseburgers.

Brett, please. Please. She squeezed her eyes shut. *Please, honey.*

"I don't know where he'd been," she could hear Denny saying. "He told me this girl lived in Chula Vista, but the cops said he was southbound on the 405, just before the Seacliff exit. Looks like maybe he fell asleep at the wheel."

"I'm not blaming you, Denny." Janna sounded as though she were crying. "But what were you thinking, letting him stay out all night? That's one thing Zoe never…"

Zoe walked away from the sounds of their voices. Her espadrilles made a slapping sound on the tiles. She'd bought them in Ensenada last year. Brett had been healthy and whole then. Why hadn't she been deliriously happy? How could anything have possibly bothered her? Voices behind her. She turned, retraced her steps. A tall, fat man in green scrubs stood in the doorway.

"Here's his mother now," Janna said from inside the room. "Come and sit down with me, honey."

"My son?" Zoe whispered.

The tall, fat man nodded. His rimless glasses reflected points of light. "Brett's had a devastating accident. Multiple injuries and we probably haven't identified them all yet. There's a lot of swelling in his brain. Until that goes down, we can't do much more than wait."

"Is he gonna make it?" Denny asked.

"The next twenty-four hours should tell us a lot, but we're not optimistic," the doctor said.

Zoe felt the room spin. Without taking her eyes from the doctor's face, she dropped into a chair. Not true, her brain was saying, not true. But her heart was pounding so hard she couldn't breathe.

"So like, what are his odds?" Denny was up on his feet. "Fifty-fifty?"

"As I said, we'll know more when the swelling goes down, but you should be aware that there's a possibility he might not wake up."

Pam began to sob.

"I don't want him kept alive on a breathing machine or something," Denny said. "My son's all boy. He's like me, always active. There's no way he'd want to go on living if he couldn't do everything just like before. If he's going to be a vegetable or something."

Zoe lost it. The effort to hold herself together exploded into rage. Hurling herself at her ex-husband, she battered his head and chest with her fists. "Bastard. Rotten, stinking bastard," she screamed. "Don't you dare use words like that. Whose fault is it—"

"Don't blame me, you crazy bitch." He caught her flailing hands. "You're the one who never let the kid do anything. He finally gets to act like a teenager instead of a mommy's boy, of course he's going to bust out. If he doesn't make it, it's *your* goddamned fault."

LATER, AFTER A social worker decided that she'd calmed down sufficiently, Zoe was allowed to see Brett. Or the bed of someone they told her was Brett. It was possible, she kept thinking, that this was all a terrible mistake. Was it just yesterday that she'd watched him leave the house? Tall and skinny, the dogs at his heels. Now there was someone lying still and silent in a hospital bed who looked nothing like her Brett. A heavy black band held his head still. Stainless steel bolts disappeared into his skull. His face and mouth were bloodied and tubes curled everywhere from his body.

There is a possibility that he might not wake up.

She could see Dr. Malcolm Thomasson's face. *Might not wake up. Might not wake up.* The words kept slamming against her. She left Brett's bedside briefly to use a pay phone outside the unit.

"I need to reach Dr. Phillip Barry. It's an emergency.

"Dr. Thomasson is handling Dr. Barry's calls," the operator told her. "Would you like to leave a message for Dr. Thomasson?"

"I want to speak to Dr. Barry." Why hadn't she asked Phillip for his home number again? "Please just get in touch with him for me."

"Dr. Thomasson—"

"I don't want Dr. Thomasson." She heard her

voice rise. "Please ask Dr. Barry to call Zoe McCann. He can reach me at Seacliff, I'll be in the Pediatric ICU. It's about my son. And please try to reach him as soon as you can."

Back in the unit again, she sat by Brett's bed and waited for Phillip to call.

People kept coming to talk to her. Telling her things. Doctors, nurses. A social worker. A chaplain. Seeing the chaplain terrified her. Chaplains were for dying people. Brett wasn't dying. Brett was going to be fine. Phillip was a miracle worker, that woman on TV had said. Phillip would work his miracle. How would you thank someone for saving your child's life? She would always be in Phillip's debt. Fine. Just make Brett whole and healthy again. I'll pay any price.

"Hey, buddy." Zoe watched Brett's face. "Listen, big boy, I'm on to your game. Don't pretend you can't hear me because I know you can. Pretty crappy excuse not to mow the lawn if you ask me. But that's okay, just open your eyes, get out of bed and all is forgiven. *Brett.*"

His hand felt cold, lifeless…no, she didn't mean that, not lifeless. That wasn't what she was thinking. Cold, though…maybe that was it. He was cold, this damn place was like a morgue…no, take that back, please, I didn't mean that. Not morgue. "Brett. Open your eyes, sweetie, it's Mom…Brett?"

"Ms. McCann," a voice behind her said.

"How about a cheeseburger?" She watched his face, willing something, anything. The blink of an eye. "A cheeseburger from Angelo's?" she said. "And some onion rings? No, no onion rings, French fries then?"

"Ms. McCann."

"Hold on, sweetie, someone needs to talk to me." She turned to see Dr. Thomasson.

He glanced at the monitors, adjusted something. Shook his head. "We'll be taking him down for another CAT scan, but if the pressure in his brain increases—"

"I have a call in to Dr. Barry. He'll be taking care of Brett."

"If the pressure in his brain increases," Thomasson continued as though she hadn't spoken, "we'll need to take him back to surgery."

"I'm expecting a call from Dr. Barry any minute now."

Thomasson closed his eyes briefly, as if summoning the patience to deal with the kind of unreasonableness that no physician of his stature should ever be exposed to, glanced again at Brett's monitors and walked out of the unit.

"This is the second time I've tried," Zoe told the hospital operator a few minutes later. "I have to speak to Dr. Barry."

"All I can do is leave a message with his answering service—"

"I can do that. What's the number for the answering service?"

"Ma'am, I can't give you—"

"You can't reach him at home? Call his cell phone or something?"

"I can leave a message, ma'am."

"Okay." Zoe spelled her first and last name, repeated the phone number twice. "It's critical," Zoe said. "I have to reach him."

MONDAY AFTERNOON, Phillip sat in the crawl of traffic heading back to Seacliff. Twice, he'd used his cell phone to call Zoe and got no answer. A vague unease that he couldn't pinpoint mingled with a more identifiable concern over Molly. She'd been released from the hospital that morning, far too soon in his opinion, but under the condition that she see the psychiatrist three times a week and continue with the new medication even though she complained that it made her feel like a zombie. And, since Molly had confessed to ransacking her mother's apartment before slashing her wrists, she would not be allowed to drive, or be in the house alone. He and Deanna had arranged their schedules to accommodate this. For now Molly would stay with Deanna in L.A. to be near the psychiatrist and he would visit on the weekends.

Any lingering illusions that Molly was just going through a few teenage problems were now gone completely.

As he drove into Orange County, his cell phone rang.

"Phillip, it's Malcolm. I'm assuming you haven't checked your answering service. Anyway, we have this kid in PICU, came in about two this morning, slammed into a windshield, split his brain—dozens of shattered skull fragments. He's got a ton of other problems—broken ribs, punctured lung, fractured legs and pelvis, and he bled into shock from a ruptured spleen. I'm not holding out much hope, but the mother's in complete denial. She's giving everyone on the unit a hard time—starting with the kid's father. She says you know her. Zoe McCann."

"HONEY." Janna was crouched on the floor beside Zoe. "Denny has been waiting out in the hallway for nearly an hour. How about we go for a walk, get a little fresh air and let him have some time with his son?"

Zoe ignored her. She tried to remember when she'd left the message for Phillip. *"I left a message for Dr. Barry,"* she kept telling people. *"Dr. Thomasson is covering Dr. Barry's calls,"* they kept responding.

"Zoe, Brett's dad is hurting, too. We all are. You've got to share Brett, sweetie. Don't try to carry this all alone."

Zoe said nothing. Why was her mother telling her all this? Brett was *her* son. Her life. What did it matter about anyone else? After a while, she realized that Janna had gone. Sometimes as she sat there, her eyes seemed stuck in a long-distance focus and she'd have to consciously adjust them to look at Brett again.

Thoughts would flit across her brain as she sat there: Who would feed the animals, pick up the mail? Water plants? Okay, Janna was feeding the animals, she knew that. Kenna had been whimpering for Brett,

Janna said. Sometimes she'd think about buying a magazine or a book. She would picture herself taking the necessary steps: retrieving money from her purse, punching the button for the elevator that would take her down to the gift shop. But from there her thoughts drifted off and people in green scrubs and white coats would come in and out and do things to Brett and glance in her direction and she'd still be there staring into space.

"Brett, sweetie. It's Mom." She touched his hand. "Brett? Can you hear me? You're in hospital, but everything's going to be okay. Brett?"

Tomorrow, maybe, she'd go home and shower. A shower would feel good. She got up, walked out of the unit and down the tile corridor to the rest room. The door had a silhouette of a woman in a triangle-shaped skirt. She pushed open the door. Inside, the light was so bright it hurt her eyes. A mirrored wall above a row of white sinks stopped her short. A hollow-eyed woman stared back at her. In the stall, a thought occurred to her. What if she left the hospital and Brett's father came in while she was gone and told them to stop keeping Brett alive?

Panic swept through her. In an instant she was running down the corridor, slapping at the metal plate outside the unit, hurrying through the swinging doors. Now there were people around Brett's bed, lots of people. Her heart thundering, she pushed between them.

"What's going on?"

"Mrs. McCann." One of the figures turned to look at her. "Please come back in a few minutes."

"I want to know what's happening to my son," she said. "I'm his mother, you can't just…Dr. Barry will be here soon and—"

"Come on, honey." A nurse led her away from the bed and out of the unit. "Someone needs to get some rest and I'm not talking about the young man in the bed back there.

With the nurse's arm around her shoulder, Zoe let herself be led into the visitors' lounge. Like an obedient child, she sat down on the couch and waited for further orders.

"Get some sleep," the nurse said, and left.

Zoe drew her legs up on the couch. She wouldn't sleep, of course, couldn't sleep even if she wanted to. But maybe if she just closed her eyes for a few moments…

"Phillip?" He watched, his heart constricting his throat as Zoe blinked then stretched out her hand to touch his face. "God, I thought I was dreaming."

"Hi." He was crouched down on the floor beside the couch where he'd found her, curled up, her hands pillowing her head. The room had been frigid, her arms mottled with chill and, he noted, track marks from her nails. He'd found a blanket, brought it back to cover her. "I came as soon as I heard," he said softly.

She started to sit up, but he put his hand on her shoulder. Given Brett's condition, her appearance shouldn't have come as a shock, but it did. She seemed tiny, shrunken almost, her eyes swollen, her face blank with exhaustion. Her nose and eyes were red, her lips cracked and her hair clung damply to her cheek. When he'd stopped in to see Brett, a nurse had corroborated his suspicion that Zoe had only succumbed to sleep at the point when she literally could not keep her eyes open any longer.

"Have you seen Brett?" she whispered, her face just inches from his.

"I stopped in for a minute."

Her eyes filled with tears. "Is he…"

"He's had a very bad accident, Zoe."

"But he'll be okay?" She leaned over and buried her face against his shoulder. "Please, tell me you can make him okay again."

He reached for her, holding her as she sobbed soundlessly, her body shaking under his hands. They stayed that way for a while, until her tears subsided.

"I'm okay now."

She reached for a box of tissues on the table beside the couch; he moved faster, grabbed the box and pulled out a handful. Her face disappeared behind the tissues as she blew her nose. Gone was the brash feistiness he'd first been drawn to, in its place a wrenching vulnerability. She was like a scared little kid, he thought, doing her best to be brave.

Meanwhile, Brett McCann might or might not survive his injuries. He might walk out of the hospital under his own steam, or he might leave contemplating a future in a wheelchair—or worse. No guarantees. All Phillip knew was that he had two patients, Brett McCann and Brett's mother. Other physicians could use their skills to help Brett, but he felt certain that only he could help Zoe through this.

"Remember that tough woman who marched into my office?" he finally asked. "We need to find her."

She wiped her eyes. "That woman's gone."

"I don't believe that. She's too strong to just cut and run."

Her eyes wide, she stared wordlessly at him.

"I'm going to do everything I can to help Brett," he told her, "but it's a team effort and I need that tough woman on the team."

Zoe nodded as though she were thinking over what he'd just said. Then she started digging around in the big yellow straw bag she'd been carrying when she first barged into his office. "I need more tissues," she said.

He grabbed the box from the low table between two couches, held it out while she continued to rummage in the bag. "Zoe."

She looked up and took the box of tissues. "Oh."

"Want to hear something funny?"

She blew her nose. "What?"

"That day you accosted me in my office, I thought you might be carrying a gun in that bag."

"A *gun*." A faint smile through her tears. "Were you scared I'd use it?"

"It crossed my mind."

The smile flickered and died. "God, that seems like a million years ago now. I was angry over Jenny and I wanted to do something about it, but...Brett was fine. Strong and healthy." Her eyes filled. "Why didn't I realize how lucky I was? How could anything else have even mattered?"

He held her again as she sobbed against his chest. "What matters now," he said after a moment, "is that you stay strong for Brett."

"I'm trying." She pulled away, palmed tears from her face. "It's so damn hard to see him like that and just sit around and do *nothing*. I've always done everything for him and it's like I'm being squeezed out of the picture."

He thought of last week's fight with Deanna. "I'm tired of putting *my* life on hold, while Molly continues to destroy her own," she had screamed at him. At this point he'd issued Deanna a long overdue ultimatum. She willingly assume responsibility for their daughter, or he'd go to court for sole custody.

All he knew now was that Zoe and Deanna were at opposite ends of a spectrum.

"Sorry." Again Zoe swiped at her tears. "That sounds crazy, I know I can't give Brett the help he needs right now. I understand it *here*." She tapped her head. "I just have to accept it emotionally."

"You're doing fine." Nothing words, he thought, throwaway words that conveyed none of what he wanted to say. His eyes went to the pair of angry red welts on her arm, and a blotch on her neck. He caught her hand, examined the rash. "Are you using something for this?"

She frowned. "Yes…I don't know, I'm out of stuff. I can't think about that, Phillip."

"You need to keep yourself well, too. I want you

to make a dermatology appointment. Explain what's going on." He made a mental note to stop by the pharmacy anyway. "Don't put it off."

"Okay, boss."

"You're a trouper."

"I *thought* I was."

"You can do this," he said, reaching out to gather her close to him. "You're stronger than any woman I know."

"Thank you, Phillip. I feel a whole lot better knowing you're here."

Phillip nodded, but couldn't come up with an adequate response. What could he say? Happy to be here? My pleasure?

"Oh, God." Zoe's hand flew to her mouth. "I'm such an idiot. How's Molly, by the way? God," she said, and grimaced. "That sounds terrible, I didn't mean, by the way…"

"It's okay. I know what you meant. She's fine." Molly had been sleeping when he'd left her at Deanna's in the care of an around-the-clock nurse. She slept constantly. The new medication, her physician had explained. Adjustment takes time. "Fine," he said again.

"What happened?"

He shook his head. "We're still trying to get to the bottom of it, but listen, you've got more than enough to think about right here."

They walked out into the hallway together. Zoe squeezed his hand one last time and then headed toward the PICU. He watched her, in her denim overalls. Despite everything, the purposeful stride. If determination alone could fix Brett McCann, Zoe would have her son walking out of the hospital tomorrow. The thought made him smile.

He was still thinking about Zoe, feeling uplifted somehow, when he saw Malcolm Thomasson and Brett's father leaving the unit. Malcolm waved him over.

"You've met Dr. Barry?" Malcolm said with a glance at the father.

"Haven't had the pleasure." The father held out his hand to Phillip. "Denny McCann."

Phillip shook his hand. Denny McCann had a shaved head and was wearing Bermudas and a T-shirt that depicted a surfer riding waves over the caption I Can Stay Up For Hours.

"I just mentioned to Mr. McCann that you would probably be taking over his son's care," Malcolm was saying. "He asked me why and..." The surgeon's plump pink face creased in a quizzical smile. "I had to tell him that, quite honestly, I didn't know."

"*I* do," Denny McCann said. "His mother's got some idea in her head that she's the only one who knows what's best for Brett. It's always been that way and I've had it up to here. I can't get in to see him, because she's always there...no offense to you, Dr. Barry, I'm sure you're as good as the next guy, but I personally don't see how it's a good thing to have Brett switch doctors, so if it's all the same to you both, I say Dr. Thomasson here stays on the case."

Thomasson said nothing then, but later that day when they were both scrubbing up, he mentioned Brett McCann to Phillip. "As if the kid didn't have problems enough, he's got a mother from hell. She doesn't listen, she's argumentative and she's in complete denial. Quite honestly, I think if I have any further interaction with her, it could get rather ugly. Frankly, I think she's got a screw loose."

Phillip, squeezing orange soap along his arms, shot a sideways glance at Thomasson. It suddenly hit him what it was that he'd never liked about Thomasson and it had nothing to do with the man's surgical skills. The man had no soul. Anyone who couldn't appreciate Zoe's uniqueness, her heart, her spirit... he stopped the thought.

"...in other words," Thomasson was saying. "You deal with her."

"Glad to," Phillip said

By ten that night, Phillip was one of three surgeons operating on Brett McCann. Brett had already had emergency surgery to deal with his spleen and his lung. Now, while Phillip worked on the boy's head, two orthopedic surgeons operated on Brett's legs and pelvis. For hours they repaired bleeds, stabilized bones and transfused blood. Just after two o'clock, Phillip thanked the staff, stripped off his gloves and left the room.

"Medically, we've done all we can right now," he told Zoe. "There's still a lot of swelling in his brain." He leaned forward slightly on the chair. "See, the brain is very soft and when Brett was thrown against the windshield his brain was pushed against the front part of the his skull, which is very hard, so there's a lot of bruising. Now it's all up to Brett."

CHAPTER EIGHTEEN

ZOE LOST TRACK OF TIME. In the pediatric intensive care unit the lights were dim but always on. There were no windows to hint at whether it was midnight or midday in the outside world. Machines beeped and buzzed and green lines and numbers flickered constantly on banks of machines.

Brett's room was an open cubicle in a semicircle of open cubicles, all visible from anywhere on the unit. She sat at Brett's bedside, reading to him, talking softly, moistening his lips with sponges dipped in ice water. Sometimes she'd look up to see nurses and figures in green scrubs conferring at a central workstation. Her mouth and teeth tasted sour and coated. She felt gritty and rumpled as though she'd been traveling for days on end, but her world had shrunk to one very small corner of the universe: this bed where banks of monitors controlled and recorded her son's every breath and movement.

People came and went, no more real than flickering images on a video screen. They were always explaining one thing or another to her, their words like an unfamiliar language she'd have to process for a moment before she could understand. Other people told her to take a break, go to the cafeteria, go home, get some sleep. They'd bring in food for her to eat.

Only Phillip really registered. Tall and solemn in his white jacket and surgical scrubs. Mornings, she'd look up to see his face and it seemed like a beam of light had suddenly penetrated the fog.

"He's in there," he'd told her one day as he leaned over to peer into Brett's eyes. "He's just waiting for the right moment."

She'd been watching her motionless son for any clue that even a spark of the real Brett burned somewhere within his brain. "Yeah, well I wish he'd make it snappy," she'd shot back.

And then Phillip had smiled at her from across the bed and she'd felt such a complicated rush of feeling that she just started bawling. "I love you," she'd told him that night before the accident, but now it was more than love. Phillip was like a vital life force, as necessary to staying alive as air or water. And that was all tangled up with this absolute confidence that only he could save Brett. *Make everything better,* she'd silently beg him. Promise me you'll never leave, *promise*. Tears streaming down her face, she'd crossed the cubicle to where he stood and just laid her head on his chest and sobbed.

"Hey, come on." He'd put his arms around her, held her for a few moments, then pulled back to look at her. "You can do this, Zoe."

Good days followed bad days, or vice versa.

Some days were good *and* bad. "One day at a time," Phillip was always telling her. "Every small improvement is a step forward."

And she'd cling to those words, saying them over and over to herself like a mantra. Days passed and then a week. People came and went. She maintained her vigil by Brett's bed.

"How're you doing?" she'd ask him. "Feeling a little better? You know what? I think you look better. Tell you what, how about if I just go on talking to you? If you want to, you can shut me out…that's what you always do." She squeezed his hand. "That was a joke, honey. Listen, we're all pulling for you. Dr. Barry's taking care of you and I feel really good about it. I mean, I'm still scared and everything…you banged yourself up pretty good, kiddo, but I feel much more confident. You know what I mean?"

"Zoe."

Someone touched her shoulder and she turned to see Rhea. Visitors streamed in and out every day—she couldn't for the life of her say who had been in—but now she looked at Rhea, who she'd always felt closer to than her own sister, and her stomach tightened with fear. *Rhea's daughter had died.* Rhea belonged to a group for parents who had lost children. Rhea was leaning over Brett's bed. She wanted to hide Brett from Rhea's view. Go away. Go away. I don't know what it's like to be in your shoes. *I* haven't lost a child. I don't want your empathy.

Rhea turned from Brett and embraced Zoe, holding her close. "How're you doing, sweetie?"

"Fine." Zoe, swallowing panic, smiled widely. She and Brett were both doing fine, really fine. "They're very optimistic. Phillip...Barry. You know," she laughed. "Dr. God. Anyway, he's really pleased with Brett's progress. He's in there somewhere," she said with a glance at her motionless son. "He's just taking his time. You know Brett, he's always done things when he's ready. No one's going to force him."

Rhea was giving her the look. The same one she'd seen Sandy and Roz give Rhea after Jenny's accident. *I feel so awful for you,* the look said. *I can't even imagine what you must be going through.*

"How about a little break?" Rhea said

"Sure, fine." She tried to sound casual, upbeat. As casual and upbeat as you could be with your son lying in a coma. *There's a possibility he might not wake up.* The fat doctor's voice. Screw the fat doctor. Phillip was in charge now. Rhea was still looking at her. "Um..." She rallied her thoughts. "Cafeteria. I think it's still open."

"I'm talking away from the hospital. How about lunch somewhere?"

She shook her head. "No. I can't leave."

"Yes, you can." Phillip's voice behind her. "The best thing you can do for yourself or Brett is to get away for a while. Doctor's orders," he said.

Rhea drove her down to Pacific Beach, where they shared a huge shrimp and artichoke-heart salad at an outdoor restaurant and watched the passing parade of Rollerbladers, strollers and dog walkers.

Phillip was right, she decided. Being away from the hospital was helping. Everything about being away from the hospital made her feel better, more optimistic.

Away from the hospital, she could imagine that Brett would come home from school that afternoon as he had hundreds of times before, raid the refrigerator, all the while complaining that he was hungry. Across the table, Rhea in a yellow sundress and dark glasses now looked as comfortably familiar as always. Zoe stirred a straw through the melting ice in her glass of tea and decided that the mini panic attack, or whatever it was, had been the result of too little sleep.

They finished the salad, *oohed* and *aahed* over the dessert menu, and agreed that sharing a slice of chocolate caramel cheesecake wouldn't break the caloric bank and anyway, they deserved it. Rhea had opened her stall at the market again, she said. Sandy was experimenting with a blackberry honey, there was other news of this and that. Underneath the banter though, Zoe sensed something uneasy hovering.

Finally Rhea pushed her salad plate away, as though she were about to get to the real reason they were there. "It's important to keep a perspective about all this," she finally said. "The twenty-four-hour vigil kind of robs you of that. Everything narrows down to one hospital bed."

Zoe sipped some tea, nodding as though she agreed. Her heart had started pounding though. Thanks for the advice, but *my* child is going to live.

"Rhea, could we just talk about something else, please? Tell me what else is going on."

"Sure." Rhea smiled, dark lenses hiding her eyes. "Let me think." An elbow on the table, she propped her chin on her hand. "Oh, I know, Roz met a guy. He stopped to buy honey and one thing led to another and the last I heard they were smearing pots of it all over each other."

Zoe laughed. "Sounds like fun."

"She seems pretty happy." Rhea sat back in her chair, folded her arms across her chest. "Um…" She hesitated. "Actually, I kind of met someone, too."

"You?"

"Well, don't look so amazed!"

"No, I didn't mean it like that," Zoe rushed to assure her. "It's just that…" We're alike, she'd been about to say. Too wrapped up in our kids to be bothered with guys. "I don't know…" She leaned forward. "So tell me about him."

"He's in my grief group," Rhea said. "One night after the group, we went out for coffee and something just clicked. We've got that common bond. He lost his s—"

"What?"

"Nothing." Rhea reached for the check. "My treat, okay? One of these days I've got to take you to this new bakery that opened in Seac—"

"Rhea. Why did you stop?"

Rhea shook her head, making a big production of digging out her credit card. "No reason, I was just babbling on and—"

"No, you weren't. You were going to say he lost his son, but you changed your mind about saying it because of Brett. That's what you meant by perspective, isn't it? That's why we're here. A reality talk because you don't think Brett's going to make it."

"That wasn't it at all." Rhea reached for Zoe's hand. "I wanted to pass along some of the things that helped me. I've been reading a lot, trying to come up with, I don't know, some sort of meaning to everything. Maybe there isn't any…who knows? But, someone said this to me. 'Happiness depends on the difference between your reality and your expectations. To be happy, accept your reality or adjust your expectations.' I had Jenny for seventeen years. That's the reality. All my expectations—of going to her wedding, having grandchildren—all of them are gone now. I have to accept that and live with the reality. For seventeen years, I had a wonderful daughter who made me very happy."

Neither of them said much on the way back to the hospital. In the lobby, she hugged Rhea and they held each other and cried a little, but she felt a new constraint between them. Not something she could think about now, she decided as she took the elevator to the unit, but when everything was back to normal, she and Rhea would have a long talk and straighten things out.

On another bad day, she and Janna were sitting in the visitor's lounge, counting the days since the accident. "Wednesday, Thursday, Friday, Saturday." She tapped her fingers, marking off the days. "Four days, Mom, and he's still…nothing's changed. No wait, it's six days. Seven, is it seven?"

"Honey, he had a really bad accident," Janna said. "It's going to take time. Listen, sweetheart, about Denny…"

"The hell with Denny."

"Zoe," Janna said gently. "Denny's torn up about this, too."

"He should be." Anger, like a hot bright light pierced the fog in her brain. "It's his fault. Brett wouldn't be lying there half…" Unable to voice the word, she bit her lip hard to stop the tears filling her throat and nose.

"That's not fair, Zoe. Don't you think Brett wanted to go out just as much—"

"Brett's a kid. Of course he *wanted* to, but his father should have had more sense."

"Honey, this doesn't help Brett."

"Nothing is helping Brett right now." Rage, white-hot now, propelled her from the couch. "He was a healthy, normal boy," she screamed. "Thanks to me. And now look at him…all because his goddamn father has the mental age of a fifteen-year-old. I can't stand it." And she'd clenched at her hair. "Why? *Why?* I'd do anything for Brett, anything. Nothing I wouldn't do. He's my life and then some idiot who doesn't have a brain…"

"Zoe, Zoe." Janna caught Zoe's flailing arms. "Come on, honey, look at me, please just look at me. You've got to calm down. Zoe, please…where's a nurse? Sweetheart, just listen to me."

ZOE KNEW when she was behaving unreasonably. She recognized the moments when she just gave way to everything, but she didn't care. Sometimes it seemed as though she were watching herself from a far-off place, a screaming and distraught woman she barely recognized. But she'd never been good at in-action and some days she'd look at Brett and feel so damn helpless to do anything that rage seemed her only vent.

Except for Phillip, she was always thinking, she would lose it completely. Even he couldn't take away the raw fear that seemed to stop her heart when she thought about tomorrow, or the next day, or anything beyond this very minute, and Phillip didn't spare her from hard-to-hear news. "There is a possibility that Brett *might* never walk again," he'd said after she'd begged him to reassure her that an overheard exchange between a couple of residents couldn't possibly apply to her son. But, just knowing Phillip was there was enough to keep her from the edge.

"Tell me he'll be okay," she'd plead.

"You know I can't promise that, Zoe. Too many things could still go wrong."

"But…you're optimistic?"

"Cautiously."

And she'd want to grab his arm, peer into his face to see if she could learn more. "Cautiously?"

"Cautiously. It's the best I can do right now. He still has a long way to go. There's a possibility that he won't be the Brett you knew, and you have to be prepared for that."

"No." Angry and a little hurt, she shook her head. "Brett's a fighter. I'm there for him, you're there for him, how could he not pull through?"

"I don't want to give you a false sense of security. He's got a long and tough road ahead of him."

"Will you go on taking care of him?"

"Along with a lot of other people."

And she'd felt her heart squeeze. "That's not what I want to hear," she'd said in a way that was supposed to be a joke, but not really. "I want you to tell me you're going to put your life on hold until Brett pulls through this."

"Zoe," he'd say, and just hold her. And she'd feel his heart beat against her chest and know that, no matter what anyone said, her Brett *would* be okay.

"YOU LOOK utterly exhausted," Deanna said when she and Molly came by the apartment ten days after Brett McCann's surgery. "I've seen you tired before, Phillip, but I'm serious, you look on the verge of collapse."

He shook his head. It had been a bad day. In the middle of surgery he'd got a page that Brett McCann's condition was deteriorating. His blood pressure had elevated, a sign of increasing pressure in his brain.

"We ran another CAT scan," a resident told him, "which pretty much confirmed things. We're going to need to get him up to surgery. His mother won't sign the consent to let anyone but you do it."

Phillip closed his eyes. He had one patient already on the table, two others scheduled back-to-back immediately afterward.

"I told her you weren't available."

"Get him up to surgery," he told the resident. "I'll talk to her."

By the time Phillip finished the operation he'd been working on before the phone call, Brett McCann was on the table being prepped. He found Zoe in the waiting room off the surgical suite. Her hand covering her mouth, she looked at him wordlessly.

"Zoe." He crouched down at her feet, took her hands. "Brett needs surgery to drain off fluid from his brain. If he doesn't have it right now, he'll die. *I* can't do it—"

"No." Her eyes wide, she pulled her hands away from his grasp. "Don't tell me that. You have to—"

"Listen to me. This is a procedure any neurosurgeon can do. I can't do it right now. You have to trust me, Zoe. Brett needs this surgery, but *I* don't have to do it. Maybe it would reassure you if I did it, but it's not necessary for Brett's survival."

Zoe stared at him. "He'll be okay?"

"He needs the surgery, sweetheart. You have to trust me." He'd brought a consent form in with him. Now he set the clipboard on her knees. "Just sign your name right there."

"I *do* trust you." Tears running down her face, she'd signed the consent. "I trust you, Phillip. Please let everything be all right."

He'd run into Zoe's mother later in the day after

Brett had been taken back to the unit. Janna had asked to speak to him.

"Not about Brett, it's Zoe," Janna had said. "She's so emotionally distraught over what happened, she's not even thinking straight. She's…irrational. Zoe's a hot-tempered girl, and I'm worried to death that she might do something foolish."

Weary, he'd just given her a blank look.

"Well…Brett's father. Zoe doesn't want him to see Brett. She's blaming him for what happened and I thought that since you and Zoe go way back and you're Brett's doctor and everything, maybe you could talk some sense into her. Try and make her understand it was no one's fault and what Brett needs more than anything is good vibes from both his parents."

Phillip had felt a wave of fatigue. If brain surgery could help Zoe forgive her ex-husband, he'd gladly take up a scalpel, but trying to understand the psychological labyrinth of relationships was way beyond his ability. Ask his ex-wife and daughter, he thought now. He'd promised to have a social worker talk to Zoe.

"God, Phillip, what do you live on?" Deanna called from the kitchen. "There's nothing in here to eat. You never cook anything for yourself? Well, I suppose we could all go out to dinner. What do you guys feel like? Thai? Indian? Just a salad would be fine with me."

Molly, who had moved to the couch beside him, gave him a sympathetic smile. From the kitchen, he could hear Deanna opening cabinets and drawers.

"Can we talk for a while, Mom?" Molly called. She moved closer to Phillip on the couch. Her feet drawn up under her, she reached out to squeeze his hand.

"Hey, Dad."

"Hey, Moll. Who loves you?"

She was still on medication, in another round of therapy, and at the moment, she seemed fine. The drugs had made her gain weight, she complained and she did look heavier. Her face was rounder, and there was a roll of fat between the top of the short black T-shirt she was wearing and her jeans. But nothing about his daughter—nothing that he could observe—hinted at the turmoil going on in her brain. His chest felt literally pummeled by the emotional roller-coaster ride of the past…week, two weeks, six weeks? He'd lost track of time.

"I'm sure these are stale, but we can nibble." Deanna set a package of crackers and a can of processed cheese on the coffee table. "Phillip?"

He shook his head, his arm still around Molly's shoulder.

"I have to tell you guys something," Molly said. "Remember that boy Brett? Dad, I told you about this industrial hemp plan we were going to do, remember?"

Phillip felt his arm tense. He nodded.

"Well see, I really liked him. We were going to do all this stuff together. He wanted us to go up to Humboldt County, or something, because his mom was so strict, she really started bugging him. So, okay, like I thought he really liked me. He was totally bummed when you guys made me go live up in L.A., I mean, he was always calling me and telling me he loved me."

"While you were staying with me?" Deanna asked. "At my apartment? Did I ever talk to him?"

"If you did, you probably forgot." Molly laughed. "You know how you guys are. Some guy could move in with me and you wouldn't notice."

Phillip glanced at Deanna, who was sitting on a black leather chair opposite him. She met his eyes for a moment, then shook her head slightly as though warning him not to speak.

"So anyway, like I heard from this kid at school that after I went up to L.A., Brett started liking this other girl, Sophie. She's French and she speaks with this accent. So like, I knew she was bad for him and he really liked me, so I pretended I was her and I called him and asked him to this party in Malibu. Except that there wasn't a party and when he got to Mom's apartment, he was so mad and we got into this humongous fight and I started throwing stuff at him and then he left."

Phillip felt the hand around his daughter's shoulder begin to tingle. He pulled it free, clasped both hands around his head, leaned back and closed his eyes. His brain refused to process the information. Like an engine low on fuel, it *whirred* but wouldn't turn over.

"I guess he's mad at me, because he never even calls and I'm trying not to call him because I promised you and Mom, but I feel so sad. I just want to tell him I'm sorry for playing the trick on him."

CHAPTER NINETEEN

"OH, BRE-ETT..." Zoe cooed softly, "Wakey wakey. Come on, I know you're in there. Come on, big boy, open your eyes. It's okay, I'm not going to make you mow the lawn."

No response. Zoe sat back in her chair. Brett was out of the PICU now, in what they called a step-down unit. The room was full of banners, flowers, balloon bouquets, pictures of Brett mugging into the camera. Pictures that she couldn't quite bring herself to look at. It takes time, Phillip kept telling her.

On the bright side, the good days were starting to outnumber the bad. The day Phillip had taken Brett off the respirator and she'd watched her son breathing on his own, she'd thrown her arms around Phillip and kissed him on the mouth.

He'd quickly released himself and they'd stood awkwardly close for a moment. "You're going to incite gossip," he finally said, and moved away.

Two days ago, Brett had opened his eyes. Dr. Thomasson had been in the room and she'd felt a tug of disappointment that it wasn't Phillip there to observe the milestone. She was trying very hard not to obsess about that sort of thing. Phillip had other patients, she knew that. Poor guy, he looked totally wiped out lately. Even when she told him the good news about Brett moving his arms and legs a little, his smile had been more weary than happy.

"Looks as though the brain stem has come all the way back," he'd said then mumbled something about getting back to surgery. Several times, she'd asked about Molly, thinking maybe that his daughter's problems were preoccupying him, but he'd just shrug and say Molly was doing fine.

"Good morning, Ms. McCann," a voice behind her said. She turned to see Thomasson again. He leaned over Brett's bed. "Can you hear me, Brett?"

Nothing.

Zoe tried. "Brett. Hey."

Nothing.

She watched Thomasson pinch Brett's chest between two pudgy pink fingers. Brett's right hand moved toward the spot. Thomasson tried the other side. Brett's left hand moved slightly. She watched Thomasson's face. He was smiling slightly.

"Localizing to pain," he said. "That's a good sign."

Thomasson was there the following day when Brett opened his eyes again, moving both of them together this time. A few days after the accident, Janna had brought in a cushion printed with a picture of him carrying his surfboard. She'd placed it at the foot of the bed. "When he wakes up, it'll be the first thing he sees," she'd said. Janna had just walked in the day Brett reached for the pillow with his toes.

Almost scared to breathe, Zoe had clutched Janna's hand and they'd both watched as Brett slowly brought the pillow up to where he could grab it with his right hand. They'd hugged and cried and Zoe had felt so relieved and happy that when Denny stopped in the waiting room that night and, seeing her there, started to leave, she called out to him.

"Look, I've been meaning to talk to you about everything. I just couldn't do it while Brett was…while we didn't know what was going to happen. I guess, I've had a whole lot of time to think." She took a deep breath. "I mean this changes everything. It's like this huge tornado has swept into our lives and nothing's ever going to be the same again. So it seems like a good time to figure out a better way for us to get along. I'm sorry I blamed you. I mean, I know I've been overprotective with him, but…well anyway, I'm trying to loosen up and everything…and I just wanted you to know that."

Denny leaned against the wall. He wore purple and black Bermudas and a black T-shirt. "Yeah, well, listen, Zoe, I'd like to say no hard feelings and all, but you gave me a pretty hard time. Like it wasn't bad enough that my son was nearly killed, you were all over me like it was all totally my fault." He paused. "But I know why you were so angry, and just so you know, I've been beating myself up over the whole thing. If I hadn't given Brett the keys that night, if I'd checked more carefully…"

"It doesn't matter." She looked him straight in the eye. "Brett is almost an adult—old enough to make a lot of his own decisions. Going up to Malibu was a bad decision. Not wearing his seat belt was another bad one. When he gets through this—and he will get through this—he'll be making much smarter decisions, and not because either you or I have anything to say about it." She paused, and looked at Denny, who was standing there with a stunned expression on his face. "Hey, I'm not going to change into Mother Teresa overnight. But I am trying to change. I mean it."

The look he gave her said he didn't quite believe her, but he wasn't crazy enough to say so. A moment passed, and he glanced down at his feet, in rubber flip-flops. "Anyway, so while we're on the subject. Me and Pam were talking about when he gets out of this place, like he's not gonna just start zipping around everywhere. He'll probably be in a wheel-chair for a while, the doctor said."

"Phillip told you that?"

"Phillip." He frowned. "You mean Dr. Barry? No, the fat one. Thompson."

"Thomasson."

"Yeah, him. Anyway, so we were thinking like our house doesn't have stairs so it would be easier for him to get about and we don't have all the junk you have everywhere, so it makes more sense for him to come and live with us. And, you might as well know this, before the accident he said that's what he wanted to do. He said you're always talking about this scholarship college stuff and he needs time to figure out what *he* wants to do."

"MAY I SIT HERE?" A tray in hand, Phillip grinned in anticipation of Zoe's surprise when she looked up to see him there. He wasn't disappointed. Her eyes went wide and she put down the spoon she'd been lifting to her mouth.

"What are you doing here?"

"Eating lunch." Phillip set his tray down. "Like you." He peered at her tray. "What the hell is that?"

"Rice pudding. Mixed with strawberry jam. My mother used to make it when I had a boo-boo."

He looked at her. As always, he had an impulse to touch her, to wrap his arms around her, to hold her hands across the table. It was an impulse he'd been training himself to ignore. As Brett continued to recover—this morning Phillip had seen him in a wheelchair on his way down to physical therapy—his own direct involvement in the case had decreased. Zoe had noticed, he'd seen it in her face. The fact that she hadn't challenged him surprised him, but this wasn't the same Zoe who had marched into his office that first day.

"And you're eating it now because…"

"Because…" She hesitated. "I was just talking to Denny. Which turned out to be sort of an emotional boo-boo. He thinks Brett should stay with him. While he goes through rehab." She stirred the rice pudding with the tip of the spoon. "They don't have stairs, so it kind of makes sense…Thomasson said Brett may be in a wheelchair for a while."

Phillip nodded.

"No one mentioned it to me."

"We think Brett's going to make a full recovery," he said. "But it's going to be another long process. Just like getting him to the point where he is now. I thought Thomasson had explained all that to you."

She shrugged. "He may have, but it was probably one of those things I didn't want to hear." Eyes down, she trailed the spoon across the pudding again. "People have told me so many things and I'm sure half of it just went in one ear and out the other." A pause. "Except when it was you talking."

Phillip watched a couple of residents in scrubs. One held a loaded tray, the other one was looking at the contents and laughing. Across the table, Zoe, stirring as though her life depended on it, had turned the rice pudding purple.

"That looks revolting," he said.

She glanced at it, then put the spoon down. "I just want you to know that I honestly couldn't have gone through this without you." Her forehead furrowed and she grabbed the back of her hair then released it. "The last few days…or weeks, I don't know how long it's been, but I've had this sense that you've been avoiding me."

"It's not that—"

"No, no, don't say anything. I know you've got other patients. I mean, I'm probably like the mother from hell, so if you were just trying to keep some distance, I understand that." Elbows on the table, she looked directly at him now. "I was going to come up to your office to tell you all this, but since you're here…thank you so much, Phillip. Not just for what you've done for Brett, which of course I can never thank you enough for, but simply for being who you are."

"Zoe…"

"Don't interrupt." She smiled, a flash of the old Zoe showing through. "I haven't finished. The other thing I wanted to say is I think you're fantastic, in-credible…and, not to embarrass you or anything, but I love you. God…" Her hand flew to her chest. "My heart is going crazy, but if I didn't say all that now, I never would. So there. It's all out on the table and I'm glad it is."

"Zoe—"

"That's fine, I can tell by your face that I was wrong. This wasn't the time to drop something like that on you."

"Listen to me." He reached for her hands. "Okay. Look at me while I tell you this." Something flick-ered in her eyes, a sudden wariness. Her hands went very still in his. "The night Brett had his accident, he was on his way back from seeing Molly. She played a trick on him. He thought it was this other girl—"

"Sophie."

"Yeah, I think that was her name. He drove up to L.A., thinking he was going to see her, but it was Molly. Evidently they had a big fight and Brett was upset when he drove home, obviously tired, too. He almost made it, but…Zoe, I'm so sorry, I don't know what to say."

Zoe looked at him for a long time. He had no idea what was running through her brain. It would be understandable if she were angry, but she hadn't pulled her hands away and her expression seemed—more than anything else—far, far away. Finally he shook their joined hands a little.

"Hey."

"Molly told you all this?"

"Yeah. She…doesn't know about Brett. She's just upset because he hasn't called her. I told you, she's got some very serious problems. I'm concerned that she might be too emotionally fragile right now to hear that kind of news."

"Poor Phillip." She freed her hand from his, leaned across the table to brush his cheek. "You've been terrified to tell me, haven't you?"

He shrugged. "Well, I wasn't exactly relishing it."

"I think," she said slowly, "that I've always had this notion of parents as sort of puppet masters. We pull the strings and make the kids dance. I don't mean it in an entirely negative way, but I certainly pulled Brett's strings and I always imagined my mom was doing the same with me. I blamed her for all the things I didn't like about my life and I resented her, too. What this accident has made me realize is that we don't control the strings. I blamed Brett's dad, as though Brett wouldn't have gone off if he'd been with me. But that was as stupid as blaming you would be. If he hadn't been going up to see Sophie or Molly, it might have been some other girl."

Relief washed over him like a wave. He shook his head. "Damn, Zoe…"

She laughed. "That was damn, Zoe, and not damn Zoe, right?"

"Actually, it was hot damn, Zoe. I love you, too."

They sat for a few minutes, hands linked but not speaking. So much had happened to all of them, words seemed inadequate somehow. Jenny Dixon's death had brought the adult Zoe into his life, his own daughter had nearly caused the death of Zoe's son. Kids, three kids. Disparate pieces of a puzzle that… He shook his head, too weary for now to follow the thought.

"Phillip." Zoe jiggled their hands. "I feel terrible about something. That first day I came to see you. I can't remember exactly what I said, but I know I blamed you for what happened to Jenny and I just want you to know—"

"Hey." Her eyes had filled with tears. "Whatever you thought about me then, trust me I was probably a whole lot harder on myself. And the tragedy of it is that Jenny wasn't the only victim. I told myself I cut back on cases so I could be there for Molly but I was too damn wrapped up in my own miseries and she ended up paying for it."

Zoe freed her hands, stuck her elbows on the table and looked at him. "Two things. One when we can all take a breath again, I think you and I and Rhea should sit down and talk about how we can create something out of what's happened. I don't know what it is yet, but I can feel an idea working away at the back of my mind."

He nodded slowly. Their thoughts were apparently working along the same lines. "And what's the other thing?"

"The past is the past. It's a memory. Good or bad there is nothing you can do about it. And tomorrow hasn't happened yet. You can plan and plan—Brett was going to medical school, I was going to do this or that, but something comes along and, boom, everything changes." She stopped to gather breath. "Projecting into the future, or living in the past. That's what we spend our lives doing. Rummaging through all the old baggage of anger and resentment. What a waste." Another pause and then a little nod as though to emphasize the point. "Well, I, for one, am going to stop doing that and you should, too. So there! I'm off my soapbox."

Phillip watched her face. Flushed and impassioned still. He wanted to smile, not at what she had said, but just because she was who she was. Zoe. "I love you," he said.

She frowned. "I know, you told me that. I love you, too. But I want you to listen to what I'm saying."

"I am listening. Essentially you're saying enjoy the moment, right?"

"Pretty much. I mean, think about it, Phillip. What else can you really count on?"

"Nothing." He got up from the table, walked around to where she sat, pulled her to her feet and led her out of the cafeteria. "So quit yakking. Let's go find a quiet spot where we can make the most of the moment. Have I ever mentioned the linen closets? They're notorious for that sort of carrying on."

CHAPTER TWENTY

THE ACCIDENT HAD CHANGED pretty much everything about his whole life, Brett was thinking. Some stuff, liking doing therapy and everything was kind of a drag and he wouldn't get to go surfing for like, six months or something. But get this, his *dad* didn't think he was ready. Not his mom, who you'd think would have got all freaked out, but his dad. His mom was kind of different, too, still hyper and everything, like right now she was trying to tie white bows on the goats and they weren't having any of it. Today was his birthday and his mom was having this big party for him and she was getting all the animals fancied up. All these kids from his old school and no one from the bunch of snobs at Country Day. That was one of the good changes. Between his medical bills and everything, his mom had finally listened to him when he told her he didn't want to go back there. He was still kind of gimping around, a leg brace that made him feel dorky, but this therapist guy promised that he'd only have to wear it another two weeks, so that was cool.

"Hey." Molly sat down on the grass next to him. "How you doing?"

"Good."

Brett thought about going to find something to

eat. His mom told him not to call Molly weird anymore because she couldn't help how she was. His
mom didn't exactly say it like that, but that's what
she meant. Molly had some sort of problem that
made her weird, but now she was on this new medication that calmed her down or something.

"Do you think your mom hates me?"

Brett looked at her. "Because of what happened?"

"Well, *duh,*" Molly said. "I guess."

"My mom doesn't hate you," Brett said. "She
doesn't hate anyone…except for my dad, and now
she doesn't even hate him." The accident had
changed all that, too. His mom not hating his dad any
more was definitely one of the good things.

"So if your mom and my dad got married or
something, I'd be your sister," Molly said.

He looked at Molly. "Who said they're getting
married?"

"Nobody. I just said if they did."

From where he sat, Brett could see his mom
standing under one of the almond trees smiling up
at Dr. Barry…Phillip, his mom said to call him.
Phillip was around a whole lot these days, which was
pretty cool. His mom seemed real happy about it,
and when his mom was happy, everything ran
smoother.

"Would you care if they got married?" he asked
Molly.

"Not really. My dad's always uptight, but when
he's around your mom he kind of loosens up. He said
she's good for him."

Brett rolled his eyes. His mom was a good person
and everything, but bottom line she was a pain in the
ass. Hard to see how she could actually be good for

someone. But his mom and Phillip were pretty old, maybe that explained it. All he knew was that now he wasn't going into the navy and he probably wasn't going to be a doctor, either, so on that score at least his mom and dad had both kind of won. And here was the way cool thing. Yesterday, Phillip had asked if one of these days, maybe next summer, he'd like to teach him to surf. Cool, huh, Brett McCann teaching Dr. Barry to surf? Weird how good things happen out of bad.

THE BED AT THE El Encante Hotel was huge. Zoe stretched her legs under the covers. Phillip was lying fully clothed on top of the bedspread where he'd flopped down, just to relax for a minute, he'd said, after their drive down to Puerta Nuevo. Their much-delayed Mexican trip. He'd fallen asleep immediately and was snoring lightly. Zoe smiled, struck by how close and intimate the sound made her feel, like an old married couple who had weathered so much together that they seemed less like two people, more like two halves of a whole.

With her toes, she touched Phillip's legs under the covers. The sheets were cold against her skin and she wanted to feel him warm and naked and curled up beside her. But she wanted to let him sleep, he needed sleep. There would be time for fun stuff later. Plenty of time. They'd booked a week at the hotel and brought very few clothes between them. Room service, champagne and walks on the beach, they'd mutually agreed.

She turned onto her side, head propped up with her hand and watched Phillip's face. They *had* weathered a lot together, an incredible storm of highs and lows, and it showed on his face, in the lines etching his mouth and eyes. A wave of overwhelming tenderness made her nose prickle with tears. She touched her finger lightly to his mouth. *I love you.*

She'd never been a weeper, but Brett's accident had produced such a huge wave of love and concern that lately tears were always right there at the surface. Nothing was the same as it once was, nor would it ever be again. On her back now, hands pillowed behind her head, she thought about all the people in her life. Brett. Her mother and sister. Rhea. Molly. There were days when she felt daunted by the things that still lay ahead: Brett still had a long road to complete recovery and Molly, she knew, might never be entirely well. There were steps to be taken, plans to be made— She thought about her new philosophy. She wouldn't go overboard on the planning stuff, but it was hard not to think ahead just a little bit. And instead of insisting on going it alone, as she'd once done, she would reach out and draw in the people who love her. It was a new reality for all of them, but they'd be all right. They would get through. Together. She closed her eyes, felt herself sinking into sleep.

Sometime later, she felt Phillip stir and then sit up. She heard the rustle of clothes coming off and then the cover being pulled back. His hand brushed her stomach and she turned to reach for him. He brought his hands to her face, his lips to her mouth and they kissed.

"'If you want my body,'" Phillip crooned against her mouth, "'and you think I'm sexy, c'mon sugar let me know.'"

So she did.

Mother and Child Reunion

A ministeries from
2003 RITA® finalist

Jean Brashear

Coming Home

Cleo Channing's dreams were simple: the stable home and big, loving family she never had as a child. Malcolm Channing walked into her life and swept her off her feet and before long, she thought she had it all—three beautiful children in a charming house she would fill to the rafters with love.

Their firstborn was a troubled girl, though, and the strain on their family grew until finally, there was nothing left to do but for them to all go their separate ways.

Now their daughter has returned, and as the days pass, awareness grows in Cleo and Malcolm that their love never truly died.

Except, the treacherous issues that drove them apart in the first place remain....

Heartwarming stories with a sense of humor, genuine charm and emotion and lots of family!

On sale starting January 2005
Available wherever Harlequin books are sold.

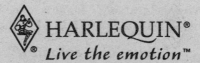
HARLEQUIN®
Live the emotion™

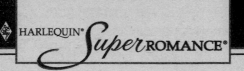

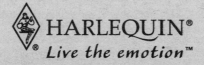

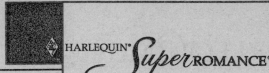

COUNT ON A COP

Forgotten Son by Linda Warren
Superromance #1250
On sale January 2005

Texas Ranger Elijah Coltrane is the forgotten son—the one his father never acknowledged. Eli's half brothers have been trying to get close to him for years, but Eli has stubbornly resisted. That is, until he meets Caroline Whitten, the woman who changes his mind about what it means to be part of a family.

By the author of *A Baby by Christmas* (Superromance #1167).

The Chosen Child by Brenda Mott
Superromance #1257
On sale February 2005

Nikki's sister survived the horrible accident caused by a hit-and-run driver, but the baby she was carrying for Nikki and her husband wasn't so lucky. The baby had been a last hope for the childless couple. Devastated, Nikki and Cody struggle to get past their tragedy. If only Cody could give up his all-consuming vendetta to find the drunk responsible—and make him pay.

Available wherever Harlequin books are sold.

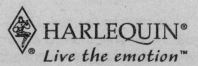

HARLEQUIN®
Live the emotion™